Diana Wynne Jones

Howl's Moving Castle

A GREENWILLOW BOOK

HarperTrophy®
An Imprint of HarperCollins Publishers

Harper Trophy® is a registered trademark of
HarperCollins Publishers Inc.

Howl's Moving Castle
Copyright © 1986 by Diana Wynne Jones

Library of Congress Cataloging-in-Publication Data
Jones, Diana Wynne. Howl's moving castle

p.   cm.

"Greenwillow Books."
Summary: Eldest of three sisters, in a land where it is considered to be a misfortune,
Sophie is resigned to her fate as a hat shop apprentice until a witch turns her into an old
woman and she finds herself in the castle of the greatly feared Wizard Howl.
ISBN 0-06-029881-2 — ISBN 0-06-441034-X (pbk.)
[1. Fantasy.] I. Title.

PZ7.J684Hp 1986   85-21981
[Fic]

Typography by Karin Paprocki

❖

First Harper Trophy edition, 2001
Visit us on the World Wide Web!
www.harperchildrens.com
12 13 14 OPM 30

Contents

1: In which Sophie talks to hats 1

2: In which Sophie is compelled to seek her fortune 18

3: In which Sophie enters into a castle and a bargain 36

4: In which Sophie discovers several strange things 49

5: Which is far too full of washing 62

6: In which Howl expresses his feelings with green slime 77

7: In which a scarecrow prevents Sophie from leaving the castle 95

8: In which Sophie leaves the castle in several directions at once 112

9: In which Michael has trouble with a spell 128

10: In which Calcifer promises Sophie a hint 142

11: In which Howl goes to a strange country in search of a spell 155

12: In which Sophie becomes Howl's old mother 172

13: In which Sophie blackens Howl's name 185

14: In which a Royal Wizard catches a cold 200

15: In which Howl goes to a funeral in disguise 218

This one is for
Stephen

The idea for this book was suggested by a boy in a school I was visiting, who asked me to write a book called *The Moving Castle*.

I wrote down his name, and put it in such a safe place, that I have been unable to find it ever since.

I would like to thank him very much.

16: In which there is a great deal of witchcraft   230

17: In which the moving castle moves house   241

18: In which the scarecrow and Miss Angorian reappear   254

19: In which Sophie expresses her feelings with weed-killer   270

20: In which Sophie finds further difficulties in
    leaving the castle   287

21: In which a contract is concluded before witnesses   306

Chapter 1:

—◆◆◆—

In which Sophie talks to hats

In the land of Ingary, where such things as seven-league boots and cloaks of invisibility really exist, it is quite a misfortune to be born the eldest of three. Everyone knows you are the one who will fail first, and worst, if the three of you set out to seek your fortunes.

Sophie Hatter was the eldest of three sisters. She was not even the child of a poor woodcutter, which might have given her some chance of success. Her parents were well to do and kept a ladies' hat shop in the prosperous town of Market Chipping. True, her own mother died when Sophie was two years old and her sister Lettie was one year old, and their father married his youngest shop assistant, a pretty blonde girl called Fanny. Fanny shortly gave birth to the third sister, Martha. This ought to have made Sophie and Lettie into Ugly Sisters, but in fact all three girls grew up very pretty indeed, though Lettie was the one everyone said was most beautiful. Fanny treated all three girls with the same kindness and did not favor Martha in the least.

Mr. Hatter was proud of his three daughters and sent them all to the best school in town. Sophie was the most studious. She read a great deal, and very soon realized how little chance she had of an interesting future. It was a disappointment to her, but she was still happy enough, looking after her sisters and grooming Martha to seek her fortune when the time came. Since Fanny was always busy in the shop, Sophie was the one who looked after the younger two. There was a certain amount of screaming and hair-pulling between those younger two. Lettie was by no means resigned to being the one who, next to Sophie, was bound to be the least successful.

"It's not fair!" Lettie would shout. "Why should Martha have the best of it just because she was born the youngest? I shall marry a prince, so there!"

To which Martha always retorted that *she* would end up disgustingly rich without having to marry anybody.

Then Sophie would have to drag them apart and mend their clothes. She was very deft with her needle. As time went on, she made clothes for her sisters too. There was one deep rose outfit she made for Lettie, the May Day before this story really starts, which Fanny said looked as if it had come from the most expensive shop in Kingsbury.

About this time everyone began talking of the

Witch of the Waste again. It was said the Witch had threatened the life of the King's daughter and that the King had commanded his personal magician, Wizard Suliman, to go into the Waste and deal with the Witch. And it seemed that Wizard Suliman had not only failed to deal with the Witch: he had got himself killed by her.

So when, a few months after that, a tall black castle suddenly appeared on the hills above Market Chipping, blowing clouds of black smoke from its four tall, thin turrets, everybody was fairly sure that the Witch had moved out of the Waste again and was about to terrorize the country the way she used to fifty years ago. People got very scared indeed. Nobody went out alone, particularly at night. What made it all the scarier was that the castle did not stay in the same place. Sometimes it was a tall black smudge on the moors to the northwest, sometimes it reared above the rocks to the east, and sometimes it came right downhill to sit in the heather only just beyond the last farm to the north. You could see it actually moving sometimes, with smoke pouring out from the turrets in dirty gray gusts. For a while everyone was certain that the castle would come right down into the valley before long, and the Mayor talked of sending to the King for help.

But the castle stayed roving about the hills, and it was learned that it did not belong to the Witch but to

Wizard Howl. Wizard Howl was bad enough. Though he did not seem to want to leave the hills, he was known to amuse himself by collecting young girls and sucking the souls from them. Or some people said he ate their hearts. He was an utterly cold-blooded and heartless wizard and no young girl was safe from him if he caught her on her own. Sophie, Lettie, and Martha, along with all the other girls in Market Chipping, were warned never to go out alone, which was a great annoyance to them. They wondered what use Wizard Howl found for all the souls he collected.

They had other things on their minds before long, however, for Mr. Hatter died suddenly just as Sophie was old enough to leave school for good. It then appeared that Mr. Hatter had been altogether too proud of his daughters. The school fees he had been paying had left the shop with quite heavy debts. When the funeral was over, Fanny sat down in the parlor in the house next door to the shop and explained the situation.

"You'll all have to leave that school, I'm afraid," she said. "I've been doing sums back and front and sideways, and the only way I can see to keep the business going *and* take care of the three of you is to see you all settled in a promising apprenticeship somewhere. It isn't practical to have you all in the shop. I can't afford it. So this is what I've decided. Lettie first—"

Lettie looked up, glowing with health and beauty which even sorrow and black clothes could not hide. "I want to go on learning," she said.

"So you shall, love," said Fanny. "I've arranged for you to be apprenticed to Cesari's, the pastry cook in Market Square. They've a name for treating their learners like kings and queens, and you should be very happy there, as well as learning a useful trade. Mrs. Cesari's a good customer and a good friend, and she's agreed to squeeze you in as a favor."

Lettie laughed in the way that showed she was not at all pleased. "Well, thank you," she said. "Isn't it lucky that I like cooking?"

Fanny looked relieved. Lettie could be awkwardly strong-minded at times. "Now Martha," she said. "I know you're full young to go out to work, so I've thought round for something that would give you a long, quiet apprenticeship and go on being useful to you whatever you decide to do after that. You know my old school friend Annabel Fairfax?"

Martha, who was slender and fair, fixed her big gray eyes on Fanny almost as strong-mindedly as Lettie. "You mean the one who talks such a lot," she said. "Isn't she a witch?"

"Yes, with a lovely house and clients all over the Folding Valley," Fanny said eagerly. "She's a good woman, Martha. She'll teach you all she knows and very likely introduce you to grand people she knows in Kingsbury. You'll be all set up in life when she's done with you."

"She's a nice lady," Martha conceded. "All right."

Sophie, listening, felt that Fanny had worked everything out just as it should be. Lettie, as the second daughter, was never likely to come to much, so Fanny had put her where she might meet a handsome young apprentice and live happily ever after. Martha, who was bound to strike out and make her fortune, would have witchcraft and rich friends to help her. As for Sophie herself, Sophie had no doubt what was coming. It did not surprise her when Fanny said, "Now, Sophie dear, it seems only right and just that you should inherit the hat shop when I retire, being the eldest as you are. So I've decided to take you on as apprentice myself, to give you a chance to learn the trade. How do you feel about that?"

Sophie could hardly say that she simply felt resigned to the hat trade. She thanked Fanny gratefully.

"So that's settled then!" Fanny said.

The next day Sophie helped Martha pack her clothes in a box, and the morning after that they all saw her off on the carrier's cart, looking small and upright and nervous. For the way to Upper Folding, where Mrs. Fairfax lived, lay over the hills past Wizard Howl's moving castle. Martha was understandably scared.

"She'll be all right," said Lettie. Lettie refused all help with the packing. When the carrier's cart was out of sight, Lettie crammed all her possessions into a pillow case and paid the neighbor's bootboy sixpence to wheel it in a wheelbarrow to Cesari's in Market Square. Lettie marched behind the wheelbarrow looking much more cheerful than Sophie expected. Indeed, she had the air of shaking the dust of the hat shop off her feet.

The bootboy brought back a scribbled note from Lettie, saying she had put her things in the girls' dormitory and Cesari's seemed great fun. A week later the carrier brought a letter from Martha to say that Martha had arrived safely and that Mrs. Fairfax was "a great dear and uses honey with everything. She keeps bees." That was all Sophie heard of her sisters for quite a while, because she started her own apprenticeship the day Martha and Lettie left.

Sophie of course knew the hat trade quite well already. Since she was a tiny child she had run in and out of the big workshed across the yard where the hats were damped and molded on blocks, and flowers and fruit and other trimmings were made from wax and silk. She knew the people who worked there. Most of them had been there when her father was a boy. She knew Bessie, the only remaining shop assistant. She knew the customers who bought the hats and the man who drove the cart which fetched raw

7

straw hats in from the country to be shaped on the blocks in the shed. She knew the other suppliers and how you made felt for winter hats. There was not really much that Fanny could teach her, except perhaps the best way to get a customer to buy a hat.

"You lead up to the right hat, love," Fanny said. "Show them the ones that won't quite do first, so they know the difference as soon as they put the right one on."

In fact, Sophie did not sell hats very much. After a day or so observing in the workshed, and another day going round the clothier and the silk merchant's with Fanny, Fanny set her to trimming hats. Sophie sat in a small alcove at the back of the shop, sewing roses to bonnets and veiling to velours, lining all of them with silk and arranging wax fruit and ribbons stylishly on the outsides. She was good at it. She quite liked doing it. But she felt isolated and a little dull. The workshop people were too old to be much fun and, besides, they treated her as someone apart who was going to inherit the business someday. Bessie treated her the same way. Bessie's only talk anyway was about the farmer she was going to marry the week after May Day. Sophie rather envied Fanny, who could bustle off to bargain with the silk merchant whenever she wanted.

The most interesting thing was the talk from the customers. Nobody can buy a hat without gossiping.

Sophie sat in her alcove and stitched and heard that the Mayor never would eat green vegetables, and that Wizard Howl's castle had moved round to the cliffs again, really that man, whisper, whisper, whisper. . . . The voices always dropped low when they talked of Wizard Howl, but Sophie gathered that he had caught a girl down the valley last month. "Bluebeard!" said the whispers, and then became voices again to say that Jane Farrier was a perfect disgrace the way she did her hair. *That* was one who would never attract even Wizard Howl, let alone a respectable man. Then there would be a fleeting, fearful whisper about the Witch of the Waste. Sophie began to feel that Wizard Howl and the Witch of the Waste should get together.

"They seem to be made for one another. Someone ought to arrange a match," she remarked to the hat she was trimming at that moment.

But by the end of the month the gossip in the shop was suddenly all about Lettie. Cesari's, it seemed, was packed with gentlemen from morning to night, each one buying quantities of cakes and demanding to be served by Lettie. She had had ten proposals of marriage, ranging in quality from the Mayor's son to the lad who swept the streets, and she had refused them all, saying she was too young to make up her mind yet.

"I call that sensible of her," Sophie said to a bonnet she was pleating silk into.

Fanny was pleased with this news. "I knew she'd be all right!" she said happily. It occurred to Sophie that Fanny was glad Lettie was no longer around.

"Lettie's bad for custom," she told the bonnet, pleating away at mushroom-colored silk. "She would make even you look glamorous, you dowdy old thing. Other ladies look at Lettie and despair."

Sophie talked to hats more and more as weeks went by. There was no one else much to talk to. Fanny was out bargaining, or trying to whip up custom, much of the day, and Bessie was busy serving and telling everyone her wedding plans. Sophie got into the habit of putting each hat on its stand as she finished it, where it sat looking almost like a head without a body, and pausing while she told the hat what the body under it ought to be like. She flattered the hats a bit, because you should flatter customers.

"You have mysterious allure," she told one that was all veiling with hidden twinkles. To a wide, creamy hat with roses under the brim she said, "You are going to have to marry money!" and to a caterpillar-green straw with a curly green feather she said, "You are young as a spring leaf." She told pink bonnets they had dimpled charm and smart hats trimmed with velvet that they were witty. She told the mushroom-pleated bonnet, "You have a heart of gold and someone in a high position will see it and fall in love with you." This was because she was sorry for that particular bonnet. It looked so fussy and plain.

Jane Farrier came into the shop next day and bought it. Her hair did look a little strange, Sophie thought, peeping out of her alcove, as if Jane had wound it round a row of pokers. It seemed a pity she had chosen that bonnet. But everyone seemed to be buying hats and bonnets around then. Maybe it was Fanny's sales talk or maybe it was spring coming on, but the hat trade was definitely picking up. Fanny began to say, a little guiltily, "I think I shouldn't have been in such a hurry to get Martha and Lettie placed out. At this rate we might have managed."

There was so much custom as April drew on toward May Day that Sophie had to put on a demure gray dress and help in the shop too. But such was the demand that she was hard at trimming hats in between customers, and every evening she took them next door to the house, where she worked by lamplight far into the night in order to have hats to sell the next day. Caterpillar-green hats like the one the Mayor's wife had were much called for, and so were pink bonnets. Then, the week before May Day, someone came in and asked for one with mushroom pleats like the one Jane Farrier had been wearing when she ran off with the Count of Catterack.

That night, as she sewed, Sophie admitted to herself that her life was rather dull. Instead of talking to the hats, she tried each one on as she finished it and looked in the mirror. This was a mistake. The staid gray dress did not suit Sophie, particularly when her eyes were red-rimmed with sewing, and, since her hair was a reddish straw color, neither did caterpillar green nor pink. The one with mushroom pleats simply made her look dreary. "Like an old maid!" said Sophie. Not that she wanted to race off with counts, like Jane Farrier, or even fancied half the town offering her marriage, like Lettie. But she wanted to do something—she was not sure what—that had a bit more interest to it than simply trimming hats. She thought she would find time next day to go and talk to Lettie.

But she did not go. Either she could not find the time, or she could not find the energy, or it seemed a great distance to Market Square, or she remembered that on her own she was in danger from Wizard Howl—anyway, every day it seemed more difficult to go and see her sister. It was very odd. Sophie had always thought she was nearly as strong-minded as Lettie. Now she was finding that there were some things she could only do when there were no excuses left. "This is absurd!" Sophie said. "Market Square is only two streets away. If I run—" And she swore to herself she would go round to Cesari's when the hat shop was closed for May Day.

Meanwhile a new piece of gossip came into the shop. The King had quarreled with his own brother,

Prince Justin, it was said, and the Prince had gone into exile. Nobody quite knew the reason for the quarrel, but the Prince had actually come through Market Chipping in disguise a couple of months back, and nobody had known. The Count of Catterack had been sent by the King to look for the Prince, when he happened to meet Jane Farrier instead. Sophie listened and felt sad. Interesting things did seem to happen, but always to somebody else. Still, it would be nice to see Lettie.

May Day came. Merrymaking filled the streets from dawn onward. Fanny went out early, but Sophie had a couple of hats to finish first. Sophie sang as she worked. After all, Lettie was working too. Cesari's was open till midnight on holidays. "I shall buy one of their cream cakes," Sophie decided. "I haven't had one for ages." She watched people crowding past the window in all kinds of bright clothes, people selling souvenirs, people walking on stilts, and felt really excited.

But when she at last put a gray shawl over her gray dress and went out into the street, Sophie did not feel excited. She felt overwhelmed. There were too many people rushing past, laughing and shouting, far too much noise and jostling. Sophie felt as if the past months of sitting and sewing had turned her into an old woman or a semi-invalid. She gathered her shawl round her and crept along close to the houses, trying to avoid being trodden on by people's best shoes or being jabbed by elbows in trailing silk sleeves. When there came a sudden volley of bangs from overhead somewhere, Sophie thought she was going to faint. She looked up and saw Wizard Howl's castle right down on the hillside above the town, so near it seemed to be sitting on the chimneys. Blue flames were shooting out of all four of the castle's turrets, bringing balls of blue fire with them that exploded high in the sky, quite horrendously. Wizard Howl seemed to be offended by May Day. Or maybe he was trying to join in, in his own fashion. Sophie was too terrified to care. She would have gone home, except that she was halfway to Cesari's by then. So she ran.

"What made me think I wanted life to be interesting?" she asked as she ran. "I'd be far too scared. It comes of being the eldest of three."

When she reached Market Square, it was worse, if possible. Most of the inns were in the Square. Crowds of young men swaggered beerily to and fro, trailing cloaks and long sleeves and stamping buckled boots they would never have dreamed of wearing on a working day, calling loud remarks and accosting girls. The girls strolled in fine pairs, ready to be accosted. It was perfectly normal for May Day, but Sophie was scared of that too. And when a young man in a fantastical blue-and-silver costume spotted Sophie and decided to accost her as well, Sophie shrank into a shop doorway and tried to hide.

The young man looked at her in surprise. "It's all right, you little gray mouse," he said, laughing rather pityingly. "I only want to buy you a drink. Don't look so scared."

The pitying look made Sophie utterly ashamed. He was such a dashing specimen too, with a bony, sophisticated face—really quite old, well into his twenties—and elaborate blonde hair. His sleeves trailed longer than any in the Square, all scalloped edges and silver insets. "Oh, no thank you, if you please, sir," Sophie stammered. "I—I'm on my way to see my sister."

"Then by all means do so," laughed this advanced young man. "Who am I to keep a pretty lady from her sister? Would you like me to go with you, since you seem so scared?"

He meant it kindly, which made Sophie more ashamed than ever. "No. No thank you, sir!" she gasped and fled away past him. He wore perfume too. The smell of hyacinths followed her as she ran. What a courtly person! Sophie thought, as she pushed her way between the little tables outside Cesari's.

The tables were packed. Inside was packed and as noisy as the Square. Sophie located Lettie among the line of assistants at the counter because of the group of evident farmers' sons leaning their elbows on it to shout remarks to her. Lettie, prettier than ever and perhaps a little thinner, was putting cakes into bags as fast as she could go, giving each bag a deft little twist and looking back under her own elbow with a smile and an answer for each bag she twisted. There was a great deal of laughter. Sophie had to fight her way through to the counter.

Lettie saw her. She looked shaken for a moment. Then her eyes and her smile widened and she shouted, "Sophie!"

"Can I talk to you?" Sophie yelled. "Somewhere," she shouted, a little helplessly, as a large, well-dressed elbow jostled her back from the counter.

"Just a moment!" Lettie screamed back. She turned to the girl next to her and whispered. The girl nodded, grinned, and came to take Lettie's place.

"You'll have to have me instead," she said to the crowd. "Who's next?"

"But I want to talk to you, Lettie!" one of the farmers' sons yelled.

"Talk to Carrie," Lettie said. "I want to talk to my sister." Nobody really seemed to mind. They jostled Sophie along to the end of the counter, where Lettie held up a flap and beckoned, and told her not to keep Lettie all day. When Sophie had edged through the flap, Lettie seized her wrist and dragged her into the back of the shop, to a room surrounded by rack upon wooden rack, each one filled with rows of cakes. Lettie pulled forward two stools. "Sit down," she said. She looked in the nearest rack, in an absentminded way, and handed Sophie a cream cake out of it. "You may need this," she said.

Sophie sank onto the stool, breathing the rich smell of cake and feeling a little tearful. "Oh, Lettie!" she said. "I am so glad to see you!"

"Yes, and I'm glad you're sitting down," said Lettie. "You see, I'm not Lettie. I'm Martha."

Chapter 2:

——— ✦ ———

In which Sophie is compelled to seek her fortune

"What?" Sophie stared at the girl on the stool opposite her. She looked just like Lettie. She was wearing Lettie's second-best blue dress, a wonderful blue that suited her perfectly. She had Lettie's dark hair and blue eyes.

"I am Martha," said her sister. "Who did you catch cutting up Lettie's silk drawers? *I* never told Lettie that. Did you?"

"No," said Sophie, quite stunned. She could see it was Martha now. There was Martha's tilt to Lettie's head, and Martha's way of clasping her hands round her knees with her thumbs twiddling. "Why?"

"I've been dreading you coming to see me," Martha said, "because I knew I'd have to tell you. It's a relief now I have. Promise you won't tell anyone. I know you won't tell if you promise. You're so honorable."

"I promise," Sophie said. "But why? How?"

"Lettie and I arranged it," Martha said, twiddling her thumbs, "because Lettie wanted to learn witchcraft and I didn't. Lettie's got brains, and she wants a future where she can use them—only try telling that to Mother! Mother's too jealous of Lettie even to admit she has brains!"

Sophie could not believe Fanny was like that, but she let it pass. "But what about you?"

"Eat your cake," said Martha. "It's good. Oh, yes, I can be clever too. It only took me two weeks at Mrs. Fairfax's to find the spell we're using. I got up at night and read her books secretly, and it was easy really. Then I asked if I could visit my family and Mrs. Fairfax said yes. She's a dear. She thought I was home-sick. So I took the spell and came here, and Lettie went back to Mrs. Fairfax pretending to be me. The difficult part was the first week, when I didn't know all the things I was supposed to know. It was awful. But I discovered that people like me—they do, you know, if *you* like *them*—and then it was all right. And Mrs. Fairfax hasn't kicked Lettie out, so I suppose she managed too."

Sophie chomped at cake she was not really tasting. "But what made you want to do this?"

Martha rocked on her stool, grinning all over Lettie's face, twirling her thumbs in a happy pink whirl. "I want to get married and have ten children."

"You're not old enough!" said Sophie.

"Not quite," Martha agreed. "But you can see I've got to start quite soon in order to fit ten children in.

And this way gives me time to wait and see if the person I want likes me for being *me*. The spell's going to wear off gradually, and I shall get more and more like myself, you see."

Sophie was so astonished that she finished her cake without noticing what kind it had been. "Why ten children?"

"Because that's how many I want," said Martha.

"I never knew!"

"Well, it wasn't much good going on about it when you were so busy backing Mother up about me making my fortune," Martha said. "You thought Mother meant it. I did too, until Father died and I saw she was just trying to get rid of us—putting Lettie where she was bound to meet a lot of men and get married off, and sending me as far away as she could! I was so angry I thought, Why not? And I spoke to Lettie and she was just as angry and we fixed it up. We're fine now. But we both feel bad about you. You're far too clever and nice to be stuck in that shop for the rest of your life. We talked about it, but we couldn't see what to do."

"I'm all right," Sophie protested. "Just a bit dull."

"All right?" Martha exclaimed. "Yes, you prove you're all right by not coming near here for months, and then turning up in a frightful gray dress and shawl, looking as if even *I* scare you! What's Mother been *doing* to you?"

"Nothing," Sophie said uncomfortably. "We've been rather busy. You shouldn't talk about Fanny that way, Martha. She *is* your mother."

"Yes, and I'm enough like her to understand her," Martha retorted. "That's why she sent me so far away, or tried to. Mother knows you don't have to be unkind to someone in order to exploit them. She knows how dutiful you are. She knows you have this thing about being a failure because you're only the eldest. She's managed you perfectly and got you slaving away for her. I bet she doesn't pay you."

"I'm still an apprentice," Sophie protested.

"So am I, but I get a wage. The Cesaris know I'm worth it," said Martha. "That hat shop is making a *mint* these days, and all because of you! You made that green hat that makes the Mayor's wife look like a stunning schoolgirl, didn't you?"

"Caterpillar green. I trimmed it," said Sophie.

"And the bonnet Jane Farrier was wearing when she met that nobleman," Martha swept on. "You're a genius with hats and clothes, and Mother knows it! You sealed your fate when you made Lettie that outfit last May Day. Now you earn the money while she goes off gadding—"

"She's out doing the buying," Sophie said.

"Buying!" Martha cried. Her thumbs whirled. "That takes her half a morning. I've seen her, Sophie, and heard the talk. She's off in a hired carriage and new clothes on your earnings, visiting all the mansions down the valley! They're saying she's going to buy that big place down at Vale End and set up in style. And where are you?"

"Well, Fanny's entitled to some pleasure after all her hard work bringing us up," Sophie said. "I suppose I'll inherit the shop."

"What a fate!" Martha exclaimed. "Listen——"

But at that moment two empty cake racks were pulled away at the other end of the room, and an apprentice stuck his head through from the back somewhere. "Thought I heard your voice, Lettie," he said, grinning in the most friendly and flirtatious way. "The new baking's just up. Tell them." His head, curly and somewhat floury, disappeared again. Sophie thought he looked a nice lad. She longed to ask if he was the one Martha really liked, but she did not get a chance. Martha sprang up in a hurry, still talking.

"I must get the girls to carry all these through to the shop," she said. "Help me with the end of this one." She dragged out the nearest rack and Sophie helped her hump it past the door into the roaring, busy shop. "You must do something about yourself, Sophie," Martha panted as they went. "Lettie kept saying she didn't know what would happen to you when we weren't around to give you some self-respect. She was right to be worried."

In the shop Mrs. Cesari seized the rack from

them in both massive arms, yelling instructions, and a line of people rushed away past Martha to fetch more. Sophie yelled goodbye and slipped away in the bustle. It did not seem right to take up more of Martha's time. Besides, she wanted to be alone to think. She ran home. There were fireworks now, going up from the field by the river where the Fair was, competing with the blue bangs from Howl's castle. Sophie felt more like an invalid than ever.

She thought and thought, most of the following week, and all that happened was that she became confused and discontented. Things just did not seem to be the way she thought they were. She was amazed at Lettie and Martha. She had misunderstood them for years. But she could not believe Fanny was the kind of woman Martha said.

There was a lot of time for thinking, because Bessie duly left to be married and Sophie was mostly alone in the shop. Fanny did seem to be out a lot, gadding or not, and trade was slack after May Day. After three days Sophie plucked up courage to ask Fanny, "Shouldn't I be earning a wage?"

"Of course, my love, with all you do!" Fanny answered warmly, fixing on a rose-trimmed hat in front of the shop mirror. "We'll see about it as soon as I've done the accounts this evening." Then she went out and did not come back until Sophie had shut the shop and taken that day's hats through to the house to trim.

Sophie at first felt mean to have listened to Martha, but when Fanny did not mention a wage, either that evening or any time later that week, Sophie began to think that Martha had been right.

"Maybe I *am* being exploited," she told a hat she was trimming with red silk and a bunch of wax cherries, "but someone has to do this or there will be no hats at all to sell." She finished that hat and started on a stark black-and-white one, very modish, and a quite new thought came to her. "Does it matter if there are no hats to sell?" she asked it. She looked round the assembled hats, on stands or waiting in a heap to be trimmed. "What good are you all?" she asked them. "You certainly aren't doing me a scrap of good."

And she was within an ace of leaving the house and setting out to seek her fortune, until she remembered she was the eldest and there was no point. She took up the hat again, sighing.

She was still discontented, alone in the shop next morning, when a very plain young woman customer stormed in, whirling a pleated mushroom bonnet by its ribbons. "Look at this!" the young lady shrieked. "You told me this was the same as the bonnet Jane Farrier was wearing when she met the Count. And you lied. Nothing has happened to me at all!"

"I'm not surprised," Sophie said, before she had caught up with herself. "If you're fool enough to wear that bonnet with a face like that, you wouldn't have the wit to spot the King himself if he came begging—if he hadn't turned to stone first just at the sight of you."

The customer glared. Then she threw the bonnet at Sophie and stormed out of the shop. Sophie carefully crammed the bonnet into the wastebasket, panting rather. The rule was: Lose your temper, lose a customer. She had just proven that rule. It troubled her to realize how very enjoyable it had been.

Sophie had no time to recover. There was the sound of wheels and horse hoofs and a carriage darkened the window. The shop bell clanged and the grandest customer she had ever seen sailed in, with a sable wrap drooping from her elbows and diamonds winking all over her dense black dress. Sophie's eyes went to the lady's wide hat first—real ostrich plume dyed to reflect the pinks and greens and blues winking in the diamonds and yet still look black. This was a wealthy hat. The lady's face was carefully beautiful. The chestnut-brown hair made her seem young, but . . . Sophie's eyes took in the young man who followed the lady in, a slightly formless-faced person with reddish hair, quite well dressed, but pale and obviously upset. He stared at Sophie with a kind of beseeching horror. He was clearly younger than the lady. Sophie was puzzled.

"Miss Hatter?" the lady asked in a musical but commanding voice.

"Yes," said Sophie. The man looked more upset than ever. Perhaps the lady was his mother.

"I hear you sell the most heavenly hats," said the lady. "Show me."

Sophie did not trust herself to answer in her present mood. She went and got out hats. None of them were in this lady's class, but she could feel the man's eyes following her and that made her uncomfortable. The sooner the lady discovered the hats were wrong for her, the sooner this odd pair would go. She followed Fanny's advice and got out the wrongest first.

The lady began rejecting hats instantly. "Dimples," she said to the pink bonnet, and "Youth" to the caterpillar-green one. To the one of twinkles and veils she said, "Mysterious allure. How very obvious. What else have you?"

Sophie got out the modish black-and-white, which was the only hat even remotely likely to interest this lady.

The lady looked at it with contempt. "This one doesn't do anything for anybody. You're wasting my time, Miss Hatter."

"Only because you came in and asked for hats," Sophie said. "This is only a small shop in a small town, Madam. Why did you—" Behind the lady, the man gasped and seemed to be trying to signal warningly. "—bother to come in?" Sophie finished, wondering what was going on.

"I always bother when someone tries to set them-selves up against the Witch of the Waste," said the lady. "I've heard of you, Miss Hatter, and I don't care for your competition or your attitude. I came to put a stop to you. There." She spread out her hand in a flinging motion toward Sophie's face.

"You mean you're the Witch of the Waste?" Sophie quavered. Her voice seemed to have gone strange with fear and astonishment.

"I am," said the lady. "And let that teach you to meddle with things that belong to me."

"I don't think I did. There must be some mistake," Sophie croaked. The man was now staring at her in utter horror, though she could not see why.

"No mistake, Miss Hatter," said the Witch. "Come, Gaston." She turned and swept to the shop door. While the man was humbly opening it for her, she turned back to Sophie. "By the way, you won't be able to tell anyone you're under a spell," she said. The shop door tolled like a funeral bell as she left.

Sophie put her hands to her face, wondering what the man had stared at. She felt soft, leathery wrinkles. She looked at her hands. They were wrinkled too, and skinny, with large veins in the back and knuckles like knobs. She pulled her gray skirt against her legs and looked down at skinny, decrepit ankles and feet which had made her shoes all knobbly. They were the legs of someone about ninety and they seemed to be real.

Sophie got herself to the mirror, and found she had to hobble. The face in the mirror was quite calm, because it was what she expected to see. It was the face of a gaunt old woman, withered and brownish, surrounded by wispy white hair. Her own eyes, yellow and watery, stared out at her, looking rather tragic.

"Don't worry, old thing," Sophie said to the face. "You look quite healthy. Besides, this is much more like you really are."

She thought about her situation, quite calmly. Everything seemed to have gone calm and remote. She was not even particularly angry with the Witch of the Waste.

"Well, of course I shall have to do for her when I get the chance," she told herself, "but meanwhile, if Lettie and Martha can stand being one another, I can stand being like this. But I can't stay here. Fanny would have a fit. Let's see. This gray dress is quite suitable, but I shall need my shawl and some food."

She hobbled over to the shop door and carefully put up the CLOSED notice. Her joints creaked as she moved. She had to walk bowed and slow. But she was relieved to discover that she was quite a hale old woman. She did not feel weak or ill, just stiff. She hobbled to collect her shawl, and wrapped it over her head and shoulders, as old women did. Then she shuffled through into the house, where she collected her purse with a few coins in it and a parcel of bread and cheese. She let herself out of the house, carefully hiding the key in the usual place, and hobbled away down the street, surprised at how calm she still felt.

She did wonder if she should say goodbye to Martha. But she did not like the idea of Martha not knowing her. It was best just to go. Sophie decided she would write to both her sisters when she got wherever she was going, and shuffled on, through the field where the Fair had been, over the bridge, and on into the country lanes beyond. It was a warm spring day. Sophie discovered that being a crone did not stop her enjoying the sight and smell of may in the hedgerows, though the sight was a little blurred. Her back began to ache. She hobbled sturdily enough, but she needed a stick. She searched the hedges as she went for a loose stake of some kind.

Evidently her eyes were not as good as they had been. She thought she saw a stick, a mile or so on, but when she hauled on it, it proved to be the bottom end of an old scarecrow someone had thrown into the hedge. Sophie heaved the thing upright. It had a withered turnip for a face. Sophie found she had some fellow feeling for it. Instead of pulling it to pieces and taking the stick, she stuck it between two branches of the hedge, so that it stood looming rakishly above the may, with the tattered sleeves on its stick arms fluttering over the hedge.

"There," she said, and her cracked old voice

surprised her into giving a cracked old cackle of laughter. "Neither of us are up to much, are we, my friend? Maybe you'll get back to your field if I leave you where people can see you." She set off up the lane again, but a thought struck her and she turned back. "Now if I wasn't doomed to failure because of my position in the family," she told the scarecrow, "you could come to life and offer me help in making my fortune. But I wish you luck anyway."

She cackled again as she walked on. Perhaps she was a little mad, but then old women often were.

She found a stick an hour or so later when she sat down on the bank to rest and eat her bread and cheese. There were noises in the hedge behind her: little strangled squeakings, followed by heavings that shook may petals off the hedge. Sophie crawled on her bony knees to peer past leaves and flowers and thorns into the inside of the hedge, and discovered a thin gray dog in there. It was hopelessly trapped by a stout stick which had somehow got twisted into a rope that was tied round its neck. The stick had wedged itself between two branches of the hedge so that the dog could barely move. It rolled its eyes wildly at Sophie's peering face.

As a girl, Sophie was scared of all dogs. Even as an old woman, she was quite alarmed by the two rows of white fangs in the creature's open jaws. But she said to herself, "The way I am now, it's scarcely worth worrying about," and felt in her sewing pocket for her scissors. She reached into the hedge with the scissors and sawed away at the rope round the dog's neck.

The dog was very wild. It flinched away from her and growled. But Sophie sawed bravely on. "You'll starve or throttle to death, my friend," she told the dog in her cracked old voice, "unless you let me cut you loose. In fact, I think someone has tried to throttle you already. Maybe that accounts for your wildness." The rope had been tied quite tightly round the dog's neck and the stick had been twisted viciously into it. It took a lot of sawing before the rope parted and the dog was able to drag itself out from under the stick.

"Would you like some bread and cheese?" Sophie asked it then. But the dog just growled at her, forced its way out through the opposite side of the hedge, and slunk away. "There's gratitude for you!" Sophie said, rubbing her prickled arms. "But you left me a gift in spite of yourself." She pulled the stick that had trapped the dog out of the hedge and found it was a proper walking stick, well trimmed and tipped with iron. Sophie finished her bread and cheese and set off walking again. The lane became steeper and steeper and she found the stick a great help. It was also something to talk to. Sophie thumped along with a will, chatting to her stick. After all, old people often talk to themselves.

"There's two encounters," she said, "and not a scrap

of magical gratitude from either. Still, you're a good stick. I'm not grumbling. But I'm surely due to have a third encounter, magical or not. In fact, I insist on one. I wonder what it will be."

The third encounter came toward the end of the afternoon when Sophie had worked her way quite high into the hills. A countryman came whistling down the lane toward her. A shepherd, Sophie thought, going home after seeing to his sheep. He was a well-set-up young fellow of forty or so. "Gracious!" Sophie said to herself. "This morning I'd have seen him as an old man. How one's point of view does alter!"

When the shepherd saw Sophie mumbling to herself, he moved rather carefully over to the other side of the lane and called out with great heartiness, "Good evening to you, Mother! Where are you off to?"

"Mother?" said Sophie. "I'm not your mother, young man!"

"A manner of speaking," the shepherd said, edging along against the opposite hedge. "I was only meaning a polite inquiry, seeing you walking into the hills at the end of the day. You won't get down into Upper Folding before nightfall, will you?"

Sophie had not considered this. She stood in the road and thought about it. "It doesn't matter really," she said, half to herself. "You can't be fussy when you're off to seek your fortune."

"Can't you indeed, Mother?" said the shepherd.

He had now edged himself downhill of Sophie and seemed to feel better for it. "Then I wish you good luck, Mother, provided your fortune don't have nothing to do with charming folks' cattle." And he took off down the road in great strides, almost running, but not quite.

Sophie stared after him indignantly. "He thought I was a witch!" she said to her stick. She had half a mind to scare the shepherd by shouting nasty things after him, but that seemed a little unkind. She plugged on uphill, mumbling. Shortly, the hedges gave way to bare banks and the land beyond became heathery upland, with a lot of steepness beyond that covered with yellow, rattling grass. Sophie kept grimly on. By now her knobby old feet ached, and her back, and her knees. She became too tired to mumble and simply plugged on, panting, until the sun was quite low. And all at once it became quite clear to Sophie that she could not walk a step further.

She collapsed onto a stone by the wayside, wondering what she would do now. "The only fortune I can think of is a comfortable chair!" she gasped.

The stone proved to be on a sort of headland, which gave Sophie a magnificent view of the way she had come. There was most of the valley spread out beneath her in the setting sun, all fields and walls and hedges, the windings of the river, and the fine mansions of rich people glowing out from clumps of trees, right down to blue mountains in the far distance. Just below her was Market Chipping. Sophie could look down into its well-known streets. There was Market Square and Cesari's. She could have tossed a stone down the chimney pots of the house next to the hat shop.

"How near it still is!" Sophie told her stick in dismay. "All that walking just to get above my own rooftop!"

It got cold on the stone as the sun went down. An unpleasant wind blew whichever way Sophie turned to avoid it. Now it no longer seemed so unimportant that she would be out on the hills during the night. She found herself thinking more and more of a comfortable chair and a fireside, and also of darkness and wild animals. But if she went back to Market Chipping, it would be the middle of the night before she got there. She might just as well go on. She sighed and stood up, creaking. It was awful. She ached all over.

"I never realized before what old people had to put up with!" she panted as she labored uphill. "Still, I don't think wolves will eat me. I must be far too dry and tough. That's one comfort."

Night was coming down fast now and the heathery uplands were blue-gray. The wind was sharper. Sophie's panting and the creaking of her limbs were so loud in her ears that it took her a while to notice that some of the grinding and puffing was not coming from herself at all. She looked up blurrily.

Wizard Howl's castle was rumbling and bumping toward her across the moorland. Black smoke was blowing up in clouds from behind its black battlements. It looked tall and thin and heavy and ugly and very sinister indeed. Sophie leaned on her stick and watched it. She was not particularly frightened. She wondered how it moved. But the main thing in her mind was that all that smoke must mean a large fireside somewhere inside those tall black walls.

"Well, why not?" she said to her stick. "Wizard Howl is not likely to want *my* soul for his collection. He only takes young girls."

She raised her stick and waved it imperiously at the castle.

"Stop!" she shrieked.

The castle obediently came to a rumbling, grinding halt about fifty feet uphill from her. Sophie felt rather gratified as she hobbled toward it.

Chapter 3:

In which Sophie enters into a castle and a bargain

There was a large black door in the black wall facing Sophie and she made for that, hobbling briskly. The castle was uglier than ever close to. It was far too tall for its height and not a very regular shape. As far as Sophie could see in the growing darkness, it was built of huge black blocks, like coal, and, like coal, the blocks were all different shapes and sizes. Chill breathed off these blocks as she got closer, but that failed to frighten Sophie at all. She just thought of chairs and firesides and stretched her hand out eagerly to the door.

Her hand could not come near it. Some invisible wall stopped her hand about a foot from the door. Sophie prodded at it with an irritable finger. When that made no difference, she prodded with her stick. The wall seemed to be all over the door from as high as her stick could reach, and right down to the heather sticking out from under the doorstep.

"Open up!" Sophie cackled at it.

That made no difference to the wall.

"Very well," Sophie said. "I'll find your back door." She hobbled off to the lefthand corner of the castle, that being both nearest and slightly downhill. But she could not get round the corner. The invisible wall stopped her again as soon as she was level with the irregular black cornerstones. At this, Sophie said a word she had learned from Martha, that neither old ladies nor young girls are supposed to know, and stumped uphill and anticlockwise to the castle's righthand corner. There was no barrier there. She turned that corner and hobbled eagerly toward the second big black door in the middle of that side of the castle.

There was a barrier over that door too.

Sophie glowered at it. "I call that very unwelcoming!" she said.

Black smoke blew down from the battlements in clouds. Sophie coughed. Now she was angry. She was old, frail, chilly, and aching all over. Night was coming on and the castle just sat and blew smoke at her. "I'll speak to Howl about this!" she said, and set off fiercely to the next corner. There was no barrier there—evidently you had to go round the castle anticlockwise—but there, a bit sideways in the next wall, was a third door. This one was much smaller and shabbier.

"The back door at last!" Sophie said.

The castle started to move again as Sophie got near the back door. The ground shook. The wall shuddered and creaked, and the door started to travel away sideways from her.

"Oh, no you don't!" Sophie shouted. She ran after the door and hit it violently with her stick. "Open up!" she yelled.

The door sprang open inward, still moving away sideways. Sophie, by hobbling furiously, managed to get one foot up on its doorstep. Then she hopped and scrambled and hopped again, while the great black blocks round the door jolted and crunched as the castle gathered speed over the uneven hillside. Sophie did not wonder the castle had a lopsided look. The marvel was that it did not fall apart on the spot.

"What a stupid way to treat a building!" she panted as she threw herself inside it. She had to drop her stick and hang on to the open door in order not to be jolted straight out again.

When she began to get her breath, she realized there was a person standing in front of her, holding the door too. He was a head taller than Sophie, but she could see he was the merest child, only a little older than Martha. And he seemed to be trying to shut the door on her and push her out of the warm, lamplit, low-beamed room beyond him, into the night again.

"Don't you have the impudence to shut the door on me, my boy!" she said.

"I wasn't going to, but you're keeping the door open," he protested. "What do you want?"

Sophie looked round at what she could see beyond the boy. There were a number of probably wizardly things hanging from the beams—strings of onions, bunches of herbs, and bundles of strange roots. There were also definitely wizardly things, like leather books, crooked bottles, and an old, brown, grinning human skull. On the other side of the boy was a fireplace with a small fire burning in the grate. It was a much smaller fire than all the smoke outside suggested, but then this was obviously only a back room in the castle. Much more important to Sophie, this fire had reached the glowing rosy stage, with little blue flames dancing on the logs, and placed beside it in the warmest position was a low chair with a cushion on it.

Sophie pushed the boy aside and dived for that chair. "Ah! My fortune!" she said, settling herself comfortably in it. It was bliss. The fire warmed her aches and the chair supported her back and she knew that if anyone wanted to turn her out now, they were going to have to use extreme and violent magic to do it.

The boy shut the door. Then he picked up Sophie's stick and politely leaned it against the chair for her. Sophie realized that there was now no sign at all that the castle was moving across the hillside: not even the ghost of a rumble or the tiniest shaking. How odd! "Tell Wizard Howl," she said to the boy, "that this castle's going to come apart round his ears if it travels much further."

"The castle's bespelled to hold together," the boy said. "But I'm afraid Howl's not here just at the moment."

This was good news to Sophie. "When will he be back?" she asked a little nervously.

"Probably not till tomorrow now," the boy said. "What do you want? Can I help you instead? I'm Howl's apprentice, Michael."

This was better news than ever. "I'm afraid only the Wizard can possibly help me," Sophie said quickly and firmly. It was probably true too. "I'll wait, if you don't mind." It was clear Michael *did* mind. He hovered over her a little helplessly. To make it plain to him that she had no intention of being turned out by a mere boy apprentice, Sophie closed her eyes and pretended to go to sleep. "Tell him the name's Sophie," she murmured. "*Old* Sophie," she added, to be on the safe side.

"That will probably mean waiting all night," Michael said. Since this was exactly what Sophie wanted, she pretended not to hear. In fact, she almost certainly fell into a swift doze. She was so tired from all that walking. After a moment Michael gave her up and went back to the work he was doing at the work-bench where the lamp stood.

So she would have a whole night's shelter, even if it was on slightly false pretenses, Sophie thought drowsily. Since Howl was such a wicked man, it probably served him right to be imposed upon. But she intended to be well away from here by the time Howl came back and raised objections. She looked sleepily and slyly across at the apprentice. It rather surprised her to find him such a nice, polite boy. After all, she had forced her way in quite rudely and Michael had not complained at all. Perhaps Howl kept him in abject servility. But Michael did not look servile. He was a tall, dark boy with a pleasant, open sort of face, and he was most respectably dressed. In fact, if Sophie had not seen him at that moment carefully pouring green fluid out of a crooked flask onto black powder in a bent glass jar, she would have taken him for the son of a prosperous farmer. How odd!

Still, things were bound to be odd where wizards were concerned, Sophie thought. And this kitchen, or workshop, was beautifully cozy and very peaceful. Sophie went properly to sleep and snored. She did not wake up when there came a flash and a muted bang from the workbench, followed by a hurriedly bitten-off swear word from Michael. She did not wake when Michael, sucking his burned fingers, put the spell aside for the night and fetched bread and cheese out of the closet. She did not stir when Michael knocked her stick down with a clatter, reaching over her for a log to put on the fire, or when Michael, looking down into Sophie's open mouth, remarked to the fireplace, "She's got all her teeth. She's not the Witch of the Waste, is she?"

"I wouldn't have let her come in if she was," the fireplace retorted.

Michael shrugged and picked Sophie's stick politely up again. Then he put a log on the fire with equal politeness and went away to bed somewhere overhead.

In the middle of the night Sophie was woken by someone snoring. She jumped upright, rather irritated to discover that she was the one who had been snoring. It seemed to her that she had only dropped off for a second or so, but Michael seemed to have vanished in those seconds, taking the light with him. No doubt a wizard's apprentice learned to do that kind of thing in his first week. And he had left the fire very low. It was giving out irritating hissings and poppings. A cold draft blew on Sophie's back. Sophie recalled that she was in a wizard's castle, and also, with unpleasant distinctness, that there was a human skull on a workbench somewhere behind her.

She shivered and cranked her stiff old neck around, but there was only darkness behind her. "Let's have a bit more light, shall we?" she said. Her cracked little voice seemed to make no more noise than the crackling of the fire. Sophie was surprised.

She had expected it to echo through the vaults of the castle. Still, there was a basket of logs beside her. She stretched out a creaking arm and heaved a log on the fire, which sent a spray of green and blue sparks flying up the chimney. She heaved on a second log and sat back, not without a nervous look or so behind her, where blue-purple light from the fire was dancing over the polished brown bone of the skull. The room was quite small. There was no one in it but Sophie and the skull.

"He's got both feet in the grave and I've only got one," she consoled herself. She turned back to the fire, which was now flaring up into blue and green flames. "Must be salt in that wood," Sophie murmured. She settled herself more comfortably, putting her knobby feet on the fender and her head into a corner of the chair, where she could stare into the colored flames, and began dreamily considering what she ought to do in the morning. But she was sidetracked a little by imagining a face in the flames. "It would be a thin blue face," she murmured, "very long and thin, with a thin blue nose. But those curly green flames on top are most definitely your hair. Suppose I didn't go until Howl gets back? Wizards can lift spells, I suppose. And those purple flames near the bottom make the mouth—you have savage teeth, my friend. You have two green tufts of flame for eyebrows. . . . " Curiously enough, the only orange flames in the fire were under

43

the green eyebrow flames, just like eyes, and they each had a little purple glint in the middle that Sophie could almost imagine was looking at her, like the pupil of an eye. "On the other hand," Sophie continued, looking into the orange flames, "if the spell was off, I'd have my heart eaten before I could turn around."

"Don't you want your heart eaten?" asked the fire.

It was definitely the fire that spoke. Sophie saw its purple mouth move as the words came. Its voice was nearly as cracked as her own, full of the spitting and whining of burning wood. "Naturally I don't," Sophie answered. "What are you?"

"A fire demon," answered the purple mouth. There was more whine than spit to its voice as it said, "I'm bound to this hearth by contract. I can't move from this spot." Then its voice became brisk and crackling. "And what are *you*?" it asked. "I can see you're under a spell."

This roused Sophie from her dreamlike state. "You see!" she exclaimed. "Can you take the spell off?"

There was a poppling, blazing silence while the orange eyes in the demon's wavering blue face traveled up and down Sophie. "It's a strong spell," it said at length. "It feels like one of the Witch of the Waste's to me."

"It is," said Sophie.

"But it seems more than that," crackled the demon. "I detect two layers. And of course you won't be able to tell anyone about it unless they know already." It gazed at Sophie a moment longer. "I shall have to study it," it said.

"How long will that take?" Sophie asked.

"It may take a while," said the demon. And it added in a soft, persuasive flicker, "How about making a bargain with me? I'll break your spell if you agree to break this contract I'm under."

Sophie looked warily at the demon's thin blue face. It had a distinctly cunning look as it made this proposal. Everything she had read showed the extreme danger of making a bargain with a demon. And there was no doubt that this one did look extraordinarily evil. Those long purple teeth. "Are you sure you're being quite honest?" she said.

"Not completely," admitted the demon. "But do you want to stay like that till you die? That spell has shortened your life by about sixty years, if I am any judge of such things."

This was a nasty thought, and one which Sophie had tried not to think about up to now. It made quite a difference. "This contract you're under," she said. "It's with Wizard Howl, is it?"

"Of course," said the demon. Its voice took on a bit of a whine again. "I'm fastened to this hearth and I can't stir so much as a foot away. I'm forced to do most of the magic around here. I have to maintain the castle and keep it moving and do all the special effects that scare people off, as well as anything else Howl wants. Howl's quite heartless, you know."

Sophie did not need telling that Howl was heartless. On the other hand, the demon was probably quite as wicked. "Don't you get anything out of this contract at all?" she said.

"I wouldn't have entered into it if I didn't," said the demon, flickering sadly. "But I wouldn't have done if I'd known what it would be like. I'm being exploited."

In spite of her caution, Sophie felt a good deal of sympathy for the demon. She thought of herself making hats for Fanny while Fanny went gadding. "All right," she said. "What are the terms of the contract? How do I break it?"

An eager purple grin spread across the demon's blue face. "You agree to a bargain?"

"If you agree to break the spell on me," Sophie said, with a brave sense of saying something fatal.

"Done!" cried the demon, his long face leaping gleefully up the chimney. "I'll break your spell the very instant you break my contract!"

"Then tell me how I break your contract," Sophie said.

The orange eyes glinted at her and looked away. "I can't. Part of the contract is that neither the Wizard nor I can say what the main clause is."

Sophie saw that she had been tricked. She opened

her mouth to tell the demon that it could sit in the fireplace until Doomsday in that case.

The demon realized she was going to. "Don't be hasty!" it crackled. "You can find out what it is if you watch and listen carefully. I implore you to try. The contract isn't doing either of us any good in the long run. And I do keep my word. The fact that I'm stuck here *shows* that I keep it!"

It was in earnest, leaping about on its logs in an agitated way. Sophie again felt a great deal of sympathy. "But if I'm to watch and listen, that means I have to stay here in Howl's castle," she objected.

"Only about a month. Remember, I have to study your spell too," the demon pleaded.

"But what possible excuse can I give for doing that?" Sophie asked.

"We'll think of one. Howl's pretty useless at most things. In fact," the demon said, venomously hissing, "he's too wrapped up in himself to see beyond his nose half the time. We can deceive him— as long as you'll agree to stay."

"Very well," Sophie said. "I'll stay. Now find an excuse."

She settled herself comfortably in the chair while the demon thought. It thought aloud, in a little crackling, flickering murmur, which reminded Sophie rather of the way she had talked to her stick when she walked here, and it blazed while it thought with such a glad and powerful roaring that she dozed again. She thought the demon did make a few suggestions. She remembered shaking her head to the notion that she should pretend to be Howl's long-lost great-aunt, and to one or two other ones even more far-fetched, but she did not remember very clearly. The demon at length fell to singing a gentle, flickering little song. It was not in any language Sophie knew—or she thought not, until she distinctly heard the word "saucepan" in it several times—and it was very sleepy-sounding. Sophie fell into a deep sleep, with a slight suspicion that she was being bewitched now, as well as beguiled, but it did not bother her particularly. She would be free of the spell soon. . . .

Chapter 4:

— ※ —

In which Sophie discovers
several strange things

When Sophie woke up, daylight was streaming across her. Since Sophie remembered no windows at all in the castle, her first notion was that she had fallen asleep trimming hats and dreamed of leaving home. The fire in front of her had sunk to rosy charcoal and white ash, which convinced her that she had certainly dreamed there was a fire demon. But her very first movements told her that there were some things she had not dreamed. There were sharp cracks from all over her body.

"Ow!" she exclaimed. "I ache all over!" The voice that exclaimed was a weak, cracked piping. She put her knobby hands to her face and felt wrinkles. At that, she discovered she had been in a state of shock all yesterday. She was very angry indeed with the Witch of the Waste for doing this to her, hugely, enormously angry. "Sailing into shops and turning people old!" she exclaimed. "Oh, *what* I won't do to her!"

Her anger made her jump up in a salvo of cracks

and creaks and hobble over to the unexpected window. It was above the workbench. To her utter astonishment, the view from it was a view of a dockside town. She could see a sloping, unpaved street, lined with small, rather poor-looking houses, and masts sticking up beyond the roofs. Beyond the masts she caught a glimmer of the sea, which was something she had never seen in her life before.

"Wherever am I?" Sophie asked the skull standing on the bench. "I don't expect you to answer that, my friend," she added hastily, remembering this was a wizard's castle, and she turned round to take a look at the room.

It was quite a small room, with heavy black beams in the ceiling. By daylight it was amazingly dirty. The stones of the floor were stained and greasy, ash was piled within the fender, and cobwebs hung in dusty droops from the beams. There was a layer of dust on the skull. Sophie absently wiped it off as she went to peer into the sink beside the workbench. She shuddered at the pink-and-gray slime in it and the white slime dripping from the pump above it. Howl obviously did not care what squalor his servants lived in.

The rest of the castle had to be beyond one or other of the four low black doors around the room. Sophie opened the nearest, in the end wall beyond the bench. There was a large bathroom beyond it. In some ways it was a bathroom you might normally find only in a palace, full of luxuries such as an indoor toilet, a shower stall, an immense bath with clawed feet, and mirrors on every wall. But it was even dirtier than the other room. Sophie winced from the toilet, flinched at the color of the bath, recoiled from green weed growing in the shower, and quite easily avoided looking at her shriveled shape in the mirrors because the glass was plastered with blobs and runnels of nameless substances. The nameless substances themselves were crowded onto a very large shelf over the bath. They were in jars, boxes, tubes, and hundreds of tattered brown packets and paper bags. The biggest jar had a name. It was called DRYING POWER in crooked letters. Sophie was not sure whether there should be a D in that or not. She picked up a packet at random. It had SKIN scrawled on it, and she put it back hurriedly. Another jar said EYES in the same scrawl. A tube stated FOR DECAY.

"It seems to work too," Sophie murmured, looking into the washbasin with a shiver. Water ran into the basin when she turned a blue-green knob that might have been brass and washed some of the decay away. Sophie rinsed her hands and face in the water without touching the basin, but she did not have the courage to use DRYING POWER. She dried the water with her skirt and then set off to the next black door.

That one opened onto a flight of rickety wooden stairs. Sophie heard someone move up there and shut the door hurriedly. It seemed only to lead to a sort of loft anyway. She hobbled to the next door. By now she was moving quite easily. She was a hale old woman, as she had discovered yesterday.

The third door opened onto a poky backyard with high brick walls. It contained a big stack of logs, and higgledy-piggledy heaps of what seemed to be scrap iron, wheels, buckets, metal sheeting, wire, mounded almost to the tops of the walls. Sophie shut that door too, rather puzzled, because it did not seem to match the castle at all. There was no castle to be seen above the brick walls. They ended at the sky. Sophie could only think that this part was round the side where the invisible wall had stopped her the night before.

She opened the fourth door and it was just a broom cupboard, with two fine but dusty velvet cloaks hanging on the brooms. Sophie shut it again, slowly. The only other door was in the wall with the window, and that was the door she had come in by last night. She hobbled over and cautiously opened that.

She stood for a moment looking out at a slowly moving view of the hills, watching heather slide past underneath the door, feeling the wind blow her wispy hair, and listening to the rumble and grind of the big black stones as the castle moved. Then she shut the door and went to the window. And there was the seaport town again. It was no picture. A woman had opened a door opposite and was sweeping dust into the street. Behind that house a grayish canvas sail was going up a mast in brisk jerks, disturbing a flock of seagulls into flying round and round against the glimmering sea.

"I don't understand," Sophie told the human skull. Then, because the fire looked almost out, she went and put on a couple of logs and raked away some of the ash.

Green flames climbed between the logs, small and curly, and shot up into a long blue face with flaming green hair. "Good morning," said the fire demon. "Don't forget we have a bargain."

So none of it was a dream. Sophie was not much given to crying, but she sat in the chair for quite a while staring at a blurred and sliding fire demon, and did not pay much attention to the sounds of Michael getting up, until she found him standing beside her, looking embarrassed and a little exasperated.

"You're still here," he said. "Is something the matter?"

Sophie sniffed. "I'm old," she began.

But it was just as the Witch had said and the fire demon had guessed. Michael said cheerfully, "Well, it comes to us all in time. Would you like some breakfast?"

Sophie discovered she was a very hale old woman indeed. After only bread and cheese at lunchtime yesterday, she was ravenous. "Yes!" she said, and when Michael went to the closet in the wall, she sprang up and peered over his shoulder to see what there was to eat.

"I'm afraid there's only bread and cheese," Michael said rather stiffly.

"But there's a whole basket of eggs in there!" Sophie said. "And isn't that bacon? What about a hot drink as well? Where's your kettle?"

"There isn't one," Michael said. "Howl's the only one who can cook."

"I can cook," said Sophie. "Unhook that frying pan and I'll show you."

She reached for the large black pan hanging on the closet wall, in spite of Michael trying to prevent her. "You don't understand," Michael said. "It's Calcifer, the fire demon. He won't bend down his head to be cooked on for anyone but Howl."

Sophie turned and looked at the fire demon. He flickered back at her wickedly. "I refuse to be exploited," he said.

"You mean," Sophie said to Michael, "that you have to do without even a hot drink unless Howl's here?" Michael gave an embarrassed nod. "Then *you're* the one that's being exploited!" said Sophie. "Give that here." She wrenched the pan from Michael's resisting fingers, plonked the bacon into it, popped a handy wooden spoon into the egg basket, and marched with the lot to the fireplace. "Now, Calcifer," she said, "let's have no more nonsense. Bend down your head."

"You can't make me!" crackled the fire demon.

"Oh, yes I can!" Sophie crackled back, with the ferocity that had often stopped both her sisters in mid-fight. "If you don't, I shall pour water on you. Or I shall pick up the tongs and take away both your logs," she added, as she got herself creakingly onto her knees by the hearth. There she whispered, "Or I can go back on our bargain, or tell Howl about it, can't I?"

"Oh, curses!" Calcifer spat. "Why did you let her in here, Michael?" Sulkily he bent his blue face forward until all that could be seen of him was a ring of curly green flames dancing on the logs.

"Thank you," Sophie said, and slapped the heavy pan onto the green ring to make sure Calcifer did not suddenly rise up again.

"I hope your bacon burns," Calcifer said, muffled under the pan.

Sophie slapped slices of bacon into the pan. It was good and hot. The bacon sizzled, and she had to wrap her skirt round her hand to hold the handle. The door opened, but she did not notice because of the sizzling. "Don't be silly," she told Calcifer. "And hold still because I want to break in the eggs."

"Oh, hello, Howl," Michael said helplessly.

Sophie turned round at that, rather hurriedly.

She stared. The tall young fellow in a flamboyant blue-and-silver suit who had just come in stopped in the act of leaning a guitar in the corner. He brushed the fair hair from his rather curious glass-green eyes and stared back. His long, angular face was perplexed.

"Who on earth are you?" said Howl. "Where have I seen you before?"

"I am a total stranger," Sophie lied firmly. After all, Howl had only met her long enough to call her a mouse before, so it was almost true. She ought to have been thanking her stars for the lucky escape she'd had then, she supposed, but in fact her main thought was, Good gracious! Wizard Howl is only a child in his twenties, for all his wickedness! It made such a difference to be old, she thought as she turned the bacon over in the pan. And she would have died rather than let this overdressed boy know she was the girl he had pitied on May Day. Hearts and souls did not enter into it. Howl was not going to know.

"She says her name's Sophie," Michael said. "She came last night."

"How did she make Calcifer bend down?" said Howl.

"She bullied me!" Calcifer said in a piteous, muffled voice from under the sizzling pan.

"Not many people can do that," Howl said thoughtfully. He propped his guitar in the corner and came over to the hearth. The smell of hyacinths mixed with the smell of bacon as he shoved Sophie firmly aside. "Calcifer doesn't like anyone but me to cook on him," he said, kneeling down and wrapping one trailing sleeve round his hand to hold the pan. "Pass me two more slices of bacon and six eggs, please, and tell me why you've come here."

Sophie stared at the blue jewel hanging from Howl's ear and passed him egg after egg. "Why I came, young man?" she said. It was obvious after what she had seen of the castle. "I came because I'm your new cleaning lady, of course."

"Are you indeed?" Howl said, cracking the eggs one-handed and tossing the shells among the logs, where Calcifer seemed to be eating them with a lot of snarling and gobbling. "Who says you are?"

"*I* do," said Sophie, and she added piously, "I can clean the dirt from this place even if I can't clean you from your wickedness, young man."

"Howl's not wicked," Michael said.

"Yes I am," Howl contradicted him. "You forget just how wicked I'm being at the moment, Michael." He jerked his chin at Sophie. "If you're so anxious to be of use, my good woman, find some knives and forks and clear the bench."

There were tall stools under the workbench. Michael was pulling them out to sit on and pushing aside all the things on top of it to make room for some knives and forks he had taken from a drawer in the side of it. Sophie went to help him. She had not expected Howl to welcome her, of course, but he had not even so far agreed to let her stay beyond breakfast. Since Michael did not seem to need help, Sophie shuffled over to her stick and put it slowly and showily in the broom cupboard. When that did not seem to attract Howl's attention, she said, "You can take me on for a month's trial, if you like."

Wizard Howl said nothing but "Plates, please, Michael," and stood up holding the smoking pan. Calcifer sprang up with a roar of relief and blazed high in the chimney.

Sophie made another attempt to pin the Wizard down. "If I'm going to be cleaning here for the next month," she said, "I'd like to know where the rest of the castle is. I can only find this one room and the bathroom."

To her surprise, both Michael and the Wizard roared with laughter.

It was not until they had almost finished breakfast that Sophie discovered what had made them laugh. Howl was not only hard to pin down. He seemed to dislike answering any questions at all. Sophie gave up asking him and asked Michael instead.

"Tell her," said Howl. "It will stop her pestering."

"There isn't any more of the castle," Michael said, "except what you've seen and two bedrooms upstairs."

"What?" Sophie exclaimed.

Howl and Michael laughed again. "Howl and Calcifer invented the castle," Michael explained, "and Calcifer keeps it going. The inside of it is really just Howl's old house in Porthaven, which is the only real part."

"But Porthaven's miles down near the sea!" Sophie said. "I call that too bad! What do you mean by having this great, ugly castle rushing about the hills and frightening everyone in Market Chipping to death?"

Howl shrugged. "What an outspoken old woman you are! I've reached that stage in my career when I need to impress everyone with my power and wickedness. I can't have the King thinking well of me. And last year I offended someone very powerful and I need to keep out of their way."

It seemed a funny way to avoid someone, but Sophie supposed wizards had different standards from ordinary people. And she shortly discovered that the castle had other peculiarities. They had finished eating and Michael was piling the plates in the slimy sink beside the bench when there came a loud, hollow knocking at the door.

Calcifer blazed up. "Kingsbury door!"

Howl, who was on his way to the bathroom, went to the door instead. There was a square wooden knob above the door, set into the lintel, with a dab of paint on each of its four sides. At that moment there was a green blob on the side that was at the bottom, but Howl turned the knob round so that it had a red blob downward before he opened the door.

Outside stood a personage wearing a stiff white wig and a wide hat on top of that. He was clothed in scarlet and purple and gold, and he held up a little staff decorated with ribbons like an infant maypole. He bowed. Scents of cloves and orange blossom blew into the room.

"His Majesty the King presents his compliments and sends payment for two thousand pair of seven-league boots," this person said.

Behind him Sophie had glimpses of a coach waiting in a street full of sumptuous houses covered with painted carvings, and towers and spires and domes beyond that, of a splendor she had barely before imagined. She was sorry it took so little time for the person at the door to hand over a long, silken, chinking purse, and for Howl to take the purse, bow back, and shut the door. Howl turned the square knob back so that the green blob was downward again and stowed the long purse in his pocket. Sophie saw Michael's eyes follow the purse in an urgent, worried way.

Howl went straight to the bathroom then, calling out, "I need hot water in here, Calcifer!" and was gone for a long, long time.

Sophie could not restrain her curiosity. "Whoever

was that at the door?" she asked Michael. "Or do I mean *wherever?*"

"That door gives on Kingsbury," Michael said, "where the King lives. I think that man was the Chancellor's clerk. And," he added worriedly to Calcifer, "I do wish he hadn't given Howl all that money."

"Is Howl going to let me stay here?" Sophie asked.

"If he is, you'll never pin him down," Michael answered. "He hates being pinned down to anything."

Chapter 5:

●━◆━●

Which is far too full of washing

The only thing to do, Sophie decided, was to show Howl that she was an excellent cleaning lady, a real treasure. She tied an old rag round her wispy white hair, she rolled the sleeves up her skinny old arms and wrapped an old tablecloth from the broom cupboard round her as an apron. It was rather a relief to think there were only four rooms to clean instead of a whole castle. She grabbed up a bucket and besom and got to work.

"What are you doing?" cried Michael and Calcifer in a horrified chorus.

"Cleaning up," Sophie replied firmly. "The place is a disgrace."

Calcifer said, "It doesn't need it," and Michael muttered, "Howl will kick you out!" but Sophie ignored them both. Dust flew in clouds.

In the midst of it there came another set of thumps at the door. Calcifer blazed up, calling, "Porthaven door!" and gave a great, sizzling sneeze which shot purple sparks through the dust clouds.

Michael left the workbench and went to the door. Sophie peered through the dust she was raising and saw that this time Michael turned the square knob over the door so that the side with a blue blob of paint on it was downward. Then he opened the door on the street you saw out of the window.

A small girl stood there. "Please, Mr. Fisher," she said, "I've come for that spell for me mum."

"Safety spell for your dad's boat, wasn't it?" Michael said. "Won't be a moment." He went back to the bench and measured powder from a jar from the shelves into a square of paper. While he was doing it, the little girl peered in at Sophie as curiously as Sophie peered out at her. Michael twisted the paper round the powder and came back saying, "Tell her to sprinkle it right along the boat. It'll last out and back, even if there's a storm."

The girl took the paper and passed over a coin. "Has the Sorcerer got a witch working for him too?" she asked.

"No," said Michael.

"Meaning me?" Sophie called. "Oh, yes, my child. I'm the best and cleanest witch in Ingary."

Michael shut the door, looking exasperated. "That will be all round Porthaven now. Howl may not like that." He turned the knob green-down again.

Sophie cackled to herself a little, quite unrepentant.

Probably she had let the besom she was using put ideas into her head. But it might persuade Howl to let her stay if everyone thought she was working for him. It was odd. As a girl, Sophie would have shriveled with embarrassment at the way she was behaving. As an old woman, she did not mind what she did or said. She found that a great relief.

She went nosily over as Michael lifted up a stone in the hearth and hid the little girl's coin under it. "What are you doing?"

"Calcifer and I try to keep a store of money," Michael said rather guiltily. "Howl spends every penny we've got if we don't."

"Feckless spendthrift!" Calcifer crackled. "He'll spend the King's money faster than I burn a log. No sense."

Sophie sprinkled water from the sink to lay the dust, which made Calcifer shrink back against the chimney. Then she swept the floor all over again. She swept her way toward the door in order to have a look at the square knob above it. The fourth side, which she had not seen used yet, had a blob of black paint on it. Wondering where that led to, Sophie began briskly sweeping the cobwebs off the beams. Michael moaned and Calcifer sneezed again.

Howl came out of the bathroom just then in a waft of steamy perfume. He looked marvelously spruce. Even the silver inlets and embroidery on his suit seemed to have become brighter. He took one look and backed into the bathroom again with a blue-and-silver sleeve protecting his head.

"Stop it, woman!" he said. "Leave those poor spiders alone!"

"These cobwebs are a disgrace!" Sophie declared, fetching them down in bundles.

"Then get them down and leave the spiders," said Howl.

Probably he had a wicked affinity with spiders, Sophie thought. "They'll only make more webs," she said.

"And kill flies, which is very useful," said Howl. "Keep that broom still while I cross my own room, please."

Sophie leaned on the broom and watched Howl cross the room and pick up his guitar. As he put his hand on the door latch, she said, "If the red blob leads to Kingsbury and the blue blob goes to Porthaven, where does the black blob take you?"

"What a nosy old woman you are!" said Howl. "That leads to my private bolt hole and you are not being told where it is." He opened the door onto the wide, moving moorland and the hills.

"When will you be back, Howl?" Michael asked a little despairingly.

Howl pretended not to hear. He said to Sophie, "You're not to kill a single spider while I'm away."

And the door slammed behind him. Michael looked meaningly at Calcifer and sighed. Calcifer crackled with malicious laughter.

Since nobody explained where Howl had gone, Sophie concluded he was off to hunt young girls again and got down to work with more righteous vigor than ever. She did not dare harm any spiders after what Howl had said. So she banged at the beams with the broom, screaming, "Out, spiders! Out of my way!" Spiders scrambled for their lives every which way, and webs fell in swathes. Then of course she had to sweep the floor yet again. After that, she got down on her knees and scrubbed it.

"I wish you'd stop!" Michael said, sitting on the stairs out of her way.

Calcifer, cowering at the back of the grate, muttered, "I wish I'd never made that bargain with you now!"

Sophie scrubbed on vigorously. "You'll be much happier when it's all nice and clean," she said.

"But I'm miserable *now!*" Michael protested.

Howl did not come back again until late that night. By that time Sophie had swept and scrubbed herself into a state when she could hardly move. She was sitting hunched up in the chair, aching all over. Michael took hold of Howl by a trailing sleeve and towed him over to the bathroom, where Sophie could hear him pouring out complaints in a passionate mutter. Phrases like "terrible old biddy" and "won't listen to a *word!*" were quite easy to hear, even though Calcifer was roaring, "Howl, stop her! She's killing us both!"

But all Howl said, when Michael let go of him, was "Did you kill any spiders?"

"Of course not!" Sophie snapped. Her aches made her irritable. "They look at me and run for their lives. What are they? All the girls whose hearts you ate?"

Howl laughed. "No, just simple spiders," he said and went dreamily away upstairs.

Michael sighed. He went into the broom cupboard and hunted until he found an old folding bed, a straw mattress, and some rugs, which he put into the arched space under the stairs. "You'd better sleep here tonight," he told Sophie.

"Does that mean Howl's going to let me stay?" Sophie asked.

"I don't know!" Michael said irritably. "Howl never commits himself to anything. I was here six months before he seemed to notice I was living here and made me his apprentice. I just thought a bed would be better than the chair."

"Then thank you very much," Sophie said gratefully. The bed was indeed more comfortable than a chair, and when Calcifer complained he was hungry in the night, it was an easy matter for Sophie to creak her way out and give him another log.

In the days that followed, Sophie cleaned her way remorselessly through the castle. She really enjoyed herself. Telling herself she was looking for clues, she washed the window, she cleaned out the oozing sink, and she made Michael clear everything off the work-bench and the shelves so that she could scrub them. She had everything out of the cupboards and down from the beams and cleaned those too. The human skull, she fancied, began to look as long-suffering as Michael. It had been moved so often. Then she tacked an old sheet to the beams nearest the fireplace and forced Calcifer to bend his head down while she swept the chimney. Calcifer hated that. He crackled with mean laughter when Sophie discovered that soot had got all over the room and she had to clean it all again. That was Sophie's trouble. She was remorseless, but she lacked method. But there was this method to her remorselessness: she calculated that she could not clean this thoroughly without sooner or later coming across Howl's hidden hoard of girls' souls, or chewed hearts—or else something that explained Calcifer's contract. Up the chimney, guarded by Calcifer, had struck her as a good hiding place. But there was noth-ing there but quantities of soot, which Sophie stored in bags in the yard. The yard was high on her list of hiding places.

Every time Howl came in, Michael and Calcifer

complained loudly about Sophie. But Howl did not seem to attend. Nor did he seem to notice the cleanliness. And nor did he notice that the food closet became very well stocked with cakes and jam and the occasional lettuce.

For, as Michael had prophesied, word had gone round Porthaven. People came to the door to look at Sophie. They called her Mrs. Witch in Porthaven and Madam Sorceress in Kingsbury. Word had gone round the capital too. Though the people who came to the Kingsbury door were better dressed than those in Porthaven, no one in either place liked to call on someone so powerful without an excuse. So Sophie was always having to pause in her work to nod and smile and take in a gift, or to get Michael to put up a quick spell for someone. Some of the gifts were nice things—pictures, strings of shells, and useful aprons. Sophie used the aprons daily and hung the shells and pictures round her cubbyhole under the stairs, which soon began to look very homelike indeed.

Sophie knew she would miss this when Howl turned her out. She became more and more afraid that he would. She knew he could not go on ignoring her forever.

She cleaned the bathroom next. That took her days, because Howl spent so long in it every day before he went out. As soon as he went, leaving it full of steam and scented spells, Sophie moved in. "Now we'll see about that contract!" she muttered at the bath, but her main target was of course the shelf of packets, jars, and tubes. She took every one of them down, on the pretext of scrubbing the shelf, and spent most of a day carefully going through them to see if the ones labeled SKIN, EYES, and HAIR were in fact pieces of girl. As far as she could tell, they were all just creams and powders and paint. If they once had been girls, then Sophie thought Howl had used the tube FOR DECAY on them and rotted them down the washbasin too thoroughly to recall. But she hoped they were only cosmetics in the packets.

She put the things back on the shelf and scrubbed. That night, as she sat aching in the chair, Calcifer grumbled that he had drained one hot spring dry for her.

"Where are the hot springs?" Sophie asked. She was curious about everything these days.

"Under the Porthaven Marshes mostly," Calcifer said. "But if you go on like this, I'll have to fetch hot water from the Waste. When are you going to stop cleaning and find out how to break my contract?"

"In good time," said Sophie. "How can I get the terms out of Howl if he's never in? Is he always away this much?"

"Only when he's after a lady," Calcifer said.

When the bathroom was clean and gleaming, Sophie scrubbed the stairs and the landing upstairs.

Then she moved on into Michael's small front room. Michael, who by this time seemed to be accepting Sophie gloomily as a sort of natural disaster, gave a yell of dismay and pounded upstairs to rescue his most treasured possessions. They were in an old box under his worm-eaten little bed. As he hurried the box protectively away, Sophie glimpsed a blue ribbon and a spun-sugar rose in it, on top of what seemed to be letters.

"So Michael has a sweetheart!" she said to herself as she flung the window open—it opened into the street in Porthaven too—and heaved his bedding across the sill to air. Considering how nosy she had lately become, Sophie was rather surprised at herself for not asking Michael who his girl was and how he kept her safe from Howl.

She swept such quantities of dust and rubbish from Michael's room that she nearly swamped Calcifer trying to burn it all.

"You'll be the death of me! You're as heartless as Howl!" Calcifer choked. Only his green hair and a blue piece of his long forehead showed.

Michael put his precious box in the drawer of the workbench and locked the drawer. "I wish Howl would listen to us!" he said. "Why is this girl taking him so long?"

The next day Sophie tried to start on the back-yard. But it was raining in Porthaven that day, driving against the window and pattering in the chimney, making Calcifer hiss with annoyance. The yard was part of the Porthaven house too, so it was pouring out there when Sophie opened the door. She put her apron over her head and rummaged a little, and before she got too wet, she found a bucket of whitewash and a large paintbrush. She took these indoors and set to work on the walls. She found an old stepladder in the broom cupboard and she whitewashed the ceiling between the beams too. It rained for the next two days in Porthaven, though when Howl opened the door with the knob green-blob-down and stepped out onto the hill, the weather there was sunny, with big cloud shadows racing over the heather faster than the castle could move. Sophie whitewashed her cubbyhole, the stairs, the landing, and Michael's room.

"What's happened in here?" Howl asked when he came in on the third day. "It seems much lighter."

"Sophie," Michael said in a voice of doom.

"I should have guessed," Howl said as he disappeared into the bathroom.

"He *noticed!*" Michael whispered to Calcifer. "The girl must be giving in at last!"

It was still drizzling in Porthaven the next day. Sophie tied on her headcloth, rolled up her sleeves, and girded on her apron. She collected her besom, her bucket, and her soap, and as soon as Howl was out of the door, she set off like an elderly avenging angel to clean Howl's bedroom.

She had left that until last for fear of what she would find. She had not even dared peep into it. And that was silly, she thought as she hobbled up the stairs. By now it was clear that Calcifer did all the strong magic in the castle and Michael did all the hackwork, while Howl gadded off catching girls and exploiting the other two just as Fanny had exploited her. Sophie had never found Howl particularly frightening. Now she felt nothing but contempt.

She arrived on the landing and found Howl standing in the doorway of his bedroom. He was leaning lazily on one hand, completely blocking her way.

"No you don't," he said quite pleasantly. "I want it dirty, thank you."

Sophie gaped at him. "Where did you come from? I saw you go out."

"I meant you to," said Howl. "You'd done your worst with Calcifer and poor Michael. It stood to reason you'd descend on me today. And whatever Calcifer told you, I *am* a wizard, you know. Didn't you think I could do magic?"

This undermined all Sophie's assumptions. She would have died rather than admit it. "Everyone knows you're a wizard, young man," she said severely. "But that doesn't alter the fact that your castle is the dirtiest place I've ever been in." She looked into the room past Howl's dangling blue-and-silver sleeve.

The carpet on the floor was littered like a bird's nest. She glimpsed peeling walls and a shelf full of books, some of them very queer-looking. There was no sign of a pile of gnawed hearts, but those were probably behind or under the huge fourposter bed. Its hangings were gray-white with dust and they prevented her from seeing what the window looked out onto.

Howl swung his sleeve in front of her face. "Uh-uh. Don't be nosy."

"I'm not being nosy!" Sophie protested. "That room—!"

"Yes, you *are* nosy," said Howl. "You're a dreadfully nosy, horribly bossy, appallingly clean old woman. Control yourself. You're victimizing us all."

"But it's a pigsty," said Sophie. "I can't help what I am!"

"Yes you can," said Howl. "And I like my room the way it is. You must admit I have a right to live in a pigsty if I want. Now go downstairs and think of something else to do. Please. I hate quarreling with people."

There was nothing Sophie could do but hobble away with her bucket clanking by her side. She was a little shaken, and very surprised that Howl had not thrown her out of the castle on the spot. But since he had not, she thought of the next thing that needed doing at once. She opened the door beside the stairs, found the drizzle had almost stopped, and sallied out into the yard, where she began vigorously sorting through piles of dripping rubbish.

There was a metallic *clash!* and Howl appeared again, stumbling slightly, in the middle of the large sheet of rusty iron Sophie had been going to move next.

"Not here either," he said. "You are a terror, aren't you? Leave this yard alone. I know just where everything is in it, and I won't be able to find the things I need for my transport spells if you tidy them up."

So there was probably a bundle of souls or a box of chewed hearts somewhere out here, Sophie thought. She felt really thwarted. "Tidying up is what I'm *here* for!" she shouted at Howl.

"Then you must think of a new meaning for your life," Howl said. For a moment it seemed as if he was going to lose his temper too. His strange, pale eyes all but glared at Sophie. But he controlled himself and said, "Now trot along indoors, you overactive old thing, and find something else to play with before I get angry. I hate getting angry."

Sophie folded her skinny arms. She did not like being glared at by eyes like glass marbles. "Of course you hate getting angry!" she retorted. "You don't like anything unpleasant, do you? You're a slitherer-outer, that's what you are! You slither away from anything you don't like!"

Howl gave a forced sort of smile. "Well now," he said. "Now we both know each other's faults. Now go back into the house. Go on. Back." He advanced on Sophie, waving her toward the door. The sleeve on his waving arm caught the edge of the rusty metal, jerked, and tore. "Damnation!" said Howl, holding up the trailing blue-and-silver ends. "Look what you've made me do!"

"I can mend it," Sophie said.

Howl gave her another glassy look. "There you go again," he said. "How you must love servitude!" He took his torn sleeve gently between the fingers of his right hand and pulled it through them. As the blue-and-silver fabric left his fingers, there was no tear in it at all. "There," he said. "Understand?"

Sophie hobbled back indoors, rather chastened. Wizards clearly had no need to work in the ordinary way. Howl had shown her he really was a wizard to be reckoned with. "Why didn't he turn me out?" she said, half to herself and half to Michael.

"It beats me," said Michael. "But I think he goes by Calcifer. Most people who come in here either don't notice Calcifer, or they're scared stiff of him."

Chapter 6:

---·—❦—·---

In which Howl expresses his feelings with green slime

Howl did not go out that day, nor for the next few days. Sophie sat quietly in the chair by the hearth, keeping out of his way and thinking. She saw that, much as Howl deserved it, she had been taking out her feelings on the castle when she was really angry with the Witch of the Waste. And she was a little upset at the thought that she was here on false pretenses. Howl might think Calcifer liked her, but Sophie knew Calcifer had simply seized on the chance to make a bargain with her. Sophie rather thought she had let Calcifer down.

This state of mind did not last. Sophie discovered a pile of Michael's clothes that needed mending. She fetched out thimble, scissors, and thread from her sewing pocket and set to work. By that evening she was cheerful enough to join in Calcifer's silly little song about saucepans.

"Happy in your work?" Howl said sarcastically.

"I need more to do," Sophie said.

"My old suit needs mending, if you have to feel busy," said Howl.

This seemed to mean that Howl was no longer annoyed. Sophie was relieved. She had been almost frightened that morning.

It was clear Howl had not yet caught the girl he was after. Sophie listened to Michael asking rather obvious questions about it, and Howl slithering neatly out of answering any of them. "He *is* a slithererouter," Sophie murmured to a pair of Michael's socks. "Can't face his own wickedness." She watched Howl being restlessly busy in order to hide his discontent. That was something Sophie understood rather well.

At the bench Howl worked a good deal harder and faster than Michael, putting spells together in an expert but slapdash way. From the look on Michael's face, most of the spells were both unusual and hard to do. But Howl would leave a spell midway and dash up to his bedroom to look after something hidden—and no doubt sinister—going on up there, and then shortly race out into the yard to tinker with a large spell out there. Sophie opened the door a crack and was rather amazed to see the elegant wizard kneeling in the mud with his long sleeves tied together behind his neck to keep them out of the way while he carefully heaved a tangle of greasy metal into a special framework of some kind.

That spell was for the King. Another overdressed

and scented messenger arrived with a letter and a long, long speech in which he wondered if Howl could possibly spare time, no doubt valuably employed in other ways, to bend his powerful and ingenious mind to a small problem experienced by His Royal Majesty——to whit, how an army might get its heavy wagons through marsh and rough ground. Howl was wonderfully polite and long-winded in reply. He said no. But the messenger spoke for a further half-hour, at the end of which he and Howl bowed to one another and Howl agreed to do the spell.

"This is a bit ominous," Howl said to Michael when the messenger had gone. "What did Suliman have to get himself lost in the Waste for? The King seems to think I'll do instead."

"He wasn't as inventive as you, by all accounts," Michael said.

"I'm too patient and too polite," Howl said gloomily. "I should have overcharged him even more."

Howl was equally patient and polite with customers from Porthaven, but, as Michael anxiously pointed out, the trouble was that Howl did not charge these people enough. This was after Howl had listened for an hour to the reasons why a seaman's wife could not pay him a penny yet, and then promised a sea captain a wind spell for almost nothing. Howl eluded Michael's arguments by giving him a magic lesson.

Sophie sewed buttons on Michael's shirts and

listened to Howl going through a spell with Michael. "I know *I'm* slapdash," he was saying, "but there's no need for you to copy me. Always read it right through, carefully, first. The shape of it should tell you a lot, whether it's self-fulfilling, or self-discovering, or simple incantation, or mixed action and speech. When you've decided that, go through again and decide which bits mean what they say and which bits are put as a puzzle. You're getting on to the more powerful kinds now. You'll find every spell of power has at least one deliberate mistake or mystery in it to prevent accidents. You have to spot those. Now take this spell . . ."

Listening to Michael's halting replies to Howl's questions, and watching Howl scribble remarks on the paper with a strange, everlasting quill pen, Sophie realized that she could learn a lot too. It dawned on her that if Martha could discover the spell to swap herself and Lettie about at Mrs. Fairfax's, then she ought to be able to do the same here. With a bit of luck, there might be no need to rely on Calcifer.

When Howl was satisfied that Michael had forgotten all about how much or little he charged people in Porthaven, he took him out into the yard to help with the King's spell. Sophie creaked to her feet and hobbled to the bench. The spell was clear enough, but Howl's scrawled remarks defeated her. "I've never *seen* such writing!" she grumbled to the human skull.

"Does he use a pen or a poker?" She sorted eagerly through every scrap of paper on the bench and examined the powders and liquids in the crooked jars. "Yes, let's admit it," she told the skull. "I snoop. And I have my proper reward. I can find out how to cure fowl pest and abate whooping cough, raise a wind and remove hairs from the face. If Martha had found this lot, she'd still be at Mrs. Fairfax's."

Howl, it seemed to Sophie, went and examined all the things she had moved when he came in from the yard. But that seemed to be only restlessness. He seemed not to know what to do with himself after that. Sophie heard him roving up and down during the night. He was only an hour in the bathroom the next morning. He seemed not to be able to contain himself while Michael put on his best plum velvet suit, ready to go to the Palace in Kingsbury, and the two of them wrapped the bulky spell up in golden paper. The spell must have been surprisingly light for its size. Michael could carry it on his own easily, with both his arms wrapped round it. Howl turned the knob over the door red-down for him and sent him out into the street among the painted houses.

"They're expecting it," Howl said. "You should only have to wait most of the morning. Tell them a child could work it. Show them. And when you come back, I'll have a spell of power for you to get to work on. So long."

He shut the door and roved round the room again. "My feet itch," he said suddenly. "I'm going for a walk on the hills. Tell Michael the spell I promised him is on the bench. And here's for you to keep busy with."

Sophie found a gray-and-scarlet suit, as fancy as the blue-and-silver one, dropped into her lap from nowhere. Howl meanwhile picked up his guitar from its corner, turned the doorknob green-down, and stepped out among the scudding heather above Market Chipping.

"*His* feet itch!" grumbled Calcifer. There was a fog down in Porthaven. Calcifer was low among his logs, moving uneasily this way and that to avoid drips in the chimney. "How does he think *I* feel, stuck in a damp grate like this?"

"Then you'll have to give me a hint at least about how to break your contract," Sophie said, shaking out the gray-and-scarlet suit. "Goodness, you're a fine suit, even if you are a bit worn! Built to pull in the girls, aren't you?"

"I *have* given you a hint!" Calcifer fizzed.

"Then you'll have to give it me again. I didn't catch it," Sophie said as she laid the suit down and hobbled to the door.

"If I give you a hint and tell you it's a hint, it will be information, and I'm not allowed to give that," Calcifer said. "Where are you going?"

"To do something I didn't dare do until they were both out," Sophie said. She twisted the square knob over the door until the black blob pointed downward. Then she opened the door.

There was nothing outside. It was neither black, nor gray, nor white. It was not thick, or transparent. It did not move. It had no smell and no feel. When Sophie put a very cautious finger out into it, it was neither hot nor cold. It felt of nothing. It seemed utterly and completely nothing.

"What *is* this?" she asked Calcifer.

Calcifer was as interested as Sophie. His blue face was leaning right out of the grate to see the door. He had forgotten the fog. "I don't know," he whispered. "I only maintain it. All I know is that it's on the side of the castle that no one can walk around. It feels quite far away."

"It feels beyond the moon!" said Sophie. She shut the door and turned the knob green-downward. She hesitated a minute and then started to hobble to the stairs.

"He's locked it," said Calcifer. "He told me to tell you if you tried to snoop again."

"Oh," said Sophie. "What has he got up there?"

"I've no idea," said Calcifer. "I don't know anything about upstairs. If you only knew how frustrating it is! I can't even really see outside the castle. Only enough to see what direction I'm going in."

Sophie, feeling equally frustrated, sat down and began mending the gray-and-scarlet suit. Michael came in quite soon after that.

"The King saw me at once," he said. "He——" He looked round the room. His eyes went to the empty corner where the guitar usually stood. "Oh, no!" he said. "Not the lady friend again! I thought she'd fallen in love with him and it was all over days ago. What's keeping her?"

Calcifer fizzed wickedly. "You got the signs wrong. Heartless Howl is finding this lady rather tough. He decided to leave her alone a few days to see if that would help. That's all."

"Bother!" said Michael. "That's bound to mean trouble. And here was I hoping Howl was almost sensible again!"

Sophie banged the suit down on her knees. "Really!" she said. "How can you both talk like that about such utter wickedness! At least, I suppose I can't blame Calcifer, since he's an evil demon. But you, Michael——!"

"I don't think I'm evil," Calcifer protested.

"But I'm not calm about it, if that's what you think!" Michael said. "If you knew the trouble we've had because Howl will keep falling in love like this! We've had lawsuits, and suitors with swords, and mothers with rolling pins, and fathers and uncles with cudgels. And aunts. Aunts are terrible. They go for you with hat pins. But the worst is when the girl herself finds out where Howl lives and turns up at the door, crying and miserable. Howl goes out through the back door and Calcifer and I have to deal with them all."

"I hate the unhappy ones," Calcifer said. "They drip on me. I'd rather have them angry."

"Now let's get this straight," Sophie said, clenching her fists knobbily in red satin. "What does Howl do to these poor females? I was told he ate their hearts and took their souls away."

Michael laughed uncomfortably. "Then you must come from Market Chipping. Howl sent me down there to blacken his name when we first set up the castle. I—er—I said that sort of thing. It's what aunts usually say. It's only true in a manner of speaking."

"Howl's very fickle," said Calcifer. "He's only interested until the girl falls in love with him. Then he can't be bothered with her."

"But he can't rest until he's made her love him," Michael said eagerly. "You can't get any sense out of him until he has. I always look forward to the time when the girl falls for him. Things get better then."

"Until they track him down," said Calcifer.

"You'd think he'd have the sense to give them a false name," Sophie said scornfully. The scorn was to hide the fact that she was feeling somewhat foolish.

"Oh, he always does," Michael said. "He loves giving false names and posing as things. He does it even when he's not courting girls. Haven't you noticed that he's Sorcerer Jenkin in Porthaven, and Wizard Pendragon in Kingsbury, as well as Horrible Howl in the castle?"

Sophie had not noticed, which made her feel more foolish still. And feeling foolish made her angry. "Well, I still think it's wicked, going round making poor girls unhappy," she said. "It's heartless and pointless."

"He's made that way," said Calcifer.

Michael pulled a three-legged stool up to the fire and sat on it while Sophie sewed, telling her of Howl's conquests and some of the trouble that had happened afterward. Sophie muttered at the fine suit. She still felt very foolish. "So you ate hearts, did you, suit? Why do aunts put things so *oddly* when they talk about their nieces? Probably fancied you themselves, my good suit. How would you feel with a raging aunt after you, eh?" As Michael told her the story of the particular aunt he had in mind, it occurred to Sophie that it was probably just as well the rumors of Howl had come to Market Chipping in those words. She could imagine a strong-minded girl like Lettie otherwise getting very interested in Howl and ending up very unhappy.

Michael had just suggested lunch and Calcifer as

usual had groaned when Howl flung the door open and came in, more discontented than ever.

"Something to eat?" said Sophie.

"No," said Howl. "Hot water in the bathroom, Calcifer." He stood moodily in the bathroom door a moment. "Sophie, have you tidied this shelf of spells in here, by any chance?"

Sophie felt more foolish than ever. Nothing would have possessed her to admit that she had gone through all those packets and jars looking for pieces of girl. "I haven't touched a thing," she replied virtuously as she went to get the frying pan.

"I hope you didn't," Michael said uneasily as the bathroom door slammed.

Rinsings and gushings came from the bathroom while Sophie fried lunch. "He's using a lot of hot water," Calcifer said from under the pan. "I think he's tinting his hair. I hope you left the hair spells alone. For a plain man with mud-colored hair, he's terribly vain about his looks."

"Oh, shut up!" snapped Sophie. "I put everything back just where I found it!" She was so cross that she emptied the pan of eggs and bacon over Calcifer.

Calcifer, of course, ate them with enormous enthusiasm and much flaring and gobbling. Sophie fried more over the spitting flames. She and Michael ate them. They were clearing away, and Calcifer was running his blue tongue round his purple lips, when the bathroom door crashed open and Howl shot out, wailing with despair.

"Look at this!" he shouted. "*Look* at it! What has that one-woman force of chaos *done* to these spells?"

Sophie and Michael whirled round and looked at Howl. His hair was wet, but, apart from that, neither of them could see that it looked any different.

"If you mean me——" Sophie began.

"I *do* mean you! Look!" Howl shrieked. He sat down with a thump on the three-legged stool and jabbed at his wet head with his finger. "Look. Survey. Inspect. My hair is ruined! I look like a pan of bacon and eggs!"

Michael and Sophie bent nervously over Howl's head. It seemed the usual flaxen color right to the roots. The only difference might have been a slight, very slight, trace of red. Sophie found that agreeable. It reminded her a little of the color her own hair should have been.

"I think it's very nice," she said.

"*Nice!*" screamed Howl. "You would! You did it on purpose. You couldn't rest until you made me miserable too. Look at it! It's *ginger!* I shall have to *hide* until it's grown out!" He spread his arms out passionately. "Despair!" he yelled. "Anguish! Horror!"

The room turned dim. Huge, cloudy, human-looking shapes bellied up in all four corners and advanced on Sophie and Michael, howling as they came. The howls began as moaning horror, and went up to despairing brays, and then up again to screams of pain and terror. Sophie pressed her hands to her ears, but the screams pressed through her hands, louder and louder still, more horrible every second. Calcifer shrank hurriedly down in the grate and flickered his way under his lowest log. Michael grabbed Sophie by her elbow and dragged her to the door. He spun the knob to blue-down, kicked the door open, and got them both out into the street in Porthaven as fast as he could.

The noise was almost as horrible out there. Doors were opening all down the road and people were running out with their hands over their ears.

"Ought we to leave him alone in that state?" Sophie quavered.

"Yes," said Michael. "If he thinks it's your fault, then definitely."

They hurried through the town, pursued by throbbing screams. Quite a crowd came with them. In spite of the fact that the fog had now become a seeping sea drizzle, everyone made for the harbor or the sands, where the noise seemed easier to bear. The gray vastness of the sea soaked it up a little. Everyone stood in damp huddles, looking out at the misty white horizon and the dripping ropes on the moored ships while the noise became a gigantic, heartbroken sobbing. Sophie reflected that she was seeing the sea close for the first time in her life. It was a pity that she was not enjoying it more.

The sobs died away to vast, miserable sighs and then to silence. People began cautiously to go back into the town. Some of them came timidly up to Sophie.

"Is something wrong with the poor Sorcerer, Mrs. Witch?"

"He's a little unhappy today," Michael said. "Come on. I think we can risk going back now."

As they went along the stone quayside, several sailors called out anxiously from the moored ships, wanting to know if the noise meant storms or bad luck.

"Not at all," Sophie called back. "It's all over now."

But it was not. They came back to the Wizard's house, which was an ordinary crooked little building from the outside that Sophie would not have recognized if Michael had not been with her. Michael opened the shabby little door rather cautiously. Inside, Howl was still sitting on the stool. He sat in an attitude of utter despair. And he was covered all over in thick green slime.

There were horrendous, dramatic, violent quantities of green slime—oodles of it. It covered Howl completely. It draped his head and shoulders in sticky dollops, heaping on his knees and hands, trickling in glops down his legs, and dripping off the stool in sticky strands. It was in oozing ponds and crawling pools over most of the floor. Long fingers of it had crept into the hearth. It smelled vile.

"Save me!" Calcifer cried in a hoarse whisper. He was down to two desperately flickering small flames. "This stuff is going to put me out!"

Sophie held up her skirt and marched as near Howl as she could get—which was not very near. "Stop it!" she said. "Stop it at once! You are behaving just like a *baby!*"

Howl did not move or answer. His face stared from behind the slime, white and tragic and wide-eyed.

"What shall we do? Is he dead?" Michael asked, jittering beside the door.

Michael was a nice boy, Sophie thought, but a bit helpless in a crisis. "No, of course he isn't," she said. "And if it wasn't for Calcifer, he could behave like a jellied eel all day for all I care! Open the bathroom door."

While Michael was working his way between pools of slime to the bathroom, Sophie threw her apron into the hearth to stop more of the stuff getting near Calcifer and snatched up the shovel. She scooped up loads of ash and dumped them in the biggest pools of slime. It hissed violently. The room filled with steam and smelled worse than ever. Sophie furled up her sleeves, bent her back to get a good purchase on the Wizard's slimy knees, and pushed Howl, stool and all, toward the bathroom. Her feet slipped and skidded in the slime, but of course the ooziness helped the stool to move too. Michael came and pulled at Howl's slime-draped sleeves. Together, they trundled him into the bathroom. There, since Howl still refused to move, they shunted him into the shower stall.

"Hot water, Calcifer!" Sophie panted grimly. "Very hot."

It took an hour to wash the slime off Howl. It took Michael another hour to persuade Howl to get off the stool and into dry clothes. Luckily, the gray-and-scarlet suit Sophie had just mended had been draped over the back of the chair, out of the way of the slime. The blue-and-silver suit was ruined. Sophie told Michael to put it in the bath to soak. Meanwhile, mumbling and grumbling, she fetched more hot water. She turned the doorknob green-down and swept all the slime out onto the moors. The castle left a trail like a snail in the heather, but it was an easy way to get rid of the slime. There were some advantages to living in a moving castle, Sophie thought as she washed the floor. She wondered if Howl's noises had been coming from the castle too. In which case, she pitied the folk of Market Chipping.

By this time Sophie was tired and cross. She knew the green slime was Howl's revenge on her, and she was not at all prepared to be sympathetic when Michael finally led Howl forth from the bathroom, clothed in gray and scarlet, and sat him tenderly in the chair by the hearth.

"That was plain stupid!" Calcifer sputtered. "Were you trying to get rid of the best part of your magic, or something?"

Howl took no notice. He just sat, looking tragic and shivering.

"I can't get him to *speak!*" Michael whispered miserably.

"It's just a tantrum," Sophie said. Martha and Lettie were good at having tantrums too. She knew how to deal with those. On the other hand, it is quite a risk to spank a wizard for getting hysterical about his hair. Anyway, Sophie's experience told her that tantrums are seldom about the thing they appear to be about. She made Calcifer move over so that she could balance a pan of milk on the logs. When it was warm, she thrust a mugful into Howl's hands. "Drink it," she said. "Now, what was all this fuss about? Is it this young lady you keep going to see?"

Howl sipped the milk dolefully. "Yes," he said. "I left her alone to see if that would make her remember me fondly, and it hasn't. She wasn't sure, even when I last saw her. Now she tells me there's another fellow."

He sounded so miserable that Sophie felt quite sorry for him. Now his hair was dry, she noticed guiltily, it really was almost pink.

"She's the most beautiful girl there ever was in these parts," Howl went on mournfully. "I love her so dearly, but she scorns my deep devotion and gets sorry for another fellow. How *can* she have another fellow after all this attention I've given her? They usually get rid of the other fellows as soon as I come along."

Sophie's sympathy shrank quite sharply. It occurred to her that if Howl could cover himself with green slime so easily, then he could just as easily turn his hair the proper color. "Then why don't you feed the girl a love potion and get it over with?" she said.

"Oh, no," said Howl. "That's not playing the game. That would spoil all the fun."

Sophie's sympathy shrank again. A game, was it? "Don't you ever give a thought for the poor girl?" she snapped.

Howl finished the milk and gazed into the mug with a sentimental smile. "I think of her all the time," he said. "Lovely, lovely Lettie Hatter."

Sophie's sympathy went for good, with a sharp bang. A good deal of anxiety took its place. Oh, Martha! she thought. You *have* been busy! So it wasn't anyone in Cesari's you were talking about!

Chapter 7:

◆

In which a scarecrow prevents Sophie from leaving the castle

Only a particularly bad attack of aches and pains prevented Sophie from setting out for Market Chipping that evening. But the drizzle in Porthaven had got into her bones. She lay in her cubbyhole and ached and worried about Martha. It might not be so bad, she thought. She only had to tell Martha that the suitor she was not sure about was none other than Wizard Howl. That would scare Martha off. And she would tell Martha that the way to scare Howl off was to announce that she was in love with him, and then perhaps to threaten him with aunts.

Sophie was still creaking when she got up next morning. "*Curse* the Witch of the Waste!" she muttered to her stick as she got it out, ready to leave. She could hear Howl singing in the bathroom as if he had never had a tantrum in his life. She tiptoed to the door as fast as she could hobble.

Howl of course came out of the bathroom before she reached it. Sophie looked at him sourly. He was all spruce and dashing, scented gently with apple blossom. The sunlight from the window dazzled off his gray-and-scarlet suit and made a faintly pink halo of his hair.

"I think my hair looks rather good this color," he said.

"Do you indeed?" grumped Sophie.

"It goes with this suit," said Howl. "You have quite a touch with your needle, don't you? You've given the suit more style somehow."

"Huh!" said Sophie.

Howl stopped with his hand on the knob above the door. "Aches and pains troubling you?" he said. "Or has something annoyed you?"

"Annoyed?" said Sophie. "Why should I be annoyed? Someone only filled the castle with rotten aspic, and deafened everyone in Porthaven, and scared Calcifer to a cinder, and broke a few hundred hearts. Why should that annoy me?"

Howl laughed. "I apologize," he said, turning the knob to red-down. "The King wants to see me today. I shall probably be kicking my heels in the Palace until evening, but I can do something for your rheumatism when I get back. Don't forget to tell Michael I left that spell for him on the bench." He smiled sunnily at Sophie and stepped out among the spires of Kingsbury.

"And you think that makes it all right!" Sophie

growled as the door shut. But the smile had mollified her. "If that smile works on *me*, then it's no wonder poor Martha doesn't know her own mind!" she muttered.

"I need another log before you go," Calcifer reminded her.

Sophie hobbled to drop another log into the grate. Then she set off to the door again. But here Michael came running downstairs and snatched the remains of a loaf off the bench as he ran to the door. "You don't mind, do you?" he said in an agitated way. "I'll bring a fresh loaf when I come back. I've got something very urgent to see to today, but I'll be back by evening. If the sea captain calls for his wind spell, it's on the end of the bench, clearly labeled." He turned the doorknob green-downward and jumped out onto the windy hillside, loaf clutched to his stomach. "See you!" he shouted as the castle trundled away past him and the door slammed.

"Botheration!" said Sophie. "Calcifer, how does a person open the door when there's no one inside the castle?"

"I'll open it for you, or Michael. Howl does it himself," said Calcifer.

So no one would be locked out when Sophie left. She was not at all sure she would be coming back, but she did not intend to tell Calcifer. She gave Michael time to get well on the way to wherever he was going and set off for the door again. This time Calcifer stopped her.

"If you're going to be away long," he said, "you might leave some logs where I can reach them."

"*Can* you pick up logs?" Sophie asked, intrigued in spite of her impatience.

For answer, Calcifer stretched out a blue arm-shaped flame divided into green fingerlike flames at the end. It was not very long, nor did it look strong. "See? I can almost reach the hearth," he said proudly.

Sophie stacked a pile of logs in front of the grate so that Calcifer could at least reach the top one. "You're not to burn them until you've got them in the grate," she warned him, and she set off for the door yet again.

This time somebody knocked on it before she got there.

It was one of those days, Sophie thought. It must be the sea captain. She put up her hand to turn the knob blue-down.

"No, it's the castle door," Calcifer said. "But I'm not sure—"

Then it was Michael back for some reason, Sophie thought as she opened the door.

A turnip face leered at her. She smelled mildew. Against the wide blue sky, a ragged arm ending in the stump of a stick wheeled round and tried to paw at her. It was a scarecrow. It was only made of sticks and rags, but it was alive, and it was trying to come in.

"Calcifer!" Sophie screamed. "Make the castle go faster!"

The stone blocks round the doorway crunched and grated. The green-brown moorland was suddenly rushing past. The scarecrow's stick arm thumped on the door, and then went scraping along the wall of the castle as the castle left it behind. It wheeled its other arm round and seemed to try to clutch at the stonework. It meant to get into the castle if it could.

Sophie slammed the door shut. This, she thought, just showed how stupid it was for an eldest child to try to seek her fortune! That was the scarecrow she had propped in the hedge on her way to the castle. She had made jokes to it. Now, as if her jokes had brought it to evil life, it had followed her all the way here and tried to paw at her face. She ran to the window to see if the thing was still trying to get into the castle.

Of course, all she could see was a sunny day in Porthaven, with a dozen sails going up a dozen masts beyond the roofs opposite, and a cloud of seagulls circling in the blue sky.

"That's the difficulty of being in several places at once!" Sophie said to the human skull on the bench.

Then, all at once, she discovered the real drawback to being an old woman. Her heart gave a leap and a little stutter, and then seemed to be trying to bang its way out of her chest. It hurt. She shook all over and her knees trembled. She rather thought she might be dying. It was all she could do to get to the chair by the hearth. She sat their panting, clutching her chest.

"Is something the matter?" Calcifer asked.

"Yes. My heart. There was a scarecrow at the door!" Sophie gasped.

"What has a scarecrow to do with your heart?" Calcifer asked.

"It was trying to get in here. It gave me a terrible fright. And my heart—but you wouldn't understand, you silly young demon!" Sophie panted. "You haven't got a heart."

"Yes I have," Calcifer said, as proudly as he had revealed his arm. "Down in the glowing part under the logs. And don't call me young. I'm a good million years older than you are! Can I reduce the speed of the castle now?"

"Only if the scarecrow's gone," said Sophie. "Has it?"

"I can't tell," said Calcifer. "It's not flesh and blood, you see. I told you I couldn't really see outside."

Sophie got up and dragged herself to the door again, feeling ill. She opened it slowly and cautiously. Green steepness, rocks, and purple slopes whirled past, making her feel dizzy, but she took a grip on the door frame and leaned out to look along the wall to the moorland they were leaving behind. The scarecrow was about fifty yards to the rear. It was hopping from clump to heather clump with a sinister sort of valiance, holding its fluttering stick arms at an angle to balance it on the hillside. As Sophie watched, the castle left it further behind. It was slow, but it was still following. She shut the door.

"It's still there," she said. "Hopping after us. Go faster."

"But that upsets all my calculations," Calcifer explained. "I was aiming to circle the hills and get back to where Michael left us in time to pick him up this evening."

"Then go twice as fast and circle the hills twice. As long as you leave that horrible thing behind!" said Sophie.

"What a fuss!" Calcifer grumbled. But he increased the castle's speed. Sophie could actually, for the first time, feel it rumbling around her as she sat huddled in her chair wondering if she was dying. She did not want to die yet, before she had talked to Martha.

As the day went on, everything in the castle began to jiggle with its speed. Bottles chinked. The skull clattered on the bench. Sophie could hear things falling off the shelf in the bathroom and splashing into the bath where Howl's blue-and-silver suit was still soaking. She began to feel a little better. She dragged herself to the door again and looked out, with her hair flying in the wind. The ground was streaking past underneath. The hills seemed to be spinning slowly as the castle sped across them. The grinding and rumbling nearly deafened her, and smoke was puffing out behind in blasts. But the scarecrow was a tiny black dot on a distant slope by then. Next time she looked, it was out of sight entirely.

"Good. Then I shall stop for the night," said Calcifer. "That was quite a strain."

The rumbling died away. Things stopped jiggling. Calcifer went to sleep, in the way fires do, sinking among the logs until they were rosy cylinders plated with white ash, with only a hint of blue and green deep underneath.

Sophie felt quite spry again by then. She went and fished six packets and a bottle out of the slimy water in the bath. The packets were soaked. She did not dare leave them that way after yesterday, so she laid them on the floor and, very cautiously, sprinkled them with the stuff labeled DRYING POWER. They were dry almost instantly. This was encouraging. Sophie let the water out of the bath and tried the POWER on Howl's suit. That dried too. It was still stained green and rather smaller than it had been, but it cheered Sophie up to find she could put at least something right.

She felt cheerful enough to busy herself getting supper. She bundled everything on the bench into a heap round the skull at one end and began chopping onions. "At least *your* eyes don't water, my friend," she told the skull. "Count your blessings."

The door sprang open.

Sophie nearly cut herself in her fright, thinking it was the scarecrow again. But it was Michael. He burst jubilantly in. He dumped a loaf, a pie, and a pink-and-white-striped box on top of the onions. Then he seized Sophie round her skinny waist and danced her round the room.

"It's all right! It's all right!" he shouted joyfully.

Sophie hopped and stumbled to keep out of the way of Michael's boots. "Steady, steady!" she gasped, giddily trying to hold the knife where it would not cut either of them. "*What* is all right?"

"Lettie loves me!" Michael shouted, dancing her almost into the bathroom and then almost into the hearth. "She's never even seen Howl! It was all a mistake!" He spun them both round in the middle of the room.

"Will you let me go before this knife cuts one of us!" Sophie squawked. "And perhaps explain a little."

"Wee-oop!" Michael shouted. He whirled Sophie to the chair and dumped her into it, where she sat gasping. "Last night I wished you'd dyed his hair *blue!*" he said. "I don't mind now. When Howl said

103

'Lettie Hatter,' I even thought of dying him blue myself. You can see the way he talks. I knew he was going to drop this girl, just like all the others, as soon as he'd got her to love him. And when I thought it was my Lettie, I—Anyway, you know he said there was another fellow, and I thought that was *me!* So I tore down to Market Chipping today. And it was all right! Howl must be after some other girl with the same name. Lettie's never even seen him."

"Let's get this straight," Sophie said dizzily. "We are talking about the Lettie Hatter who works in Cesari's pastry shop, are we?"

"Of course we are!" Michael said jubilantly. "I've loved her ever since she started work there, and I almost couldn't believe it when she said she loved *me.* She has hundreds of admirers. I wouldn't have been surprised if Howl was one of them. I'm so *relieved!* I got you a cake from Cesari's to celebrate. Where did I put it? Oh, here it is."

He thrust the pink-and-white box at Sophie. Onion fell off it into her lap.

"How old are you, my child?" Sophie asked.

"Fifteen last May Day," said Michael. "Calcifer sent fireworks up from the castle. Didn't you, Calcifer? Oh, he's asleep. You're probably thinking I'm too young to be engaged—I've still got three years of my apprenticeship to run, and Lettie's got even longer—but we promised one another, and we don't mind waiting."

Then Michael was about the right age for Martha, Sophie thought. And she knew by now he was a nice, steady lad with a career as a wizard ahead of him. Bless Martha's heart! When she thought back to that bewildering May Day, she realized that Michael had been one of that shouting group leaning on the counter in front of Martha. But Howl had been outside in Market Square.

"Are you sure your Lettie was telling the truth about Howl?" she asked anxiously.

"Positive," said Michael. "I know when she's lying. She stops twiddling her thumbs."

"She does too!" said Sophie, chuckling.

"How do *you* know?" Michael asked in surprise.

"Because she's my sis-ter—er—sister's grand-daughter," said Sophie, "and as a small girl she was not always terribly truthful. But she's quite young and—er ... Well, suppose she changes as she grows. She—er—may not look quite the same in a year or so."

"Neither will I," said Michael. "People our age change all the time. It won't worry us. She'll still be Lettie."

In a manner of speaking, Sophie thought. "But suppose she was telling the truth," she went on anxiously, "and she just knew Howl under a false name?"

"Don't worry, I thought of that!" said Michael. "I described Howl—you must admit he's pretty rec-ognizable—and she really hadn't seen him or his wretched guitar. I didn't even have to tell her he doesn't know how to play the thing. She never set eyes on him, and she twiddled her thumbs all the time she said she hadn't."

"That's a relief!" Sophie said, lying stiffly back in her chair. And it certainly was a relief about Martha. But it was not much of a relief, because Sophie was positive that the only other Lettie Hatter in the district was the real one. If there had been another, someone would have come into the hat shop and gossiped about it. It sounded like strong-minded Lettie, not giving in to Howl. What worried Sophie was that Lettie had told Howl her real name. She might not be sure about him, but she liked him enough to trust him with an important secret like that.

"Don't look so anxious!" Michael laughed, leaning on the back of the chair. "Have a look at the cake I brought you."

As Sophie started opening the box, it dawned on her that Michael had gone from seeing her as a natural disaster to actually liking her. She was so pleased and grateful that she decided to tell Michael the whole truth about Lettie and Martha and herself too. It was only fair to let him know the sort of family he meant to marry into. The box came open. It was Cesari's most luscious cake, covered in cream and cherries and little curls of chocolate. "Oh!" said Sophie.

The square knob over the door clicked round to red-blob-down of its own accord and Howl came in. "What a marvelous cake! My favorite kind," he said. "Where did you get it?"

"I—er—I called in at Cesari's," Michael said in a sheepish, self-conscious way. Sophie looked up at Howl. Something was always going to interrupt her when she decided to say she was under a spell. Even a wizard, it seemed.

"It looks worth the walk," Howl said, inspecting the cake. "I've heard Cesari's is better than any of the cake shops in Kingsbury. Stupid of me never to have been in the place. And is that a pie I see on the bench?" He went over to look. "Pie in a bed of raw onions. Human skull looking put-upon." He picked up the skull and knocked an onion ring out of its eye-socket. "I see Sophie has been busy again. Couldn't you have restrained her, my friend?"

The skull yattered its teeth at him. Howl looked startled and put it down rather hastily.

"Is something the matter?" Michael asked. He seemed to know the signs.

"There is," said Howl. "I shall have to find someone to blacken my name to the King."

"Was there something wrong with the wagon spell?" said Michael.

"No. It worked perfectly. That's the trouble," Howl said, restlessly twiddling an onion ring on one finger. "The King's trying to pin me down to do something else now. Calcifer, if we're not very careful, he's going to appoint me Royal Magician." Calcifer did not answer. Howl roved back to the fireside and realized Calcifer was asleep. "Wake him up, Michael," he said. "I need to consult him."

Michael threw two logs on Calcifer and called him. Nothing happened, apart from a thin spire of smoke.

"Calcifer!" Howl shouted. That did no good either. Howl gave Michael a mystified look and picked up the poker, which was something Sophie had never seen him do before. "Sorry, Calcifer," he said, jabbing under the unburned logs. "Wake *up!*"

One thick black cloud of smoke rolled up, and stopped. "Go away," Calcifer grunted. "I'm tired."

At this, Howl looked thoroughly alarmed. "What's wrong with him? I've never known him like this before!"

"I think it was the scarecrow," Sophie said.

Howl swiveled round on his knees and leveled his glass-marble eyes at her. "What have you done *now?*" He went on staring while Sophie explained. "A scarecrow?" he said. "Calcifer agreed to speed up the castle because of a *scarecrow?* Dear Sophie, do please tell me how you bully a fire demon into being that obliging. I'd dearly love to know!"

"I didn't bully him," said Sophie. "It gave me a

turn and he was sorry for me."

"It gave her a turn and Calcifer was sorry for her," Howl repeated. "My good Sophie, Calcifer is never sorry for anyone. Anyway, I hope you enjoy raw onions and cold pie for your supper, because you've almost put Calcifer out."

"There's the cake," Michael said, trying to make peace.

The food did seem to improve Howl's temper, although he kept casting anxious looks at the unburning logs in the hearth all the time they were eating. The pie was good cold, and the onions were quite tasty when Sophie had soaked them in vinegar. The cake was superb. While they were eating it, Michael risked asking Howl what the King had wanted.

"Nothing definite yet," Howl said gloomily. "But he was sounding me out about his brother, quite ominously. Apparently they had a good old argument before Prince Justin stormed off, and people are talking. The King obviously wanted me to volunteer to look for his brother. And like a fool I went and said I didn't think Wizard Suliman was dead, and that made matters worse."

"Why do you want to slither out of looking for the Prince?" Sophie demanded. "Don't you think you can find him?"

"Rude as well as a bully, aren't you?" Howl said. He had still not forgiven her about Calcifer. "I want to get out of it because I know I *can* find him, if you must know. Justin was great buddies with Suliman, and the argument was because he told the King he was going to look for him. He didn't think the King should have sent Suliman to the Waste in the first place. Now, even you must know there is a certain lady in the Waste who is very bad news. She promised to fry me alive last year, and she sent a curse out after me that I've only avoided so far because I had the sense to give her a false name."

Sophie was almost awed. "You mean you jilted the Witch of the Waste?"

Howl cut himself another lump of cake, looking sad and honorable. "That is not the way to put it. I admit I thought I was fond of her for a time. She is in some ways a very sad lady, very unloved. Every man in Ingary is scared stiff of her. *You* ought to know how that feels, Sophie dear."

Sophie's mouth opened in utter indignation. Michael said quickly, "Do you think we should move the castle? That's why you invented it, wasn't it?"

"That depends on Calcifer." Howl looked over his shoulder at the barely smoking logs again. "I must say, if I think of the King and the Witch both after me, I get a craving for planting the castle on a nice, frowning rock a thousand miles away."

Michael obviously wished he had not spoken. Sophie could see he was thinking that a thousand miles was a terribly long way from Martha. "But what happens to your Lettie Hatter," she said to Howl, "if you up and move?"

"I expect that will be all over by then," Howl said absently. "But if I could only think of a way to get the King off my back . . . I know!" He lifted his fork, with a melting hunk of cream and cake on it, and pointed it at Sophie. "*You* can blacken my name to the King. You can pretend to be my old mother and plead for your blue-eyed boy." He gave Sophie the smile which had no doubt charmed the Witch of the Waste and possibly Lettie too, firing it along the fork, across the cream, straight into Sophie's eyes, dazzlingly. "If you can bully Calcifer, the King should give you no trouble at all."

Sophie stared through the dazzle and said nothing. This, she thought, was where *she* slithered out. She was leaving. It was too bad about Calcifer's contract. She had had enough of Howl. First green slime, then glaring at her for something Calcifer had done quite freely, and now this! Tomorrow she would slip off to Upper Folding and tell Lettie all about it.

Chapter 8:

❖

In which Sophie leaves the castle in several directions at once

To Sophie's relief, Calcifer blazed up bright and cheerful next morning. If she had not had enough of Howl, she would have been almost touched by how glad Howl was to see Calcifer. "I thought she'd done for you, you old ball of gas," Howl said, kneeling at the hearth with his sleeves trailing in the ash.

"I was only tired," Calcifer said. "There was some kind of drag on the castle. I'd never taken it that fast before."

"Well, don't let her make you do it again," said Howl. He stood up, gracefully brushing ash off his gray-and-scarlet suit. "Make a start on that spell today, Michael. And if anyone comes from the King, I'm away on urgent private business until tomorrow. I'm going to see Lettie, but you needn't tell him that." He picked up his guitar and opened the door with the knob green-down, onto the wide, cloudy hills.

The scarecrow was there again. When Howl opened the door, it pitched sideways across him with its turnip face in his chest. The guitar uttered an awful *twang-oing*. Sophie gave a faint squawk of terror and hung on to the chair. One of the scarecrow's stick arms was scraping stiffly round to get a purchase on the door. From the way Howl's feet were braced, it was clear he was being shoved quite hard. There was no doubt that the thing was determined to get into the castle.

Calcifer's blue face leaned out of the grate. Michael stood stock still beyond. "There really *is* a scarecrow!" they both said.

"Oh, is there? Do tell!" Howl panted. He got one foot up against the door frame and heaved. The scarecrow flew lumpishly away backward, to land with a light rustle in the heather some yards off. It sprang up instantly and came hopping toward the castle again. Howl hurriedly laid the guitar on the doorstep and jumped down to meet it. "No you don't, my friend," he said with one hand out. "Go back where you came from." He walked forward slowly, still with his hand out. The scarecrow retreated a little, hopping slowly and warily backward. When Howl stopped, the scarecrow stopped too, with its one leg planted in the heather and its ragged arms tilting this way and that like a person sparring for an opening. The rags fluttering on its arms seemed a mad imitation of Howl's sleeves.

"So you won't go?" Howl said. And the turnip

head slowly moved from side to side. No. "I'm afraid you'll have to," Howl said. "You scare Sophie, and there's no knowing what she'll do when she's scared. Come to think of it, you scare me too." Howl's arms moved, heavily, as if he was lifting a large weight, until they were raised high above his head. He shouted out a strange word, which was half hidden in a crack of sudden thunder. And the scarecrow went soaring away. Up and backward it went, rags fluttering, arms wheeling in protest, up and out, and on and on, until it was a soaring speck in the sky, then a vanishing point in the clouds, and then not to be seen at all.

Howl lowered his arms and came back to the doorway, mopping his face on the back of his hand. "I take back my hard words, Sophie," he said, panting. "That thing was alarming. It may have been dragging the castle back all yesterday. It had some of the strongest magic I've met. Whatever was it—all that was left of the last person you cleaned for?"

Sophie gave a weak little cackle of laughter. Her heart was behaving badly again.

Howl realized something was wrong with her. He jumped indoors across his guitar, took hold of her elbow, and sat her in the chair. "Take it easy now!" Something happened between Howl and Calcifer then. Sophie felt it, because she was being held by Howl, and Calcifer was still leaning out of the grate. Whatever it was, her heart began to behave properly almost at once. Howl looked at Calcifer, shrugged, and turned away to give Michael a whole lot of instructions about making Sophie keep quiet for the rest of the day. Then he picked up the guitar and left at last.

Sophie lay in the chair and pretended to feel twice as ill as she did. She had to let Howl get out of sight. It was a nuisance he was going to Upper Folding as well, but she would walk so much more slowly that she would arrive around the time he started back. The important thing was not to meet him on the way. She watched Michael slyly while he spread out the spell and scratched his head over it. She waited until he dragged big leather books off the shelves and began making notes in a frantic, depressed sort of way. When he seemed properly absorbed, Sophie muttered several times, "Stuffy in here!"

Michael took no notice. "Terribly stuffy," Sophie said, getting up and shambling to the door. "Fresh air." She opened the door and climbed out. Calcifer obligingly stopped the castle dead while she did. Sophie landed in the heather and took a look round to get her bearings. The road over the hills to Upper Folding was a sandy line through the heather just downhill from the castle. Naturally. Calcifer would not make things inconvenient for Howl. Sophie set off toward it. She felt a little sad. She was going to miss Michael and Calcifer.

She was almost at the road when there was shouting behind her. Michael came bounding down the hillside after her, and the tall black castle came bobbling along behind him, shedding anxious puffs of smoke from all four turrets.

"What are you *doing?*" Michael said when he caught up. From the way he looked at her, Sophie could see he thought the scarecrow had sent her wrong in the head.

"I'm perfectly all right," Sophie said indignantly. "I'm simply going to see my other sister's granddaughter. She's called Lettie Hatter too. Now do you understand?"

"Where does she live?" Michael demanded, as if he thought Sophie might not know.

"Upper Folding," said Sophie.

"But that's over ten miles away!" Michael said. "I promised Howl I'd make you rest. I can't let you go. I told him I wouldn't let you out of my sight."

Sophie did not look very kindly on this. Howl thought she was useful now because he wanted her to see the King. Of course he did not want her to leave the castle. "Huh!" she said.

"Besides," said Michael, slowly grasping the situation, "Howl must have gone to Upper Folding too."

"I'm quite sure he has," said Sophie.

"Then you're anxious about this girl, if she's your great-niece," Michael said, arriving at the point at last.

"I see! But I can't let you go."

"I'm going," said Sophie.

"But if Howl sees you there, he'll be furious," Michael went on, working things out. "Because I promised him, he'll be mad with both of us. You ought to rest." Then, when Sophie was almost ready to hit him, he exclaimed, "Wait! There's a pair of seven-league boots in the broom cupboard!"

He took Sophie by her skinny old wrist and towed her uphill to the waiting castle. She was forced to give little hops in order not to catch her feet in the heather. "But," she panted, "seven leagues is twenty-one miles! I'd be halfway to Porthaven in two strides!"

"No, it's ten and a half miles a step," said Michael. "That makes Upper Folding almost exactly. If we each take one boot and go together, then I won't be letting you out of my sight and you won't be doing anything strenuous, and we'll get there before Howl does, so he won't even know we've been. That solves all our problems beautifully!"

Michael was so pleased with himself that Sophie did not have the heart to protest. She shrugged and supposed Michael had better find out about the two Letties before they changed looks again. It was more honest this way. But when Michael fetched the boots from the broom cupboard, Sophie began to have doubts. Up to now she had thought they were two leather buckets that had somehow lost their handles and then got a little squashed.

"You're supposed to put your foot in them, shoe and all," Michael explained as he carried the two heavy, bucket-shaped things to the door. "These are the prototypes of the boots Howl made for the King's army. We managed to get the later ones a bit lighter and more boot-shaped." He and Sophie sat on the doorstep and each put one foot in a boot. "Point yourself toward Upper Folding before you put the boot down," Michael warned her. He and Sophie stood up on the foot which was in an ordinary shoe and carefully swung themselves round to face Upper Folding. "Now tread," said Michael.

Zip! The landscape instantly rushed past them so fast it was only a blur, a gray-green blur for the land and a blue-gray blur for the sky. The wind of their going tore at Sophie's hair and dragged every wrinkle in her face backward until she thought she would arrive with half her face behind each ear.

The rushing stopped as suddenly as it had begun. Everything was calm and sunny. They were knee-deep in buttercups in the middle of Upper Folding village common. A cow nearby stared at them. Beyond it, thatched cottages drowsed under trees. Unfortunately, the bucketlike boot was so heavy that Sophie staggered as she landed.

"Don't put that foot down!" Michael yelled, too late.

There was another zipping blur and more rushing wind. When it stopped, Sophie found herself right down the Folding Valley, almost into Marsh Folding. "Oh, drat!" she said, and hopped carefully round on her shoe and tried again.

Zip! Blur. And she was back on Upper Folding green again, staggering forward with the weight of the boot. She had a glimpse of Michael diving to catch her—

Zip! Blur. "Oh, bother!" wailed Sophie. She was up in the hills again. The crooked black shape of the castle was drifting peacefully nearby. Calcifer was amusing himself blowing black smoke rings from one turret. Sophie saw that much before her shoe caught in the heather and she stumbled forward again.

Zip! Zip! This time Sophie visited in rapid succession the Market Square of Market Chipping and the front lawn of a very grand mansion. "Blow!" she cried. "Drat!" One word for each place. And she was off again with her own momentum and another Zip! right down at the end of that valley in a field somewhere. A large red bull raised its ringed nose from the grass and thoughtfully lowered its horns.

"I'm just leaving, my good beast!" Sophie cried, hopping herself round frantically.

Zip! Back to the mansion. Zip! to Market Square. Zip! and there was the castle yet again. She was getting the hang of it. Zip! Here was Upper Folding—

but how did you stop? Zip!

"Oh, *confound* it!" Sophie cried, almost in Marsh Folding again.

This time she hopped round very carefully and trod with great deliberation. Zip! And fortunately the boot landed in a cowpat and she sat down with a thump. Michael sprinted up before Sophie could move and dragged the boot off her foot. "Thank you!" Sophie cried breathlessly. "There seemed no reason why I should ever stop!"

Sophie's heart pounded a bit as they walked across the common to Mrs. Fairfax's house, but only in the way hearts do when you have done a lot rather quickly. She felt very grateful for whatever Howl and Calcifer had done.

"Nice place," Michael remarked as he hid the boots in Mrs. Fairfax's hedge.

Sophie agreed. The house was the biggest in the village. It was thatched, with white walls between the black beams, and, as Sophie remembered from visits as a child, you walked up to the porch through a garden crowded with flowers and humming with bees. Over the porch a honeysuckle and a white climbing rose were competing as to which could give most work to the bees. It was a perfect, hot summer morning down here in Upper Folding.

Mrs. Fairfax answered the door herself. She was one of those plump, comfortable ladies, with swathes of butter-colored hair coiled round her head, who made you feel good with life just to look at her. Sophie felt just the tiniest bit envious of Lettie. Mrs. Fairfax looked from Sophie to Michael. She had seen Sophie last a year ago as a girl of seventeen, and there was no reason for her to recognize her as an old woman of ninety. "Good morning to you," she said politely.

Sophie sighed. Michael said, "This is Lettie Hatter's great-aunt. I brought her here to see Lettie."

"Oh, I *thought* the face looked familiar!" Mrs. Fairfax exclaimed. "There's quite a family likeness. Do come in. Lettie's a little bit busy just now, but have some scones and honey while you wait."

She opened her front door wider. Instantly a large collie dog squeezed past Mrs. Fairfax's skirts, barged between Sophie and Michael, and ran across the nearest flower bed, snapping off flowers right and left.

"Oh, stop him!" Mrs. Fairfax gasped, flying off in pursuit. "I don't want him out just now!"

There was a minute or so of helter-skelter chase, in which the dog ran hither and thither, whining in a disturbed way, and Mrs. Fairfax and Sophie ran after the dog, jumping flower beds and getting in one another's way, and Michael ran after Sophie crying, "Stop! You'll make yourself ill!" Then the dog set off loping round one corner of the house. Michael realized that the way to stop Sophie was to stop the dog. He made a crosswise dash through the flower beds, plunged round the house after the dog, and seized it by two handfuls of its thick coat just as it reached the orchard at the back.

Sophie hobbled up to find Michael pulling the dog away backward and making such strange faces at her that she thought at first he was ill. But he jerked his head so often toward the orchard that she realized he was only trying to tell her something. She stuck her face round the corner of the house, expecting to see a swarm of bees.

Howl was there with Lettie. They were in a grove of mossy apple trees in full bloom, with a row of beehives in the distance. Lettie sat in a white garden seat. Howl was kneeling on one knee in the grass at her feet, holding one of her hands and looking noble and ardent. Lettie was smiling lovingly at him. But the worst of it, as far as Sophie was concerned, was that Lettie did not look like Martha at all. She was her own extremely beautiful self. She was wearing a dress of the same kind of pinks and white as the crowded apple blossom overhead. Her dark hair trailed in glossy curls over one shoulder and her eyes shone with devotion for Howl.

Sophie brought her head back round the corner and looked with dismay at Michael holding the whining collie dog. "He must have had a speed spell with him," Michael whispered, equally dismayed.

Mrs. Fairfax caught them up, panting and trying to pin back a loose coil of her buttery hair. "Bad dog!" she said in a fierce whisper to the collie. "I'll put a spell on you if you do that once more!" The dog blinked and crouched down. Mrs. Fairfax pointed a stern finger. "Into the house! Stay in the house!" The collie shook himself free of Michael's hands and slunk away round the house again. "Thank you so much," Mrs. Fairfax said to Michael as they all followed it. "He *will* keep trying to bite Lettie's visitor. *Inside!*" she shouted sternly in the front garden, as the collie seemed to be thinking of going round the house and getting to the orchard the other way. The dog gave her a woeful look over its shoulder and crawled dismally indoors through the porch.

"That dog may have the right idea," Sophie said. "Mrs. Fairfax, do you know who Lettie's visitor is?"

Mrs. Fairfax chuckled. "The Wizard Pendragon, or Howl, or whatever he calls himself," she said. "But Lettie and I don't let on we know. It amused me when he first turned up, calling himself Sylvester Oak, because I could see he'd forgotten me, though I hadn't forgotten him, even though his hair used to be black in his student days." Mrs. Fairfax by now had her hands folded in front of her and was standing bolt upright, prepared to talk all day, as Sophie had often seen her do before. "He was my old tutor's very last pupil, you know, before she retired. When Mr. Fairfax was alive, he used to like me to transport us both to Kingsbury to see a show from time to time. I can manage two very nicely if I take it slowly. And I always used to drop in on old Mrs. Pentstemmon while I was there. She likes her old pupils to keep in touch. And one time she introduced this young Howl to us. Oh, she was proud of him. She taught Wizard Suliman too, you know, and she said Howl was twice as good—"

"But don't you know the reputation Howl has?" Michael interrupted.

Getting into Mrs. Fairfax's conversation was rather like getting into a turning skipping rope. You had to choose the exact moment, but once you were in, you were in. Mrs. Fairfax turned herself slightly to face Michael.

"Most of it's just talk, to my mind," she said. Michael opened his mouth to say that it was not, but he was in the skipping rope then and it went on turning. "And I said to Lettie, 'Here's your big chance, my love.' I knew Howl could teach her twenty times more than I could—for I don't mind telling you, Lettie's brains go way beyond mine, and she could end up in the same league as the Witch of the Waste, only in a *good* way. Lettie's a good girl and I'm fond of her. If Mrs. Pentstemmon was still teaching, I'd have Lettie to her tomorrow. But she isn't. So I said, 'Lettie, here's Wizard Howl courting you and you could do worse than fall in love with him yourself and let him be your teacher. The pair of you will go far.' I don't think Lettie was too keen on the idea at first, but she's been softening lately, and today it seems to be going beautifully."

Here Mrs. Fairfax paused to beam benevolently at Michael, and Sophie dashed into the skipping rope for her turn. "But someone told me Lettie was fond of someone else," she said.

"Sorry for him, you mean," said Mrs. Fairfax. She lowered her voice. "There's a terrible disability there," she whispered suggestively, "and it's asking too much of any girl. I told him so. I'm sorry for him myself—"

Sophie managed a mystified "Oh?"

"—but it's a fearsomely strong spell. It's very sad," Mrs. Fairfax wound on. "I had to tell him that there's no way someone of my abilities can break anything that's put on by the Witch of the Waste. Howl might, but of course he can't ask Howl, can he?"

Here Michael, who kept looking nervously to the corner of the house in case Howl came round it and discovered them, managed to trample through the skipping rope and stop it by saying, "I think we'd better be going."

"Are you sure you won't come in for a taste of my honey?" asked Mrs. Fairfax. "I use it in nearly all my spells, you know." And she was off again, this time about the magical properties of honey. Michael and

Sophie walked purposefully down the path to the gate and Mrs. Fairfax drifted behind them, talking away and sorrowfully straightening plants that the dog had bent as she talked. Sophie meanwhile racked her brains for a way to find out how Mrs. Fairfax knew Lettie was Lettie, without upsetting Michael. Mrs. Fairfax paused to gasp a bit as she heaved a large lupine upright.

Sophie took the plunge. "Mrs. Fairfax, wasn't it my niece Martha who was supposed to come to you?"

"Naughty girls!" Mrs. Fairfax said, smiling and shaking her head as she emerged from the lupine. "As if I wouldn't recognize one of my own honey-based spells! But as I said to her at the time, 'I'm not one to keep anyone against their will and I'd always rather teach someone who wants to learn. Only,' I said to her, 'I'll have no pretense here. You stay as your own self or not at all.' And it's worked out very happily, as you see. Are you sure you won't stay and ask her for yourself?"

"I think we'd better go," Sophie said.

"We have to get back," Michael added, with another nervous look toward the orchard. He collected the seven-league boots from the hedge and set one down outside the gate for Sophie. "And I'm going to hold on to you this time," he said.

Mrs. Fairfax leaned over her gate while Sophie inserted her foot in the boot. "Seven-leaguers," she said. "Would you believe, I've not seen any of those for years. Very useful things for someone your age, Mrs. Er—I wouldn't mind a pair myself these days. So it's you Lettie inherits her witchcraft from, is it? Not that it necessarily runs in families, but as often as not—"

Michael took hold of Sophie's arm and pulled. Both boots came down and the rest of Mrs. Fairfax's talk vanished in the Zip! and rush of air. Next moment Michael had to brace his feet in order not to collide with the castle. The door was open. Inside, Calcifer was roaring, "Porthaven door! Someone's been banging on it ever since you left."

Chapter 9:

⟶⊱⟨⊰⟵

In which Michael has trouble
with a spell

It was the sea captain at the door, come for his wind spell at last, and not at all pleased at having to wait. "If I miss my tide, boy," he said to Michael, "I shall have a word with the Sorcerer about you. I don't like lazy boys."

Michael, in Sophie's opinion, was far too polite to him, but she was feeling too dejected to interfere. When the captain had gone, Michael went to the bench to frown over his spell again and Sophie sat silently mending her stockings. She had only the one pair and her knobby feet had worn huge holes in them. Her gray dress by this time was frayed and dirty. She wondered whether she dared cut the least-stained bits out of Howl's ruined blue-and-silver suit to make herself a new skirt with. But she did not quite dare.

"Sophie," Michael said, looking up from his eleventh page of notes, "how many nieces have you?"

Sophie had been afraid Michael would start asking questions. "When you get to my age, my lad," she said, "you lose count. They all look so alike. Those two Letties could be twins, to my mind."

"Oh, no, not really," Michael said, to her surprise. "The niece in Upper Folding isn't as pretty as *my* Lettie." He tore up the eleventh page and made a twelfth. "I'm glad Howl didn't meet *my* Lettie," he said. He began on his thirteenth page and tore that up too. "I wanted to laugh when that Mrs. Fairfax said she knew who Howl was, didn't you?"

"No," said Sophie. It had made no difference to Lettie's feelings. She thought of Lettie's bright, adoring face under the apple blossom. "I suppose there's no chance," she asked hopelessly, "that Howl could be properly in love this time?"

Calcifer snorted green sparks up the chimney.

"I was afraid you'd start thinking that," Michael said. "But you'd be deceiving yourself, just like Mrs. Fairfax."

"How do you know?" said Sophie.

Calcifer and Michael exchanged glances. "Did he forget to spend at least an hour in the bathroom this morning?" Michael asked.

"He was in there two hours," said Calcifer, "putting spells on his face. Vain fool!"

"There you are, then," said Michael. "The day Howl forgets to do that will be the day I believe he's really in love, and not before."

Sophie thought of Howl on one knee in the

orchard, posing to look as handsome as possible, and she knew they were right. She thought of going to the bathroom and tipping all Howl's beauty spells down the toilet. But she did not quite dare. Instead, she hobbled up and fetched the blue-and-silver suit, which she spent the rest of the day cutting little blue triangles out of in order to make a patchwork sort of skirt.

Michael patted her shoulder kindly as he came to throw all seventeen pages of his notes onto Calcifer. "Everyone gets over things in the end, you know," he said.

By this time it was clear Michael was having trouble with his spell. He gave up the notes and scraped some soot off the chimney. Calcifer craned round to watch him in a mystified way. Michael took a withered root from one of the bags hanging on the beams and put it in the soot. Then, after much thought, he turned the doorknob blue-down and vanished for twenty minutes into Porthaven. He came back with a large, whorled seashell and put that with the root and the soot. After that he tore up pages and pages of paper and put those in too. He put the lot in front of the human skull and stood blowing on it, so that soot and bits of paper whirled all over the bench.

"What's he doing, do you think?" Calcifer asked Sophie.

Michael gave up blowing and started mashing

everything, paper and all, with a pestle and mortar, looking at the skull expectantly from time to time. Nothing happened, so he tried different ingredients from bags and jars.

"I feel bad about spying on Howl," he announced as he pounded a third set of ingredients to death in a bowl. "He may be fickle to females, but he's been awfully good to me. He took me in when I was just an unwanted orphan sitting on his doorstep in Porthaven."

"How did that come about?" asked Sophie as she snipped out another blue triangle.

"My mother died and my father got drowned in a storm," Michael said. "And nobody wants you when that happens. I had to leave our house because I couldn't pay rent, and I tried to live in the streets, but people kept turning me off doorsteps and out of boats until the only place I could think of to go was somewhere everyone was too scared of to interfere with. Howl had just started up in a small way as Sorcerer Jenkin then. But everyone said his house had devils in it, so I slept on his doorstep for a couple of nights until Howl opened the door one morning on his way to buy bread and I fell inside. So he said I could wait indoors while he got something to eat. I went in, and there was Calcifer, and I started talking to him because I'd never met a demon before."

"What did you talk about?" said Sophie,

wondering if Calcifer had asked Michael to break his contract too.

"He told me his troubles and dripped on me. Didn't you?" said Calcifer. "It didn't seem to occur to him that I might have troubles as well."

"I don't think you have. You just grumble a lot," Michael said. "You were quite nice to me that morning, and I think Howl was impressed. But you know how he is. He didn't tell me I could stay. He just didn't tell me to go. So I started being useful wherever I could, like looking after money so that he didn't spend it all as soon as he'd got it, and so on."

The spell gave a sort of *whuff* then and exploded mildly. Michael brushed soot off the skull, sighing, and tried new ingredients. Sophie began making a patchwork of blue triangles round her feet on the floor.

"I did make lots of stupid mistakes when I first started," Michael went on. "Howl was awfully nice about it. I thought I'd got over that now. And I think I do help with money. Howl buys such expensive clothes. He says no one's going to employ a wizard who looks as if he can't make money at the trade."

"That's just because he likes clothes," said Calcifer. His orange eyes watched Sophie at work rather meaningly.

"This suit was spoiled," Sophie said.

"It isn't just clothes," Michael said. "Remember

last winter when we were down to your last log and Howl went off and bought the skull and that stupid guitar? I was really annoyed with him. He said they *looked* good."

"What did you do about logs?" Sophie asked.

"Howl conjured some from someone who owed him money," Michael said. "At least, he said they did, and I just hoped he was telling the truth. And we ate seaweed. Howl says it's good for you."

"Nice stuff," murmured Calcifer. "Dry and crackly."

"I hate it," said Michael, staring abstractedly at his bowl of pounded stuff. "I don't know—there should be seven ingredients, unless it's seven processes, but let's try it in a pentacle anyway." He put the bowl on the floor and chalked a sort of five-pointed star round it.

The powder exploded with a force that blew Sophie's triangles into the hearth. Michael swore and hurriedly rubbed out the chalk marks.

"Sophie," he said, "I'm stuck in this spell. You don't think you could possibly help me, do you?"

Just like someone bringing their homework to their granny, Sophie thought, collecting triangles and patiently laying them out again. "Let's have a look," she said cautiously. "I don't know anything about magic, you know."

Michael eagerly thrust a strange, slightly shiny

paper into her hand. It looked unusual, even for a spell. It was printed in bold letters, but they were slightly gray and blurred, and there were gray blurs, like retreating stormclouds, round all the edges. "See what you think," said Michael.

Sophie read:

> "Go and catch a falling star,
>   Get with child a mandrake root,
>   Tell me where all past years are,
>   Or who cleft the Devil's foot.
>   Teach me to hear the mermaids singing,
>   Or to keep off envy's stinging,
>   And find
>   What wind
> Serves to advance an honest mind.
>
> Decide what this is about
> Write a second verse yourself"

It puzzled Sophie exceedingly. It was not quite like any of the spells she had snooped at before. She plowed through it twice, not really helped by Michael eagerly explaining as she tried to read. "You know Howl told me that advanced spells have a puzzle in them? Well, I decided at first that every line was meant to be a puzzle. I used soot with sparks in it for the falling star, and a seashell for the mermaids singing. And I thought *I* might count as a child, so I got a mandrake root down, and I wrote out lists of past years from the almanacs, but I wasn't sure about that—maybe that's where I went wrong—and could the thing that stops stinging be dock leaf? I hadn't thought of that before—anyway, none of it *works!*"

"I'm not surprised," said Sophie. "It looks to me like a set of impossible things to do."

But Michael was not having that. If the things were impossible, he pointed out reasonably, no one would ever be able to do the spell. "And," he added, "I'm so ashamed of spying on Howl that I want to make up for it by getting this spell right."

"Very well," said Sophie. "Let's start with 'Decide what this is about.' That ought to start things moving, if deciding is part of the spell anyway."

But Michael was not having that either. "No," he said. "It's the sort of spell that reveals itself as you do it. That's what the last line means. When you write the second half, saying what the spell means, that makes it work. Those kind are very advanced. We have to crack the first bit first."

Sophie collected her blue triangles into a pile again. "Let's ask Calcifer," she suggested. "Calcifer, who—?"

But this was yet another thing Michael did not let her do. "No, be quiet. I think Calcifer's part of the spell. Look at the way it says 'Tell me' and 'Teach me.'

I thought at first it meant teach the skull, but that didn't work, so it must be Calcifer."

"You can do it by yourself, if you sit on everything I have to say!" Sophie said. "Anyway, surely Calcifer must know who cleft his own foot!"

Calcifer flared up a little at this. "I haven't got any feet. I'm a demon, not a devil." Saying which, he retreated right under his logs, where he could be heard chinking about, muttering, "Lot of nonsense!" all the rest of the time Sophie and Michael were discussing the spell. By this time the puzzle had got a grip on Sophie. She packed away her blue triangles, fetched pen and paper, and started making notes in the same sort of quantities that Michael had. For the rest of the day she and Michael sat staring into the distance, nibbling quills and throwing out suggestions at one another.

An average page of Sophie's notes read:

> Does garlic keep off envy? I could cut a star out of paper and drop it. Could we tell it to Howl? Howl would like mermaids better than Calcifer. Do not think Howl's mind honest. Is Calcifer's? Where <u>are</u> past years anyway? Does it mean one of those dry roots must bear fruit? Plant it? Next to dock leaf? In seashell? Cloven hoof, most things but horses. Shoe a horse with a clove of garlic? Wind? Smell? Wind of seven-league boots? Is Howl devil? Cloven toes in seven-league boots? Mermaids in boots?

As Sophie wrote this, Michael asked equally desperately, "Could the 'wind' be some sort of pulley? An honest man being hanged? That's *black* magic, though."

"Let's have supper," said Sophie.

They ate bread and cheese, still staring into distance. At last Sophie said, "Michael, for goodness' sake, let's give up guessing and try doing just what it says. Where's the best place to catch a shooting star? Out on the hills?"

"Porthaven Marshes are flatter," Michael said. "*Can* we? Shooting stars go awfully fast."

"So can we, in seven-league boots," Sophie pointed out.

Michael sprang up, full of relief and delight. "I think you've got it!" he said, scrambling for the boots. "Let's go and try."

This time Sophie prudently took her stick and her shawl, since it was now quite dark. Michael was turning the doorknob blue-down when two strange things happened. On the bench the teeth of the skull started clattering. And Calcifer blazed right up the chimney. "I don't want you to go!" he said.

"We'll be back soon," Michael said soothingly.

They went out into the street in Porthaven. It was a bright, balmy night. As soon as they had reached the end of the street, however, Michael remembered that

Sophie had been ill that morning and began worrying about the effect of the night air on her health. Sophie told him not to be silly. She stumped gamely along with her stick until they left the lighted windows behind and the night became wide and damp and chilly. The marshes smelled of salt and earth. The sea glittered and softly swished to the rear. Sophie could feel, more than see, the miles and miles of flatness stretching away in front of them. What she could see were bands of low bluish mist and pale glimmers of marshy pools, over and over again, until they built into a pale line where the sky started. The sky was everywhere else, huger still. The Milky Way looked like a band of mist risen from the marshes, and the keen stars twinkled through it.

Michael and Sophie stood, each with a boot ready on the ground in front of them, waiting for one of the stars to move.

After about an hour Sophie had to pretend she was not shivering, for fear of worrying Michael.

Half an hour later Michael said, "May is not the right time of year. August or November is best."

Half an hour after that, he said in a worried way, "What do we do about the mandrake root?"

"Let's see to this part before we worry about that," Sophie said, biting her teeth together while she spoke, for fear they would chatter.

Some time later Michael said, "You go home,

Sophie. It's my spell, after all."

Sophie had her mouth open to say that this was a very good idea, when one of the stars came unstuck from the firmament and darted in a white streak down the sky. "*There's* one!" Sophie shrieked instead.

Michael thumped his foot into his boot and was off. Sophie braced herself with her stick and was off a second later. Zip! Squash. Down far out in the marshes with mist and emptiness and dull-glimmering pools in all directions. Sophie stabbed her stick into the ground and managed to stand still. Michael's boot was a dark blot standing just beside her. Michael himself was a sploshy sound of madly running feet somewhere ahead.

And there was the falling star. Sophie could see it, a little white descending flame shape a few yards beyond the dark movements that were Michael. The bright shape was coming down slowly now, and it looked as if Michael might catch it.

Sophie dragged her shoe out of the boot. "Come on, stick!" she crowed. "Get me there!" And she set off at top hobble, leaping across tussocks and staggering through pools, with her eyes on that little white light.

By the time she caught up, Michael was stalking the star with soft steps, both arms out to catch it. Sophie could see him outlined against the star's light. The star was drifting level with Michael's hands and only a step or so beyond. It was looking back at him nervously. How odd! Sophie thought. It was made of light, it lit up a white ring of grass and reeds and black pools round Michael, and yet it had big, anxious eyes peering backward at Michael, and a small, pointed face.

Sophie's arrival frightened it. It gave an erratic swoop and cried out in a shrill, crackling voice, "What *is* it? What do you want?"

Sophie tried to say to Michael, Do stop—it's terrified! But she had no breath left to speak with.

"I only want to catch you," Michael explained. "I won't hurt you."

"No! No!" the star crackled desperately. "That's wrong! I'm supposed to die!"

"But I could save you if you'd let me catch you," Michael told it gently.

"No!" cried the star. "I'd rather die!" It dived away from Michael's fingers. Michael plunged for it, but it was too quick for him. It swooped for the nearest marsh pool, and the black water leaped into a blaze of whiteness for just an instant. Then there was a small, dying sizzle. When Sophie hobbled over, Michael was standing watching the last light fade out of a little round lump under the dark water.

"That was sad," Sophie said.

Michael sighed. "Yes. My heart sort of went out to it. Let's go home. I'm sick of this spell."

It took them twenty minutes to find the boots. Sophie thought it was a miracle they found them at all.

"You know," Michael said, as they trudged dejectedly through the dark streets of Porthaven, "I can tell I'll never be able to do this spell. It's too advanced for me. I shall have to ask Howl. I hate giving in, but at least I'll get some sense out of Howl now this Lettie Hatter's given in to him."

This did not cheer Sophie up at all.

Chapter 10:

━━◆━━

In which Calcifer promises
Sophie a hint

Howl must have come back while Sophie and Michael were out. He came out of the bathroom while Sophie was frying breakfast on Calcifer, and sat gracefully in the chair, groomed and glowing and smelling of honeysuckle.

"Dear Sophie," he said. "Always busy. You were hard at work yesterday, weren't you, in spite of my advice? Why have you made a jigsaw puzzle of my best suit? Just a friendly inquiry, you know."

"You jellied it the other day," said Sophie. "I'm making it over."

"I can do that," said Howl. "I thought I showed you. I can also make you a pair of seven-league boots of your own if you give me your size. Something practical in brown calf, perhaps. It's amazing the way one can take a step ten and a half miles long and still always land in a cowpat."

"It may have been a bullpat," said Sophie. "I daresay you found mud from the marshes on them too. A person my age needs a lot of exercise."

"You were even busier than I realized, then," said Howl. "Because when I happened to tear my eyes from Lettie's lovely face for an instant yesterday, I could have sworn I saw your long nose poking round the corner of the house."

"Mrs. Fairfax is a family friend," said Sophie. "How was I to know you would be there too?"

"You have an instinct, Sophie, that's how," said Howl. "Nothing is safe from you. If I were to court a girl who lived on an iceberg in the middle of an ocean, sooner or later—probably sooner—I'd look up to see you swooping overhead on a broomstick. In fact, by now I'd be disappointed in you if I *didn't* see you."

"Are you off to the iceberg today?" Sophie retorted. "From the look on Lettie's face yesterday, there's nothing that need keep you there!"

"You wrong me, Sophie," Howl said. He sounded deeply injured. Sophie looked suspiciously sideways. Beyond the red jewel swinging in Howl's ear, his profile looked sad and noble. "Long years will pass before I leave Lettie," he said. "And in fact I'm off to see the King again today. Satisfied, Mrs. Nose?"

Sophie was not sure she believed a word of this, though it was certainly to Kingsbury, with the doorknob red-down, that Howl departed after breakfast, waving Michael aside when Michael tried to consult him about the perplexing spell. Michael, since he had nothing to do, left too. He said he might as well go to Cesari's.

Sophie was left alone. She still did not truly believe what Howl had said about Lettie, but she had been wrong about him before, and she had only Michael and Calcifer's word for Howl's behavior, after all. She collected up all the little blue triangles of cloth and began guiltily sewing them back into the silver fishing net which was all that was left of the suit. When someone knocked at the door, she started violently, thinking it was the scarecrow again.

"Porthaven door," Calcifer said, flickering a purple grin at her.

That should be all right, then. Sophie hobbled over and opened it, blue-down. There was a cart horse outside. The young fellow of fifty who was leading it wondered if Mrs. Witch had something which might stop it casting shoes all the time.

"I'll see," said Sophie. She hobbled over to the grate. "What shall I *do?*" she whispered.

"Yellow powder, fourth jar along on the second shelf," Calcifer whispered back. "Those spells are mostly belief. Don't look uncertain when you give it to him."

So Sophie poured yellow powder into a square of paper as she had seen Michael do, twisted it smartly, and hobbled to the door with it. "There you are, my boy," she said. "That'll stick the shoes on harder than any hundred nails. Do you hear me, horse? You won't need a smith for the next year. That'll be a penny, thank you."

It was quite a busy day. Sophie had to put down her sewing and sell, with Calcifer's help, a spell to unblock drains, another to fetch goats, and something to make good beer. The only one that gave her any trouble was the customer who pounded on the door in Kingsbury. Sophie opened it red-down to find a richly dressed boy not much older than Michael, white-faced and sweating, wringing his hands on the doorstep.

"Madam Sorceress, for pity's sake!" he said. "I have to fight a duel at dawn tomorrow. Give me something to make sure I win. I'll pay any sum you ask!"

Sophie looked over her shoulder at Calcifer, and Calcifer made faces back, meaning that there was no such thing ready-made. "That wouldn't be right at all," Sophie told the boy severely. "Besides, dueling is wrong."

"Then just give me something that lets me have a fair chance!" the lad said desperately.

Sophie looked at him. He was very undersized and clearly in a great state of fear. He had that hopeless look a person has who always loses at everything. "I'll see what I can do," Sophie said. She hobbled over to the shelves and scanned the jars. The red one labeled CAYENNE looked the most likely. Sophie poured a generous heap of it on a square of paper. She stood the human skull beside it. "Because you must know more about this than I do," she muttered at it. The young man was leaning anxiously round the door to watch. Sophie took up a knife and made what she hoped would look like mystic passes over the heap of pepper. "You are to make it a fair fight," she mumbled. "A fair fight. Understand?" She screwed the paper up and hobbled to the door with it. "Throw this in the air when the duel starts," she told the undersized young man, "and it will give you the same chance as the other man. After that, whether you win or not depends on you."

The undersized young man was so grateful that he tried to give her a gold piece. Sophie refused to take it, so he gave her a two-penny bit instead and went away whistling happily. "I feel a fraud," Sophie said as she stowed the money under the hearthstone. "But I would like to be there at that fight!"

"So would I!" crackled Calcifer. "When are you going to release me so that I can go and see things like that?"

"When I've got even a hint about this contract," Sophie said.

"You may get one later today," said Calcifer.

Michael breezed in toward the end of the after-noon. He took an anxious look round to make sure Howl had not come home first and went to the bench, where he got things out to make it look as if he had been busy, singing cheerfully while he did.

"I envy you being able to walk all that way so easily," Sophie said, sewing a blue triangle to silver braid. "How was Ma—my niece?"

Michael gladly left the workbench and sat on the stool by the hearth to tell her all about his day. Then he asked about Sophie's. The result was that when Howl shouldered the door open with his arms full of parcels, Michael was not even looking busy. He was rolling around on the stool laughing at the duel spell.

Howl backed into the door to shut it and leaned there in a tragic attitude. "Look at you all!" he said. "Ruin stares me in the face. I slave all day for you all. And not one of you, even Calcifer, can spare time to say hello!"

Michael sprang up guiltily and Calcifer said, "I never *do* say hello."

"Is something wrong?" asked Sophie.

"That's better," said Howl. "Some of you are pretending to notice me at last. How kind of you to ask, Sophie. Yes, something *is* wrong. The King has asked me officially to find his brother for him—with a strong hint that destroying the Witch of the Waste would come in handy too—and you all sit there and laugh!"

By now it was clear that Howl was in a mood to produce green slime any second. Sophie hurriedly put her sewing away. "I'll make some hot buttered toast," she said.

"Is that all you can do in the face of tragedy?" Howl asked. "Make toast! No, don't get up. I've trudged here laden with stuff for you, so the least you can do is show polite interest. Here." He tipped a shower of parcels into Sophie's lap and handed another to Michael.

Mystified, Sophie unwrapped things: several pairs of silk stockings; two parcels of the finests cambric petticoats, with flounces, lace, and satin insets; a pair of elastic-sided boots in dove-gray suede; a lace shawl; and a dress of gray watered silk trimmed with lace that matched the shawl. Sophie took one professional look at each and gasped. The lace alone was worth a fortune. She stroked the silk of the dress, awed.

Michael unwrapped a handsome new velvet suit. "You must have spent every bit that was in the silk purse!" he said ungratefully. "I don't need this. You're the one who needs a new suit."

Howl hooked his boot into what remained of the blue-and-silver suit and held it up ruefully. Sophie had been working hard, but it was still more hole than suit. "How selfless I am," he said. "But I can't send you and Sophie to blacken my name to the King in rags. The King would think I didn't look after my old mother properly. Well, Sophie? Are the boots the right size?"

Sophie looked up from her awed stroking. "Are you being kind," she said, "or cowardly? Thank you very much and no I won't."

"What ingratitude!" Howl exclaimed, spreading out both arms. "Let's have green slime again! After which I shall be forced to move the castle a thousand miles away and never see my lovely Lettie again!"

Michael looked at Sophie imploringly. Sophie glowered. She saw well enough that the happiness of both her sisters depended on her agreeing to see the King. With green slime in reserve. "You haven't asked me to do anything yet," she said. "You've just said I'm going to."

Howl smiled. "And you *are* going to, aren't you?"

"All right. When do you want me to go?" Sophie said.

"Tomorrow afternoon," said Howl. "Michael can go as your footman. The King's expecting you." He sat on the stool and began explaining very clearly and soberly just what Sophie was to say. There was no trace of the green-slime mood, now things were going Howl's way, Sophie noticed. She wanted to slap him. "I want you to do a very delicate job," Howl explained, "so that the King will go on giving me work like the transport spells, but not trust me with anything like finding his brother. You must tell him how I've angered the Witch of the Waste and explain what a good son I am to you, but I want you to do it in such a way that he'll understand I'm really quite useless."

Howl explained in great detail. Sophie clasped her hands round the parcels and tried to take it all in, though she could not help thinking, If I was the King, I wouldn't understand a word of what the old woman was driving at!

Michael meanwhile was hovering at Howl's elbow, trying to ask him about the perplexing spell. Howl kept thinking of new, delicate details to tell the King and waving Michael away. "Not now, Michael. And it occurred to me, Sophie, that you might want some practice in order not to find the Palace overwhelming. We don't want you coming over queer in the middle of the interview. Not yet, Michael. So I arranged for you to pay a call to my old tutor, Mrs. Pentstemmon. She's a grand old thing. In some ways she's grander than the King. So you'll be quite used to that kind of thing by the time you get to the Palace."

By this time Sophie was wishing she had never agreed. She was heartily relieved when Howl at last turned to Michael.

"Right, Michael. Your turn now. What is it?"

Michael waved the shiny gray paper and explained in an unhappy rush how impossible the spell seemed to do.

Howl seemed faintly astonished to hear this, but he took the paper, saying, "Now, where was your problem?" and spread it out. He stared at it. One of his eyebrows shot up.

"I tried it as a puzzle and I tried doing it just as it says," Michael explained. "But Sophie and I couldn't catch the falling star—"

"Great gods above!" Howl exclaimed. He started to laugh, and bit his lip to stop himself. "But, Michael, this isn't the spell I left you. Where did you find it?"

"On the bench, in that heap of things Sophie piled round the skull," said Michael. "It was the only new spell there, so I thought—"

Howl leaped up and sorted among the things on the bench. "Sophie strikes again," he said. Things skidded right and left as he searched. "I might have known! No, the proper spell's not here." He tapped the skull thoughtfully on its brown, shiny dome. "Your doing, friend? I have a notion you come from there. I'm sure the guitar does. Er— Sophie dear—"

"What?" said Sophie.

"Busy old fool, unruly Sophie," said Howl. "Am I right in thinking that you turned my doorknob black-side-down and stuck your long nose out through it?"

"Just my finger," Sophie said with dignity.

"But you opened the door," said Howl, "and the thing Michael thinks is a spell must have got through.

Didn't it occur to either of you that it doesn't look like spells usually do?"

"Spells often look peculiar," Michael said. "What is it really?"

Howl gave a snort of laughter. "'Decide what this is about. Write a second verse'! Oh, lord!" he said and ran for the stairs. "I'll show you," he called as his feet pounded up them.

"I think we wasted our time rushing around the marshes last night," Sophie said. Michael nodded gloomily. Sophie could see he was feeling a fool. "It was my fault," she said. "I opened the door."

"What was outside?" Michael asked with great interest.

But Howl came charging downstairs just then. "I haven't got that book after all," he said. He seemed upset now. "Michael, did I hear you say you went out and tried to catch a shooting star?"

"Yes, but it was scared stiff and fell in a pool and drowned," Michael said.

"Thank goodness for that!" said Howl.

"It was very sad," Sophie said.

"Sad, was it?" said Howl, more upset than ever. "It was *your* idea, was it? It *would* be! I can just see you hopping about the marshes, encouraging him! Let me tell you, that was the most stupid thing he's ever done in his life. He'd have been more than sad if he'd chanced to catch the thing! And you——"

Calcifer flickered sleepily up the chimney. "What's all this fuss about?" he demanded. "You caught one yourself, didn't you?"

"Yes, and I—!" Howl began, turning his glass-marble glare on Calcifer. But he pulled himself together and turned to Michael instead. "Michael, promise me you'll never try to catch one again."

"I promise," Michael said willingly. "What is that writing, if it's not a spell?"

Howl looked at the gray paper in his hand. "It's called 'Song'—and that's what it is, I suppose. But it's not all here and I can't remember the rest of it." He stood and thought, as if a new idea had struck him, one which obviously worried him. "I think the next verse was important," he said. "I'd better take it back and see—" He went to the door and turned the knob black-down. Then he paused. He looked round at Michael and Sophie, who were naturally enough both staring at the knob. "All right," he said. "I know Sophie will squirm through somehow if I leave her behind, and that's not fair to Michael. Come along, both of you, so I've got you where I can keep my eye on you."

He opened the door on the nothingness and walked into it. Michael fell over the stool in his rush to follow. Sophie shed parcels right and left into the hearth as she sprang up too. "Don't let any sparks get on those!" she said hurriedly to Calcifer.

"If you promise to tell me what's out there," Calcifer said. "You had your hint, by the way."

"Did I?" said Sophie. She was in too much of a hurry to attend.

Chapter 11:

❖

In which Howl goes to a strange country in search of a spell

The nothingness was only inch-thick after all. Beyond it, in a gray, drizzling evening, was a cement path down to a garden gate. Howl and Michael were waiting at the gate. Beyond that was a flat, hard-looking road lined with houses on both sides. Sophie looked back at where she had come from, shivering rather in the drizzle, and found the castle had become a house of yellow brick with large windows. Like all the other houses, it was square and new, with a front door of wobbly glass. Nobody seemed to be about among the houses. That may have been due to the drizzle, but Sophie had a feeling that it was really because, in spite of there being so many houses, this was somewhere at the edge of a town.

"When you've quite finished nosing," Howl called. His gray-and-scarlet finery was all misted with drizzle. He was dangling a bunch of strange keys, most of which were flat and yellow and seemed to match the houses. When Sophie came down the path, he said, "We need to be dressed in keeping with this place." His finery blurred, as if the drizzle round him had suddenly become a fog. When it came into focus again, it was still scarlet-and-gray, but quite a different shape. The dangling sleeves had gone and the whole outfit was baggier. It looked worn and shabby.

Michael's jacket had become a waist-length padded thing. He lifted his foot, with a canvas shoe on it, and stared at the tight blue things encasing his legs. "I can hardly bend my knee," he said.

"You'll get used to it," said Howl. "Come on, Sophie."

To Sophie's surprise, Howl led the way back up the garden path toward the yellow house. The back of his baggy jacket, she saw, had mysterious words on it: WELSH RUGBY. Michael followed Howl, walking in a kind of tight strut because of the things on his legs. Sophie looked down at herself and saw twice as much skinny leg showing above her knobby shoes. Otherwise, not much about her had changed.

Howl unlocked the wavy-glass door with one of his keys. It had a wooden notice hanging beside it on chains. RIVENDELL, Sophie read, as Howl pushed her into a neat, shiny hall space. There seemed to be people in the house. Loud voices were coming from behind the nearest door. When Howl opened that door, Sophie realized that the voices were coming from magic colored pictures moving on the front of a big, square box.

"Howell!" exclaimed a woman who was sitting there knitting.

She put down her knitting, looking a little annoyed, but before she could get up, a small girl, who had been watching the magic picture very seriously with her chin in her hands, leaped up and flung herself at Howl. "Uncle Howell!" she screamed, and jumped halfway up Howl with her legs wrapped round him.

"Mari!" Howl bawled in reply. "How are you, cariad? Been a good girl, then?" He and the little girl broke into a foreign language then, fast and loud. Sophie could see they were very special to one another. She wondered about the language. It sounded the same as Calcifer's silly saucepan song, but it was hard to be sure. In between bursts of foreign chatter, Howl managed to say, as if he were a ventriloquist, "This is my niece, Mari, and my sister, Megan Parry. Megan, this is Michael Fisher and Sophie—er—"

"Hatter," said Sophie.

Megan shook hands with both of them in a restrained, disapproving way. She was older than Howl, but quite like him, with the same long, angular face, but her eyes were blue and full of anxieties, and her hair was darkish. "Quiet now, Mari!" she said in a voice that cut through the foreign chatter. "Howell, are you staying long?"

"Just dropped in for a moment," Howl said, lowering Mari to the floor.

"Gareth isn't in yet," Megan said in a meaning sort of way.

"What a pity! We can't stay," Howl said, smiling a warm, false smile. "I just thought I'd introduce you to my friends here. And I want to ask you something that may sound silly. Has Neil by any chance lost a piece of English homework lately?"

"*Funny* you should say that!" Megan exclaimed. "Looking everywhere for it, he was, last Thursday! He's got this new English teacher, see, and she's very strict, doesn't just worry about spelling either. Puts the fear of God into them about getting work in on time. Doesn't do Neil any harm, lazy little devil! So here he is on Thursday, hunting high and low, and all he can find is a funny old piece of writing—"

"Ah," said Howl. "What did he do with that writing?"

"I told him to hand it in to this Miss Angorian of his," Megan said. "Might show her he tried for once."

"And did he?" Howl asked.

"*I* don't know. Better ask Neil. He's up in the front bedroom with that machine of his," said Megan. "But you won't get a word of sense out of him."

"Come on," Howl said to Michael and Sophie, who were both staring round the shiny brown-and-orange room. He took Mari's hand and led them all out of the room and up the stairs. Even those had a carpet, a pink-and-green one. So the procession led by Howl made hardly any noise as it went along the pink-and-green passage upstairs and into a room with a blue-and-yellow carpet. But Sophie was not sure the two boys crouched over the various magic boxes on a big table by the window would have looked up even for an army with a brass band. The main magic box had a glass front like the one downstairs, but it seemed to be showing writing and diagrams more than pictures. All the boxes grew on long, floppy white stalks that appeared to be rooted in the wall at one side of the room.

"Neil!" said Howl.

"Don't interrupt," one of the boys said. "He'll lose his life."

Seeing it was a matter of life and death, Sophie and Michael backed toward the door. But Howl, quite unperturbed at killing his nephew, strode over to the wall and pulled the boxes up by the roots. The picture on the box vanished. Both boys said words which Sophie did not think even Martha knew. The second boy spun round, shouting, "Mari! I'll get you for that!"

"Wasn't me this time. So!" Mari shouted back.

Neil whirled further round and stared accusingly at Howl. "How do, Neil?" Howl said pleasantly.

"Who is he?" the other boy asked.

"My no-good uncle," Neil said. He glowered at Howl. He was dark, with thick eyebrows, and his glower was impressive. "What do you want? Put that plug back in."

"There's a welcome in the valleys!" said Howl. "I'll put it back when I've asked you something and you've answered."

Neil sighed. "Uncle Howell, I'm in the middle of a computer game."

"A new one?" asked Howl.

Both the boys looked discontented. "No, it's one I had for Christmas," Neil said. "You ought to know the way they go on about wasting time and money on useless things. They won't give me another till my birthday."

"Then that's easy," said Howl. "You won't mind stopping if you've done it before, and I'll bribe you with a new one—"

"Really?" both boys said eagerly, and Neil added, "Can you make it another of those that nobody else has got?"

"Yes. But just take a look at this first and tell me what it is," Howl said, and he held the shiny gray paper out in front of Neil.

Both boys looked at it. Neil said, "It's a poem," in the way most people would say, "It's a dead rat."

"It's the one Miss Angorian set for last week's homework," said the other boy. "I remember 'wind' and 'finned.' It's about submarines."

While Sophie and Michael blinked at this new theory, wondering how they had missed it, Neil exclaimed, "Hey! It's my long-lost homework. Where did you find it? Was that funny writing that turned up *yours*? Miss Angorian said it was interesting—lucky for me—and she took it home with her."

"Thank you," said Howl. "Where does she live?"

"That flat over Mrs. Phillips' tea shop. Cardiff Road," said Neil. "When will you give me the new tape?"

"When you remember how the rest of the poem goes," said Howl.

"That's not fair!" said Neil. "I can't even remember the bit that was written down now. That's just playing with a person's feelings——!" He stopped when Howl laughed, felt in one baggy pocket, and handed him a flat packet. *"Thanks!"* Neil said devoutly, and without more ado he whirled round to his magic boxes. Howl planted the bundle of roots back in the wall, grinning, and beckoned Michael and Sophie out of the room. Both boys began a flurry of mysterious activity, into which Mari somehow squeezed herself, watching with her thumb in her mouth.

Howl hurried away to the pink-and-green stairs, but Michael and Sophie both hung about near the door of the room, wondering what the whole thing was about. Inside, Neil was reading aloud. "You are in an enchanted castle with four doors. Each opens on a different dimension. In Dimension One the castle is moving constantly and may arrive at a hazard at any time. . . ."

Sophie wondered at the familiarity of this as she hobbled to the stairs. She found Michael standing halfway down, looking embarrassed. Howl was at the foot of the stairs having an argument with his sister.

"What do you mean, you've sold all my books?" she heard Howl saying. "I needed one of them particularly. They weren't yours to sell."

"Don't keep interrupting!" Megan answered in a low, ferocious voice. "*Listen* now! I've told you before I'm not a storehouse for your property. You're a disgrace to me and Gareth, lounging about in those clothes instead of buying a proper suit and looking respectable for once, taking up with riffraff and layabouts, bringing them to this house! Are you trying to bring me down to your level? You had all that education, and you don't even get a decent job, you just hang around, wasting all that time at college, wasting all those sacrifices other people made, wasting your money . . . "

Megan would have been a match for Mrs. Fairfax. Her voice went on and on. Sophie began to understand how Howl had acquired the habit of slithering out. Megan was the kind of person who made you want to back quietly out of the nearest door. Unfortunately,

Howl was backed up against the stairs, and Sophie and Michael were bottled up behind him.

" . . . never doing an honest day's work, never getting a job I could be proud of, bringing shame on me and Gareth, coming here and spoiling Mari rotten," Megan ground on remorselessly.

Sophie pushed Michael aside and stumped downstairs, looking as stately as she could manage. "Come, Howl," she said grandly. "We really must be on our way. While we stand here, money is ticking away and your servants are probably selling the gold plate. *So* nice to meet you," she said to Megan as she arrived at the foot of the stairs, "but we must rush. Howl is such a busy man."

Megan gulped a bit and stared at Sophie. Sophie gave her a stately nod and pushed Howl toward the wavy-glass front door. Michael's face was bright red. Sophie saw that because Howl turned back to ask Megan, "Is my old car still in the shed, or have you sold that too?"

"You've got the only set of keys," Megan answered dourly.

That seemed to be the only goodbye. The front door slammed and Howl took them to a square white building at the end of the flat black road. Howl did not say anything about Megan. He said, as he unlocked a wide door in the building, "I suppose the fierce English teacher is bound to have a copy of that book."

Sophie wished to forget the next bit. They rode in a carriage without horses that went at a terrifying speed, smelling and growling and shaking as it tore down some of the steepest roads Sophie had ever seen—roads so steep that she wondered why the houses lining them did not slide into a heap at the bottom. She shut her eyes and clung to some of the pieces that had torn off the seats, and simply hoped it would be over soon.

Luckily, it was. They arrived in a flatter road with houses crammed in on both sides, beside a large window filled with a white curtain and a notice that said: TEAS CLOSED. But, despite this forbidding notice, when Howl pressed a button at a small door beside the window, Miss Angorian opened the door. They all stared at her. For a fierce schoolteacher, Miss Angorian was astonishingly young and slender and good-looking. She had sheets of blue-black hair hanging round her olive-brown heart-shaped face, and enormous dark eyes. The only thing which suggested fierceness about her was the direct and clever way those enormous eyes looked and seemed to sum them up.

"I'll take a small guess that you may be Howell Jenkins," Miss Angorian said to Howl. She had a low, melodious voice that was nevertheless rather amused and quite sure of itself.

Howl was taken aback for an instant. Then his smile snapped on. And that, Sophie thought, was goodbye to the pleasant dreams of Lettie and Mrs. Fairfax. For Miss Angorian was exactly the kind of lady someone like Howl could be trusted to fall in love with on the spot. And not only Howl. Michael was staring admiringly too. And though all the houses around were apparently deserted, Sophie had no doubt that they were full of people who all knew both Howl and Miss Angorian and were watching with interest to see what would happen. She could feel their invisible eyes. Market Chipping was like that too.

"And you must be Miss Angorian," said Howl. "I'm sorry to bother you, but I made a stupid mistake last week and carried off my nephew's English homework instead of a rather important paper I had with me. I gather Neil gave it to you as proof that he wasn't shirking."

"He did," said Miss Angorian. "You'd better come in and collect it."

Sophie was sure the invisible eyes in all the houses goggled and the invisible necks craned as Howl and Michael and she trooped in through Miss Angorian's door and up a flight of stairs to Miss Angorian's tiny, severe living room.

Miss Angorian said considerately to Sophie, "Won't you sit down?"

Sophie was still shaking from that horseless carriage. She sat down gladly on one of the two chairs. It was not very comfortable. Miss Angorian's room was not designed for comfort but for study. Though many of the things in it were strange, Sophie understood the walls of books, and the piles of paper on the table, and the folders stacked on the floor. She sat and watched Michael staring sheepishly and Howl turning on his charm.

"How is it you come to know who I am?" Howl asked beguilingly.

"You seem to have caused a lot of gossip in this town," Miss Angorian said, busy sorting through papers on the table.

"And what have those people who gossip told you?" Howl asked. He leaned languishingly on the end of the table and tried to catch Miss Angorian's eye.

"That you disappear and turn up rather unpredictably, for one thing," Miss Angorian said.

"And what else?" Howl followed Miss Angorian's movements with such a look that Sophie knew Lettie's only chance was for Miss Angorian to fall instantly in love with Howl too.

But Miss Angorian was not that kind of lady. She said, "Many other things, few of them to your credit," and caused Michael to blush by looking at him and then at Sophie in a way that suggested these things were not fit for their ears. She held a yellowish wavy-edged paper out to Howl. "Here it is," she said severely. "Do you know what it is?"

"Of course," said Howl.

"Then please tell me," said Miss Angorian.

Howl took the paper. There was a bit of a scuffle as he tried to take Miss Angorian's hand with it. Miss Angorian won the scuffle and put her hands behind her back. Howl smiled meltingly and passed the paper to Michael. "*You* tell her," he said.

Michael's blushing face lit up as soon as he looked at it. "It's the spell! Oh, I can do this one— it's enlargement, isn't it?"

"That's what I thought," Miss Angorian said rather accusingly. "I'd like to know what you were doing with such a thing."

"Miss Angorian," said Howl, "if you have heard all those things about me, you must know I wrote my doctoral thesis on charms and spells. You look as if you suspect me of working black magic! I assure you, I never worked any kind of spell in my life." Sophie could not stop herself making a small snort at this blatant lie. "With my hand on my heart," Howl added, giving Sophie an irritated frown, "this spell is for study purposes only. It's very old and rare. That's why I wanted it back."

"Well, you have it back," Miss Angorian said briskly. "Before you go, would you mind giving me my homework sheet in return? Photocopies cost money."

Howl brought out the gray paper willingly and held it just out of reach. "This poem now," he said.

"It's been bothering me. Silly, really!——but I can't remember the rest of it. By Walter Raleigh, isn't it?"

Miss Angorian gave him a withering look. "Certainly not. It's by John Donne and it's very well known indeed. I have the book with it in here, if you want to refresh your memory."

"Please," said Howl, and from the way his eyes followed Miss Angorian as she went to her wall of books, Sophie realized that this was the real reason why Howl had come into this strange land where his family lived. But Howl was not above killing two birds with one stone. "Miss Angorian," he said pleadingly, following her contours as she stretched for the book, "would you consider coming out for some supper with me tonight?"

Miss Angorian turned round with a large book in her hands, looking more severe than ever. "I would not," she said. "Mr. Jenkins, I don't know what you've heard about me, but you must have heard that I still consider myself engaged to Ben Sullivan——"

"Never heard of him," said Howl.

"My fiancé," said Miss Angorian. "He disappeared some years back. Now, do you wish me to read this poem out to you?"

"Do that," Howl said, quite unrepentant. "You have such a lovely voice."

"Then I'll start with the second verse," Miss Angorian said, "since you have the first verse there in your hand." She read very well, not only melodiously, but in a way which made the second verse fit the rhythm of the first, which in Sophie's opinion it did not do at all:

> "If thou beest born to strange sights,
>   Things invisible to see,
> Ride ten thousand days and nights
> Till age snow white hairs on thee.
> Thou, when thou returnest, wilt tell me
> All strange wonders that befell thee,
>   And swear
>   No where
> Lives a woman true, and fair.
>
> If thou—"

Howl had gone a terrible white. Sophie could see sweat standing on his face. "Thank you," he said. "Stop there. I won't trouble you for the rest. Even the good woman is untrue in the last verse, isn't she? I remember now. Silly of me. John Donne, of course." Miss Angorian lowered the book and stared at him. He forced up a smile. "We must be going now. Sure you won't change your mind about supper?"

"I will not," said Miss Angorian. "Are you quite well, Mr. Jenkins?"

"In the pink," Howl said, and he hustled Michael

and Sophie away down the stairs and into the horrible horseless carriage. The invisible watchers in the houses must have thought Miss Angorian was chasing them with a saber, if they judged from the speed with which Howl packed them into it and drove off.

"What's the matter?" Michael asked as the carriage went roaring and grinding uphill again and Sophie clung to bits of seat for dear life. Howl pretended not to hear. So Michael waited until Howl was locking it into its shed and asked again.

"Oh, nothing," Howl said airily, leading the way back to the yellow house called RIVENDELL. "The Witch of the Waste has caught up with me with her curse, that's all. Bound to happen sooner or later." He seemed to be calculating or doing sums in his head while he opened the garden gate. "Ten thousand," Sophie heard him murmur. "That brings it to about Midsummer Day."

"What is brought to Midsummer Day?" asked Sophie.

"The time I'll be ten thousand days old," Howl said. "And that, Mrs. Nose," he said, swinging into the garden of RIVENDELL, "is the day I shall have to go back to the Witch of the Waste." Sophie and Michael hung back on the path, staring at Howl's back, so mysteriously labeled WELSH RUGBY. "If I keep clear of mermaids," they heard him mutter, "and don't touch a mandrake root——"

Michael called out, "Do we have to go back into that house?" and Sophie called, "What will the Witch do?"

"I shudder to think," Howl said. "You don't have to go back in, Michael."

He opened the wavy-glass door. Inside was the familiar room of the castle. Calcifer's sleepy flames were coloring the walls faintly blue-green in the dusk. Howl flung back his long sleeves and gave Calcifer a log.

"She caught up, old blueface," he said.

"I know," said Calcifer. "I felt it take."

Chapter 12:

---◆◆◆---

In which Sophie becomes
Howl's old mother

Sophie did not see much point in blackening Howl's name to the King, now that the Witch had caught up with him. But Howl said it was more important than ever. "I shall need everything I've got just to escape the Witch," he said. "I can't have the King after me as well."

So the following afternoon Sophie put on her new clothes and sat feeling very fine, if rather stiff, waiting for Michael to get ready and for Howl to finish in the bathroom. While she waited, she told Calcifer about the strange country where Howl's family lived. It took her mind off the King.

Calcifer was very interested. "I knew he came from foreign parts," he said. "But this sounds like another world. Clever of the Witch to send the curse in from there. Very clever all round. That's magic I admire, using something that exists anyway and turning it round into a curse. I did wonder about it when you and Michael were reading it the other day. That fool Howl told her too much about himself."

Sophie gazed at Calcifer's thin blue face. It did not surprise her to find Calcifer admired the curse, any more than it surprised her when he called Howl a fool. He was always insulting Howl. But she never could work out if Calcifer really hated Howl. Calcifer looked so evil anyway that it was hard to tell.

Calcifer moved his orange eyes to look into Sophie's. "I'm scared too," he said. "I shall suffer with Howl if the Witch catches him. If you don't break the contract before she does, I won't be able to help you at all."

Before Sophie could ask more, Howl came dashing out of the bathroom looking his very finest, scenting the room with roses and yelling for Michael. Michael clattered downstairs in his new blue velvet. Sophie stood up and collected her trusty stick. It was time to go.

"You look wonderfully rich and stately!" Michael said to her.

"She does me credit," said Howl, "apart from that awful old stick."

"Some people," said Sophie, "are thoroughly self-centered. This stick goes with me. I need it for moral support."

Howl looked at the ceiling, but he did not argue.

They took their stately way into the streets of Kingsbury. Sophie of course looked back to see what the castle was like here. She saw a big, arched gateway surrounding a small black door. The rest of the castle seemed to be a blank stretch of plastered wall between two carved stone houses.

"Before you ask," said Howl, "it's really just a disused stable. This way."

They walked through the streets, looking at least as fine as any of the passersby. Not that many people were about. Kingsbury was a long way south and it was a bakingly hot day there. The pavements shimmered. Sophie discovered another disadvantage to being old: you felt queer in hot weather. The elaborate buildings wavered in front of her eyes. She was annoyed, because she wanted to look at the place, but all she had was a dim impression of golden domes and tall houses.

"By the way," Howl said, "Mrs. Pentstemmon will call you Mrs. Pendragon. Pendragon's the name I go under here."

"Whatever for?" said Sophie.

"For disguise," said Howl. "Pendragon's a lovely name, much better than Jenkins."

"I get by quite well with a plain name," Sophie said as they turned into a blessedly narrow, cool street.

"We can't all be Mad Hatters," said Howl.

Mrs. Pentstemmon's house was gracious and tall, near the end of the narrow street. It had orange trees in tubs on either side of its handsome front door. This door was opened by an elderly footman in black velvet, who led them into a wonderfully cool black-and-white checkered marble hall, where Michael tried secretly to wipe sweat off his face. Howl, who always seemed to be cool, treated the footman as an old friend and made jokes to him.

The footman passed them on to a page boy in red velvet. Sophie, as the boy led them ceremoniously up polished stairs, began to see why this made good practice for meeting the King. She felt as if she were in a palace already. When the boy ushered them into a shaded drawing room, she was sure even a palace could not be this elegant. Everything in the room was blue and gold and white, and small and fine. Mrs. Pentstemmon was finest of all. She was tall and thin, and she sat bolt upright in a blue-and-gold embroidered chair, supporting herself rigidly with one hand, in a gold-mesh mitten, on a gold-topped cane. She wore old-gold silk, in a very stiff and old-fashioned style, finished off with an old-gold headdress not unlike a crown, which tied in a large old-gold bow beneath her gaunt eagle face. She was the finest and most frightening lady Sophie had ever seen.

"Ah, my dear Howell," she said, holding out a gold-mesh mitten.

Howl bent and kissed the mitten, as he was obviously supposed to. He did it very gracefully, but it was rather spoiled from back view by Howl flapping his other hand furiously at Michael behind his back. Michael, a little too slowly, realized he was supposed to stand by the door beside the page boy. He backed there in a hurry, only too pleased to get as far away from Mrs. Pentstemmon as he could.

"Mrs. Pentstemmon, allow me to present my old mother," Howl said, waving his hand at Sophie. Since Sophie felt just like Michael, Howl had to flap his hand at her too.

"Charmed. Delighted," said Mrs. Pentstemmon, and she held her gold mitten out to Sophie. Sophie was not sure if Mrs. Pentstemmon meant her to kiss the mitten as well, but she could not bring herself to try. She laid her own hand on the mitten instead. The hand under it felt like an old, cold claw. After feeling it, Sophie was quite surprised that Mrs. Pentstemmon was alive. "Forgive my not standing up, Mrs. Pendragon," Mrs. Pentstemmon said. "My health is not good. It forced me to retire from teaching three years ago. Pray sit down, both of you."

Trying not to shake with nerves, Sophie sat grandly in the embroidered chair opposite Mrs. Pentstemmon's, supporting herself on her stick in what she hoped was the same elegant way. Howl spread himself gracefully in a chair next to it. He looked quite at home, and Sophie envied him.

"I am eighty-six," Mrs. Pentstemmon announced.

"How old are you, my dear Mrs. Pendragon?"

"Ninety," Sophie said, that being the first high number that came into her head.

"So old?" Mrs. Pentstemmon said with what may have been slight, stately envy. "How lucky you are to move so nimbly still."

"Oh, yes, she's so wonderfully nimble," Howl agreed, "that sometimes there's no stopping her."

Mrs. Pentstemmon gave him a look which told Sophie she had been a teacher at least as fierce as Miss Angorian. "I am talking to your mother," she said. "I daresay she is as proud of you as I am. We are two old ladies who both had a hand in forming you. You are, one might say, our joint creation."

"Don't you think I did any of me myself, then?" Howl asked. "Put in just a few touches of my own?"

"A few, and those not altogether to my liking," Mrs. Pentstemmon replied. "But you will not wish to sit here and hear yourself being discussed. You will go down and sit on the terrace, taking your page boy with you, where Hunch will bring you both a cool drink. Go along."

If Sophie had not been so nervous herself, she might have laughed at the expression on Howl's face. He had obviously not expected this to happen at all. But he got up, with only a slight shrug, made a slight warning face at Sophie, and shooed Michael out of the room ahead of him. Mrs. Pentstemmon

177

turned her rigid body very slightly to watch them go. Then she nodded at the page boy, who scuttled out of the room too. After that, Mrs. Pentstemmon turned herself back toward Sophie, and Sophie felt more nervous than ever.

"I prefer him with black hair," Mrs. Pentstemmon announced. "That boy is going to the bad."

"Who? Michael?" Sophie said, bewildered.

"Not the servitor," said Mrs. Pentstemmon. "I do not think he is clever enough to cause me concern. I am talking about Howell, Mrs. Pendragon."

"Oh," said Sophie, wondering why Mrs. Pentstemmon only said "going." Howl had surely arrived at the bad long ago.

"Take his whole appearance," Mrs. Pentstemmon said sweepingly. "Look at his clothes."

"He *is* always very careful about his appearance," Sophie agreed, and wondered why she was putting it so mildly.

"And always was. I am careful about my appearance too, and I see no harm in that," said Mrs. Pentstemmon. "But what call has he to be walking around in a charmed suit? It is a dazzling attraction charm, directed at ladies—very well done, I admit, and barely detectable even to my trained eye, since it appears to have been darned into the seams—and one which will render him almost irresistible to ladies. This represents a downward trend into black arts which must surely cause you some motherly concern, Mrs. Pendragon."

Sophie thought uneasily about the gray-and-scarlet suit. She had darned the seams without noticing it had anything particular about it. But Mrs. Pentstemmon was an expert on magic, and Sophie was only an expert on clothes.

Mrs. Pentstemmon put both gold mittens on top of her stick and canted her stiff body so that both her trained and piercing eyes stared into Sophie's. Sophie felt more and more nervous and uneasy. "My life is nearly over," Mrs. Pentstemmon announced. "I have felt death tiptoeing close for some time now."

"Oh, I'm sure that isn't so," Sophie said, trying to sound soothing. It was hard to sound like anything with Mrs. Pentstemmon staring at her like that.

"I assure you it is so," said Mrs. Pentstemmon. "This is why I was anxious to see you, Mrs. Pendragon. Howell, you see, was my last pupil and by far my best. I was about to retire when he came to me out of a foreign land. I thought my work was done when I trained Benjamin Sullivan—whom you probably know better as Wizard Suliman, rest his soul!—and procured him the post of Royal Magician. Oddly enough, he came from the same country as Howell. Then Howell came, and I saw at a glance that he had twice the imagination and twice the abilities, and, though I admit he had some faults of character, I knew he was a force for good. *Good*, Mrs. Pendragon. But what is he now?"

"What indeed?" Sophie said.

"Something has happened to him," Mrs. Pentstemmon said, still staring piercingly at Sophie. "And I am determined to put that right before I die."

"What do you think has happened?" Sophie asked uncomfortably.

"I must rely on you to tell me that," said Mrs. Pentstemmon. "My feeling is that he has gone the same way as the Witch of the Waste. They tell me she was not wicked once—though I have this only on hearsay, since she is older than either of us and keeps herself young by her arts. Howell has gifts in the same order as hers. It seems as if those of high ability cannot resist some extra, dangerous stroke of cleverness, which results in a fatal flaw and begins a slow decline to evil. Do you, by any chance, have a clue what it might be?"

Calcifer's voice came into Sophie's mind, saying, "The contract isn't doing either of us any good in the long run." She felt a little chilly, in spite of the heat of the day blowing through the open windows of the shaded, elegant room. "Yes," she said. "He's made some sort of contract with his fire demon."

Mrs. Pentstemmon's hands shook a little on her stick. "That will be it. You must break that contract, Mrs. Pendragon."

"I would if I knew how," Sophie said.

"Surely your maternal feelings and your own strong magic gift will tell you how," Mrs. Pentstemmon said. "I have been looking at you, Mrs. Pendragon, though you may not have noticed—"

"Oh, I noticed, Mrs. Pentstemmon," Sophie said.

"—and I like your gift," said Mrs. Pentstemmon. "It brings life to things, such as that stick in your hand, which you have evidently talked to, to the extent that it has become what the layman would call a magic wand. I think you would not find it too hard to break that contract."

"Yes, but I need to know what the terms of it are," Sophie said. "Did Howl tell you I was a witch, because if he did—"

"He did not. There is no need to be coy. You can rely on my experience to know these things," said Mrs. Pentstemmon. Then, to Sophie's relief, she shut her eyes. It was like a strong light being turned off. "I do not know, nor do I wish to know, about such contracts," she said. Her cane wobbled again, as if she might be shuddering. Her mouth quirked into a line, suggesting she had unexpectedly bitten on a peppercorn. "But I now see," she said, "what has happened to the Witch. She made a contract with a fire demon and, over the years, that demon has taken control of her. Demons do not understand good and evil. But they can be bribed into a contract, provided the human offers them something valuable, something only humans have. This prolongs the life of both human and demon, and the human gets the demon's magic power to add to his or her own." Mrs. Pentstemmon opened her eyes again. "That is all I can bear to say on the subject," she said, "except to advise you to find out what that demon got. Now I must bid you farewell. I have to rest awhile."

And like magic, which it probably was, the door opened and the page boy came in to usher Sophie out of the room. Sophie was extremely glad to go. She was all but squirming with embarrassment by then. She looked back at Mrs. Pentstemmon's rigid, upright form as the door closed and wondered if Mrs. Pentstemmon would have made her feel this bad if she had really and truly been Howl's old mother. Sophie rather thought she would. "I take my hat off to Howl for standing her as a teacher for more than a day!" she murmured to herself.

"Madam?" asked the page boy, thinking Sophie was talking to him.

"I said, go slowly down the stairs or I can't keep up," Sophie told him. Her knees were wobbling. "You young boys dash about so," she said.

The page boy took her slowly and considerately down the shiny stairs. Halfway down, Sophie recovered enough from Mrs. Pentstemmon's personality to think of some of the things Mrs. Pentstemmon had actually said. She had said Sophie was a witch. Oddly enough, Sophie accepted this without any trouble at all. That explained the popularity of certain hats, she thought. It explained Jane Farrier's Count Whatsit. It possibly explained the jealousy of the Witch of the Waste. It was as if Sophie had always known this. But she had thought it was not proper to have a magic gift because she was the eldest of three. Lettie had been far more sensible about such things.

Then she thought of the gray-and-scarlet suit and nearly fell downstairs with dismay. She was the one who had put the charm on that. She could hear herself now, murmuring to it. "Built to pull in the girls!" she had told it. And of course it did. It had charmed Lettie that day in the orchard. Yesterday, somewhat disguised, it must have had its secret effect on Miss Angorian too.

Oh, dear! Sophie thought. I've gone and doubled the number of hearts he'll have broken! I must get that suit off him somehow!

Howl, in that same suit, was waiting in the cool black-and-white hall with Michael. Michael nudged Howl in a worried way as Sophie came slowly down the stairs behind the page boy. Howl looked saddened. "You seem a bit ragged," he said. "I think we'd better skip seeing the King. I'll go and blacken my own name when I make your excuses. I can say my wicked ways have made you ill. That could be true, from the look of you."

Sophie certainly did not wish to see the King. But she thought of what Calcifer had said. If the King commanded Howl to go into the Waste and the Witch caught him, Sophie's own chance of being young again would have gone too.

She shook her head. "After Mrs. Pentstemmon," she said, "the King of Ingary will seem just like an ordinary person."

Chapter 13:

In which Sophie blackens
Howl's name

Sophie was feeling decidedly queer again when they reached the Palace. Its many golden domes dazzled her. The way to the front entrance was up a huge flight of steps, with a soldier in scarlet standing guard every six steps. The poor boys must have been near fainting in the heat, Sophie thought as she puffed her way dizzily up past them. At the top of the steps were archways, halls, corridors, lobbies, one after another. Sophie lost count of how many. At every archway a splendidly dressed person wearing white gloves—still somehow white in spite of the heat—inquired their business and then led them on to the next personage in the next archway.

"Mrs. Pendragon to see the King!" the voice of each echoed down the halls.

About halfway, Howl was politely detached and told to wait. Michael and Sophie went on being handed from person to person. They were taken upstairs, after which the splendid persons were dressed in blue instead of red, and handed on again until they came to an anteroom paneled in a hundred different-colored woods. There Michael was peeled off and made to wait too. Sophie, who by this time was not at all sure whether she was not having some strange dream, was ushered through huge double doors, and this time the echoing voice said, "Your Majesty, here is Mrs. Pendragon to see you."

And there was the King, not on a throne, but sitting in a rather square chair with only a little gold leaf on it, near the middle of a large room, and dressed much more modestly than the persons who waited on him. He was quite alone, like an ordinary person. True, he sat with one leg thrust out in a kingly sort of manner, and he was handsome in a plump, slightly vague way, but to Sophie he seemed quite youthful and just a touch too proud of being a king. She felt he ought, with that face, to have been more unsure of himself.

He said, "Well, what does Wizard Howl's mother want to see me about?"

And Sophie was suddenly overwhelmed by the fact that she was standing talking to the King. It was, she thought dizzily, as if the man sitting there and the huge, important thing which was kingship were two separate things that just happened to occupy the same chair. And she found she had forgotten every word of the careful, delicate things Howl had told her to say. But she had to say something.

"He sent me to tell you he's not going to look for your brother," she said. "Your Majesty."

She stared at the King. The King stared back. It was a disaster.

"Are you sure?" asked the King. "The Wizard seemed quite willing when I talked to him."

The one thing Sophie had left in her head was that she was here to blacken Howl's name, so she said, "He lied about that. He didn't want to annoy you. He's a slitherer-outer, if you know what I mean, Your Majesty."

"And he hopes to slither out of finding my brother Justin," said the King. "I see. Won't you sit down, since I see you are not young, and tell me the Wizard's reasons?"

There was another plain chair rather a long way from the King. Sophie creaked herself down into it and sat with her hands propped on her stick like Mrs. Pentstemmon, hoping that would make her feel better. But her mind was still simply a roaring white blank of stage fright. All she could think of to say was "Only a coward would send his old mother along to plead for him. You can see what he's like just from that, Your Majesty."

"It is an unusual step," the King said gravely. "But I told him that I'd make it worth his while if he agreed."

"Oh, he doesn't care about money," Sophie said.

"But he's scared stiff of the Witch of the Waste, you see. She put a curse on him and it's just caught up with him."

"Then he has every reason to be scared," the King said with a slight shiver. "But tell me more, please, about the Wizard."

More about Howl? Sophie thought desperately. I have to blacken his name! Her mind was such a blank that for a second it actually seemed to her that Howl had no faults at all. How stupid! "Well, he's fickle, careless, selfish, and hysterical," she said. "Half the time I think he doesn't care what happens to anyone as long as *he's* all right—but then I find out how awfully kind he's been to someone. Then I think he's kind just when it suits him—only then I find out he undercharges poor people. I don't know, Your Majesty. He's a mess."

"My impression," said the King, "was that Howl is an unprincipled, slippery rogue with a glib tongue and a clever mind. Would you agree?"

"How well you put it!" Sophie said heartily. "But you left out how vain he is and——" She looked suspiciously at the King across the yards of carpet. He seemed so surprisingly ready to help her blacken Howl's name.

The King was smiling. It was the slightly uncertain smile that went with the person he was, rather than the king he ought to be. "Thank you, Mrs.

Pendragon," he said. "Your outspokenness has taken a weight off my mind. The Wizard agreed to look for my brother so readily that I thought I had picked the wrong man after all. I feared he was someone who was either unable to resist showing off or would do anything for money. But you have shown me he is just the man I need."

"Oh, confound it!" Sophie cried out. "He sent me to tell you he wasn't!"

"And so you did." The King hitched his chair an inch toward Sophie's. "Let me be equally outspoken now," he said. "Mrs. Pendragon, I need my brother back badly. It is not just that I am fond of him and regret the quarrel we had. It is not even that certain people are whispering that I did away with him myself—which anyone who knows us both knows to be perfect nonsense. No, Mrs. Pendragon. The fact is, my brother Justin is a brilliant general and, with High Norland and Strangia about to declare war on us, I can't do without him. The Witch has threatened me too, you know. Now that all reports agree that Justin did indeed go into the Waste, I am certain that the Witch meant me to be without him when I needed him most. I think she took Wizard Suliman as bait to fetch Justin. And it follows that I need a fairly clever and unscrupulous wizard to get him back."

"Howl will just run away," Sophie warned the King.

"No," said the King. "I don't think he will. The fact that he sent you tells me that. He did it to show me he was too much of a coward to care what I thought of him, isn't that right, Mrs. Pendragon?"

Sophie nodded. She wished she could have remembered all Howl's delicate remarks. The King would have understood them even if she did not.

"Not the act of a vain man," the King said. "But no one would do that except as a last resort, which shows me that Wizard Howl will do what I want if I make it clear to him that his last resort has failed."

"I think you may be—er—taking delicate hints that aren't there, Your Majesty," Sophie said.

"I think not." The King smiled. His slightly vague features had all firmed up. He was sure he was right. "Tell Wizard Howl, Mrs. Pendragon, that I am appointing him Royal Wizard as from now, with our Royal Command to find Prince Justin, alive or dead, before the year is out. You have our leave to go now."

He held out his hand to Sophie, just like Mrs. Pentstemmon, but a little less royally. Sophie levered herself up, wondering if she was meant to kiss this hand or not. But since she felt more like raising her stick and beating the King over the head with it, she shook the King's hand and gave a creaking little curtsy. It seemed to be the right thing to do. The King gave her a friendly smile as she hobbled away to the double doors.

"Oh, curses!" she muttered to herself. It was not only exactly what Howl did not want. Howl would now move the castle a thousand miles away. Lettie, Martha, and Michael would all be miserable, and no doubt there would be torrents of green slime into the bargain as well. "It comes of being the eldest," she muttered while she was shoving the heavy doors open. "You just can't win!"

And here was another thing which had gone wrong. In her annoyance and disappointment, Sophie had somehow come out through the wrong set of double doors. This anteroom had mirrors all round it. In them she could see her own little bent, hobbling shape in its fine gray dress, a great many people in blue Court dress, others in suits as fine as Howl's, but no Michael. Michael of course was hanging about in the anteroom paneled in a hundred kinds of wood.

"Oh, drat!" said Sophie.

One of the courtiers hastened up to her and bowed. "Madam Sorceress! Can I be of assistance?"

He was an undersized young man, rather red-eyed. Sophie stared at him. "Oh, good gracious!" she said. "So the spell worked!"

"It did indeed," said the small courtier a little ruefully. "I disarmed him while he was sneezing and he is now suing me. But the important thing"——his face spread into a happy smile——"is that my dear Jane has come back to me! Now, what can I do for you? I feel responsible for your happiness."

"I'm not sure that it mightn't be the other way round," Sophie said. "Are you by any chance the Count of Catterack?"

"At your service," said the small courtier, bowing.

Jane Farrier must be a good foot taller than he is! Sophie thought. It is all definitely my fault. "Yes, you *can* help me," she said, and explained about Michael.

The Count of Catterack assured her that Michael would be fetched and brought down to the entrance hall to meet her. It was no trouble at all. He took Sophie to a gloved attendant himself and handed her over with much bowing and smiling. Sophie was handed to another attendant, then another, just as before, and eventually hobbled her way down to the stairs guarded by the soldiers.

Michael was not there. Nor was Howl, but that was small relief to Sophie. She thought she might have guessed it would be like this! The Count of Catterack was obviously a person who never got a thing right, and she was another herself. It was probably lucky she had even found the way out. By now she was so tired and hot and dejected that she decided not to wait for Michael. She wanted to sit down in the fireside chair and tell Calcifer the mess she had made of things.

She hobbled down the grand staircase. She hobbled down a grand avenue. She stumped along another, where spires and towers and gilded roofs circled around in giddy profusion. And she realized it was worse than she had thought. She was lost. She had absolutely no idea how to find the disguised stable where the castle entrance was. She turned up another handsome thoroughfare at random, but she did not recognize that either. By now she did not even know the way back to the Palace. She tried asking people she met. Most of them seemed as hot and tired as she was. "Wizard Pendragon?" they said. "Who is he?"

Sophie hobbled on hopelessly. She was near giving up and sitting on the next doorstep for the night, when she passed the end of the narrow street where Mrs. Pentstemmon's house was. Ah! she thought. I can go and ask the footman. He and Howl were so friendly that he must know where Howl lives. So she turned down the street.

The Witch of the Waste was coming up it toward her.

How Sophie recognized the Witch would be hard to say. Her face was different. Her hair, instead of being orderly chestnut curls, was a rippling mass of red, hanging almost to her waist, and she was dressed in floating flutters of auburn and pale yellow. Very cool and lovely she looked. Sophie knew her at once. She almost stopped, but not quite.

There's no reason she should remember me, Sophie thought. I must be just one of hundreds of people she's enchanted. And Sophie stumped boldly on, thumping her stick on the cobbles and reminding herself, in case of trouble, that Mrs. Pentstemmon had said that same stick had become a powerful object.

That was another mistake. The Witch came floating up the little street, smiling, twirling her parasol, followed by two sulky-looking page boys in orange velvet. When she came level with Sophie, she stopped, and tawny perfume filled Sophie's nose. "Why, it's Miss Hatter!" the Witch said, laughing. "I never forget a face, particularly if I've made it myself! What are you doing here, dressed up all so fine? If you're thinking of calling on that Mrs. Pentstemmon, you can save yourself the trouble. The old biddy's dead."

"Dead?" said Sophie. She had a silly impulse to add, But she was alive an hour ago! And she stopped herself, because death is like that: people *are* alive until they die.

"Yes. Dead," said the Witch. "She refused to tell me where someone was that I want to find. She said, 'Over my dead body!' so I took her at her word."

She's looking for Howl! Sophie thought. *Now* what do I do? If she had not been so very hot and tired, Sophie would have been almost too scared to think. For a witch who could kill Mrs. Pentstemmon would have no trouble with Sophie, stick or no stick. And if she suspected for a moment that Sophie knew where Howl was, that could be the end of Sophie.

Perhaps it was just as well Sophie could not remember where the castle entrance was.

"I don't know who this person is that you've killed," she said, "but that makes you a wicked murderess."

But the Witch did seem to suspect anyway. She said, "But I thought you said you were going to call on Mrs. Pentstemmon?"

"No," said Sophie. "It was you said that. I don't have to know her to call you wicked for killing her."

"Then where were you going?" said the Witch.

Sophie was tempted to tell the Witch to mind her own business. But that was asking for trouble. So she said the only other thing she could think of. "I'm going to see the King," she said.

The Witch laughed disbelievingly. "But will the King see *you*?"

"Yes, of course," Sophie declared, trembling with terror and anger. "I made an appointment. I'm— going to petition him for better conditions for hatters. I keep going, you see, even after what you did to me."

"Then you're going in the wrong direction," said the Witch. "The Palace is behind you."

"Oh? Is it?" said Sophie. She did not have to pretend to be surprised. "Then I must have got turned around. I've been a little vague about directions ever since you made me like this."

The Witch laughed heartily and did not believe a

word of it. "Then come with me," she said, "and I'll show you the way to the Palace."

There seemed nothing Sophie could do but turn round and stump beside the Witch, with the two page boys trudging sullenly behind them both. Anger and hopelessness settled over Sophie. She looked at the Witch floating gracefully beside her and remembered Mrs. Pentstemmon had said the Witch was an old woman really. It's not fair! Sophie thought, but there was nothing she could do about it.

"Why *did* you make me like this?" she demanded as they went up a grand thoroughfare with a fountain at the top of it.

"You were preventing me getting some information I needed," the Witch said. "I got it in the end, of course." Sophie was quite mystified by this. She was wondering whether it would do any good to say there must be some mistake, when the Witch added, "Though I daresay you had no idea you were," and laughed, as if that was the funniest part of it. "Have you heard of a land called Wales?" she asked.

"No," said Sophie. "Is it under the sea?"

The Witch found this funnier than ever. "Not at the moment," she said. "It's where Wizard Howl comes from. You know Wizard Howl, don't you?"

"Only by hearsay," Sophie lied. "He eats girls. He's as wicked as you." But she felt rather cold. It did not seem to be due to the fountain they were passing at that moment. Beyond the fountain, across a pink marble plaza, were the stone stairs with the Palace at the top.

"There you are. There's the Palace," said the Witch. "Are you sure you can manage all those stairs?"

"None the better for you," said Sophie. "Make me young again and I'll run up them, even in this heat."

"That wouldn't be half so funny," said the Witch. "Up you go. And if you do persuade the King to see you, remind him that his grandfather sent me to the Waste and I bear him a grudge for that."

Sophie looked hopelessly up the long flight of stairs. At least there was nobody but soldiers on them. With the luck she was having today, it would not have surprised her to find Michael and Howl on their way down. Since the Witch was obviously going to stand there and make sure she went up, Sophie had no choice but to climb them. Up she hobbled, past the sweating soldiers, all the way to the Palace entrance again, hating the Witch more with every step. She turned round, panting, at the top. The Witch was still there, a floating russet shape at the foot, with two small orange figures beside her, waiting to see her thrown out of the Palace.

"Drat her!" said Sophie. She hobbled over to the guards at the archway. Her bad luck still held. There was no sign of Michael or Howl in the reaches beyond. She was forced to say to the guards, "There was something I forgot to tell the King."

They remembered her. They let her inside, to be received by a personage in white gloves. And before Sophie had collected her wits, the Palace machinery was in motion again and she was being handed from person to person, just like the first time, until she arrived at the same double doors and the same person in blue was announcing, "Mrs. Pendragon to see you again, Your Majesty."

It was like a bad dream, Sophie thought as she went into the same large room. She seemed to have no choice but to blacken Howl's name again. The trouble was, what with all that had happened, and stagefright again into the bargain, her mind was blanker than ever. The King, this time, was standing at a large desk in one corner, rather anxiously moving flags about on a map. He looked up and said pleasantly, "They tell me there was something you forgot to say."

"Yes," said Sophie. "Howl says he'll only look for Prince Justin if you promise him your daughter's hand in marriage." What put *that* into my head? she thought. He'll have us both executed!

The King gave her a concerned look. "Mrs. Pendragon, you must know that's quite out of the question," he said. "I can see you must be very worried about your son to suggest it, but you can't keep him tied to your apron strings forever, you know, and my mind is made up. Please come and sit in this chair. You seem tired."

Sophie tottered to the low chair the King pointed to and sank into it, wondering when the guards would arrive to arrest her.

The King looked vaguely around. "My daughter was here just now," he said. To Sophie's considerable surprise, he bent down and looked under the desk. "Valeria," he called. "Vallie, come on out. This way, there's a good girl."

There was a shuffling noise. After a second, Princess Valeria shunted herself out from under the desk in sitting position, grinning benignly. She had four teeth. But she was not old enough to have grown a proper head of hair. All she had was a ring of wispy whiteness above her ears. When she saw Sophie, she grinned wider yet and reached out with the hand she had just been sucking and took hold of Sophie's dress. Sophie's dress responded with a spreading wet stain as the princess hauled herself to her feet on it. Staring up into Sophie's face, Valeria addressed a friendly remark to her in what was clearly a private foreign language.

"Oh," said Sophie, feeling an awful fool.

"I understand how a parent feels, Mrs. Pendragon," said the King.

Chapter 14:

- ← →⊱⊰← → -

In which a Royal Wizard
catches a cold

Sophie rode back to the castle's Kingsbury entrance in one of the King's coaches, drawn by four horses. On it also were a coachman, a groom, and a footman. A sergeant and six Royal Troopers went with it to guard it. The reason was Princess Valeria. She had climbed into Sophie's lap. As the coach clattered the short way downhill, Sophie's dress was still covered with the wet marks of Valeria's royal approval. Sophie smiled a little. She thought Martha might have a point after all, wanting children, although ten Valerias struck her as a bit much. As Valeria had scrambled over her, Sophie remembered hearing that the Witch had threatened Valeria in some way, and she found herself saying to Valeria, "The Witch shan't hurt you. I won't let her!"

The King had not said anything about that. But he had ordered out a royal coach for Sophie.

The equipage drew to a very noisy halt outside the disguised stable. Michael shot out of the door and got in the way of the footman who was helping

Sophie down. "Where did you get to?" he said. "I've been so worried! And Howl's terribly upset—"

"I'm sure he is," Sophie said apprehensively.

"Because Mrs. Pentstemmon's dead," said Michael.

Howl came to the door too. He looked pale and depressed. He was holding a scroll with red-and-blue royal seals dangling off it, which Sophie eyed guiltily. Howl gave the sergeant a gold piece and did not say a word until the coach and the Troopers had gone clattering away. Then he said, "I make that four horses and ten men just to get rid of one old woman. What did you *do* to the King?"

Sophie followed Howl and Michael indoors, expecting to find the room covered with green slime. But it was not, and there was Calcifer flaring up the chimney, grinning his purple grin. Sophie sank into the chair. "I think the King got sick of me turning up and blackening your name. I went twice," she said. "Everything went wrong. And I met the Witch on her way from killing Mrs. Pentstemmon. What a day!"

While Sophie described some of what had happened, Howl leaned on the mantelpiece, dangling the scroll as if he was thinking of feeding it to Calcifer. "Behold the new Royal Wizard," he said. "My name is very black." Then he began to laugh, much to the surprise of Sophie and Michael. "And what did she do to the Count of Catterack?" he laughed. "I should never have let her near the King!"

"I did blacken your name!" Sophie protested.

"I know. It was my miscalculation," Howl said. "Now, how am I going to go to poor Mrs. Pentstemmon's funeral without the Witch knowing? Any ideas, Calcifer?"

It was clear that Howl was far more upset about Mrs. Pentstemmon than anything else.

Michael was the one who worried about the Witch. He confessed next morning that he had had nightmares all night. He had dreamed she came through all the castle entrances at once. "Where's Howl?" he asked anxiously.

Howl had gone out very early, leaving the bathroom full of the usual scented steam. He had not taken his guitar, and the doorknob was turned to green-down. Even Calcifer knew no more than that. "Don't open the door to anyone," Calcifer said. "The Witch knows about all the entrances except the Porthaven one."

This so alarmed Michael that he fetched some planks from the yard and wedged them crosswise over the door. Then he got to work at last on the spell they had got back from Miss Angorian.

Half an hour later the doorknob turned sharply to black-down. The door began to bounce about. Michael clutched at Sophie. "Don't be afraid," he said shakily. "I'll keep you safe."

The door bounced powerfully for a while. Then it stopped. Michael had just let go of Sophie in great relief when there came a violent explosion. The planks clattered to the floor. Calcifer plunged to the bottom of the grate and Michael plunged into the broom cupboard, leaving Sophie standing there as the door burst open and Howl stormed in.

"This is a bit much, Sophie!" he said. "I do live here." He was soaking wet. The gray-and-scarlet suit was black-and-brown. His sleeves and the ends of his hair were dripping.

Sophie looked at the doorknob, still turned to black-down. Miss Angorian, she thought. And he went to see her in that charmed suit. "Where have you been?" she said.

Howl sneezed. "Standing in the rain. None of your business," he said hoarsely. "What were those planks in aid of?"

"I did them," Michael said, edging out of the broom cupboard. "The Witch—"

"You must think I don't know my business," Howl said irritably. "I have so many misdirection spells out that most people wouldn't find us at all. I give even the Witch three days. Calcifer, I need a hot drink."

Calcifer had been climbing up among his logs, but as Howl went over to the fireplace, he plunged down again. "Don't come near me like that! You're wet!" he hissed.

"Sophie," Howl said pleadingly.

Sophie folded her arms pitilessly. "What about Lettie?" she said.

"I'm soaked through," said Howl. "I should have a hot drink."

"And I said, What about Lettie Hatter?" Sophie said.

"Bother you, then!" said Howl. He shook himself. The water fell off him in a neat ring on the floor. Howl stepped out of it with his hair gleaming dry and his suit gray-and-scarlet and not even damp, and went to fetch the saucepan. "The world is full of hard-hearted women, Michael," he said. "I can name three without stopping to think."

"One of them being Miss Angorian?" asked Sophie.

Howl did not answer. He ignored Sophie grandly for the rest of the morning while he discussed moving the castle with Michael and Calcifer. Howl really was going to run away, just as she had warned the King he would, Sophie thought as she sat and sewed more triangles of blue-and-silver suit together. She knew she must get Howl out of that gray-and-scarlet suit as soon as possible.

"I don't think we need move the Porthaven entrance," Howl said. He conjured himself a handkerchief out of the air and blew his nose with a hoot which made Calcifer flicker uneasily. "But I want the moving castle well away from anywhere it's been before and the Kingsbury entrance shut down."

Someone knocked on the door then. Sophie noticed that Howl jumped and looked round as nervously as Michael. Neither of them answered the door. Coward! Sophie thought scornfully. She wondered why she had gone to all that trouble for Howl yesterday. "I must have been mad!" she muttered to the blue-and-silver suit.

"What about the black-down entrance?" Michael asked when the person knocking seemed to have gone away.

"That stays," Howl said, and conjured himself another handkerchief with a final sort of flick.

It would! Sophie thought. Miss Angorian is outside it. Poor Lettie!

By the middle of the morning Howl was conjuring handkerchiefs in twos and threes. They were floppy squares of paper really, Sophie saw. He kept sneezing. His voice grew hoarser. He was conjuring handkerchiefs by the half-dozen soon. Ashes from the used ones were piled all round Calcifer.

"Oh, why is it that whenever I go to Wales I always come back with a cold!" Howl croaked, and conjured himself a whole wad of tissues.

Sophie snorted.

"Did you say something?" Howl croaked.

"No, but I was thinking that people who run away

from everything deserve every cold they get," Sophie said. "People who are appointed to do something by the King and go courting in the rain instead have only themselves to blame."

"You don't know everything I do, Mrs. Moralizer," Howl said. "Want me to write out a list before I go out another time? I have *looked* for Prince Justin. Courting isn't the only thing I do when I go out."

"When have you looked?" said Sophie.

"Oh, how your ears flap and your long nose twitches!" Howl croaked. "I looked when he first disappeared, of course. I was curious to know what Prince Justin was doing up this way, when everyone knew Suliman had gone to the Waste. I think someone must have sold him a dud finding spell, because he went right over into the Folding Valley and bought another from Mrs. Fairfax. And that fetched him back this way, fairly naturally, where he stopped at the castle and Michael sold him another finding spell and a disguise spell—"

Michael's hand went over his mouth. "Was that man in the green uniform Prince *Justin?*"

"Yes, but I didn't mention the matter before," said Howl, "because the King might have thought you should have had the sense to sell him another dud. I had a conscience about it. Conscience. Notice that word, Mrs. Longnose. I had a conscience." Howl conjured another wad of handkerchiefs and glowered at Sophie over them out of eyes that were now red-rimmed and watery. Then he stood up. "I feel ill," he announced. "I'm going to bed, where I may die." He tottered piteously to the stairs. "Bury me beside Mrs. Pentstemmon," he croaked as he went up them to bed.

Sophie applied herself to her sewing harder than ever. Here was her chance to get the gray-and-scarlet suit off Howl before it did more damage to Miss Angorian's heart—unless, of course, Howl went to bed in his clothes, which she did not put past him. So Howl must have been looking for Prince Justin when he went to Upper Folding and met Lettie. Poor Lettie! Sophie thought, putting brisk, tiny stitches round her fifty-seventh blue triangle. Only another forty or so to go.

Howl's voice was presently heard shouting weakly, "Help me, someone! I'm dying from neglect up here!"

Sophie snorted. Michael left off working on his new spell and ran up and down stairs. Things became very restless. In the time it took Sophie to sew ten more blue triangles Michael ran upstairs with lemon and honey, with a particular book, with cough mixture, with a spoon to take the cough mixture with, and then with nose drops, throat pastilles, gargle, pen, paper, three more books, and an infusion of willow bark. People kept knocking at the door too, making Sophie jump and Calcifer flicker uneasily. When no one opened the door, some of the people went on hammering for five minutes or so, rightly thinking they were being ignored.

By this time Sophie was becoming worried about the blue-and-silver suit. It was getting smaller and smaller. One cannot sew in that number of triangles without taking up quite a lot of cloth in the seams. "Michael," she said when Michael came rushing downstairs again because Howl fancied a bacon sandwich for lunch. "Michael, is there a way of making small clothes larger?"

"Oh, yes," said Michael. "That's just what my new spell is—when I get a chance to work on it. He wants six slices of bacon in the sandwich. Could you ask Calcifer?"

Sophie and Calcifer exchanged speaking looks. "I don't think he's dying," Calcifer said.

"I'll give you the rinds to eat if you bend your head down," Sophie said, laying down her sewing. It was easier to bribe Calcifer than bully him.

They had bacon sandwiches for lunch, but Michael had to rush upstairs in the middle of eating his. He came down with the news that Howl wanted him to go into Market Chipping now, to get some things he needed for moving the castle.

"But the Witch—is it safe?" Sophie asked.

Michael licked bacon grease off his fingers and dived into the broom cupboard. He came out with one of the dusty velvet cloaks slung round his shoulders. At last, the person who came out wearing the cloak was a burly man with a red beard. This person licked his fingers and said with Michael's voice, "Howl thinks I'll be safe enough like this. It's misdirection as well as disguise. I wonder if Lettie will know me." The burly man opened the door green-down and jumped out onto the slowly moving hills.

Peace descended. Calcifer settled and chinked. Howl had evidently realized that Sophie was not going to run about after him. There was silence upstairs. Sophie got up and cautiously hobbled to the broom cupboard. This was her chance to go and see Lettie. Lettie must be very miserable by now. Sophie was fairly sure Howl had not been near her since that day in the orchard. It might just do some good if Sophie were to tell her that her feelings were caused by a charmed suit. Anyway, she owed it to Lettie to tell her.

The seven-league boots were not in the cupboard. Sophie could not believe it at first. She turned everything out. And there was nothing there but ordinary buckets, brooms, and the other velvet cloak. "Drat the man!" Sophie exclaimed. Howl had obviously made sure she would not follow him anywhere again.

She was putting everything back into the cupboard when someone knocked at the door. Sophie, as usual, jumped and hoped they would go away. But this person seemed more determined than most. Whoever it was went on knocking—or perhaps hurling him or herself at the door, for the sound was more a steady whump, whump, whump than proper knocking. After five minutes they were still doing it.

Sophie looked at the uneasy green flickers which were all she could see of Calcifer. "Is it the Witch?"

"No," said Calcifer, muffled among his logs. "It's the castle door. Someone must be running along beside us. We're going quite fast."

"Is it the scarecrow?" Sophie asked, and her chest gave a tremor at the mere idea.

"It's flesh and blood," Calcifer said. His blue face climbed up into the chimney, looking puzzled. "I'm not sure what it is, except that it wants to come in badly. I don't think it means any harm."

Since the whump, whump just kept on, giving Sophie an irritable feeling of urgency, she decided to open the door and put a stop to it. Besides, she was curious about what it was. She still had the second velvet cloak in her hand from turning out the broom cupboard, so she threw it round her shoulders as she went to the door. Calcifer stared. Then, for the first time since she had known him, he bent his head down voluntarily. Great crackles of laughter came from under the curly green flames. Wondering what the cloak had turned her into, Sophie opened the door.

A huge, spindly greyhound leaped off the hillside

between the grinding black blocks of the castle and landed in the middle of the room. Sophie dropped the cloak and backed away hurriedly. She had always been nervous of dogs, and greyhounds are not reassuring to look at. This one put itself between her and the door and stared at her. Sophie looked longingly at the wheeling rocks and heather outside and wondered whether it would do any good to yell for Howl.

The dog bent its already bent back and somehow hoisted itself onto its lean hind legs. That made it almost as tall as Sophie. It held its front legs stiffly out and heaved upward again. Then, as Sophie had her mouth open to yell to Howl, the creature put out what was obviously an enormous effort and surged upward into the shape of a man in a crumpled brown suit. He had gingerish hair and a pale, unhappy face.

"Came from Upper Folding!" panted this dog-man. "Love Lettie—Lettie sent me—Lettie crying and very unhappy—sent me to you—told me to stay—" He began to double up and shrink before he had finished speaking. He gave a dog howl of despair and annoyance. "Don't tell Wizard!" he whined and dwindled away inside reddish curly hair into a dog again. A different dog. This time he seemed to be a red setter. The red setter waved its fringed tail and stared earnestly at Sophie from melting, miserable eyes.

"Oh, dear," said Sophie as she shut the door.

"You do have troubles, my friend. You were that collie dog, weren't you? Now I see what Mrs. Fairfax was
talking about. That Witch wants slaying, she really
does! But why has Lettie sent you *here*? If you don't
want me to tell Wizard Howl——"

The dog growled faintly at the name. But it also
wagged its tail and stared appealingly.

"All right. I won't tell him," Sophie promised. The
dog seemed reassured. He trotted to the hearth, where
he gave Calcifer a somewhat wary look and lay down
beside the fender in a skinny red bundle. "Calcifer,
what do you think?" Sophie said.

"This dog is a bespelled human," Calcifer said
unnecessarily.

"I know, but can you take the spell off him?"
Sophie asked. She supposed Lettie must have heard,
like so many people, that Howl had a witch working
for him now. And it seemed rather important to turn
the dog into a man again and send him back to Upper
Folding before Howl got out of bed and found him
there.

"No. I'd need to be linked with Howl for that,"
Calcifer said.

"Then I'll try it myself," Sophie said. Poor Lettie!
Breaking her heart for Howl, and her only other lover
a dog most of the time! Sophie laid her hand on the
dog's soft, rounded head. "Turn back into the man
you should be," she said. She said it quite often, but

its only effect seemed to be to send the dog deeply to sleep. It snored and twitched against Sophie's legs.

Meanwhile a certain amount of moaning and groaning was coming from upstairs. Sophie kept muttering to the dog and ignored it. A loud, hollow coughing followed, dying away into more moaning. Sophie ignored that too. Crashing sneezes followed the coughing, each one rattling the window and all the doors. Sophie found those harder to ignore, but she managed. Pooot-pooooot! went a blown nose, like a bassoon in a tunnel. The coughing started again, mingled with moans. Sneezes mixed with the moans and the coughs, and the sounds rose to a crescendo in which Howl seemed to be managing to cough, groan, blow his nose, sneeze, and wail gently all at the same time. The doors rattled, the beams in the ceiling shook, and one of Calcifer's logs rolled off onto the hearth.

"All right, all right, I get the message!" Sophie said, dumping the log back into the grate. "It'll be green slime next. Calcifer, make sure that dog stays where it is." And she climbed the stairs, muttering loudly, "Really, these wizards! You'd think no one had ever had a cold before! Well, what is it?" she asked, hobbling through the bedroom door onto the filthy carpet.

"I'm dying of boredom," Howl said pathetically. "Or maybe just dying."

He was lying propped on dirty gray pillows, looking quite poorly, with what might have been a patchwork coverlet over him, except that it was all one color with dust. The spiders he seemed to like so much were spinning busily in the canopy above him.

Sophie felt his forehead. "You do have a bit of a fever," she admitted.

"I'm delirious," said Howl. "Spots are crawling before my eyes."

"Those are spiders," said Sophie. "Why can't you cure yourself with a spell?"

"Because there *is* no cure for a cold," Howl said dolefully. "Things are going round and round in my head—or maybe my head is going round and round in things. I keep thinking of the terms of the Witch's curse. I hadn't realized she could lay me bare like that. It's a bad thing to be laid bare, even though the things that are true so far are all my own doing. I keep waiting for the rest to happen."

Sophie thought back to the puzzling verse. "What things? 'Tell me where all past years are'?"

"Oh, I know that," said Howl. "My own, or anyone else's. They're all there, just where they always were. I could go and play bad fairy at my own christening if I wanted. Maybe I did and that's my trouble. No, there are only three things I'm waiting for: the mermaids, the mandrake root, and the wind to advance an honest mind. And whether I get white hairs, I suppose, only

I'm not going to take the spell off to see. There's only about three weeks left for them to come true in, and the Witch gets me as soon as they do. But the Rugby Club Reunion is Midsummer Eve, so I shall get to that at least. The rest had all happened long ago."

"You mean the falling star and never being able to find a woman true and fair?" said Sophie. "I'm not surprised, the way you go on. Mrs. Pentstemmon told me you were going to the bad. She was right, wasn't she?"

"I must go to her funeral if it kills me," Howl said sadly. "Mrs. Pentstemmon always thought far too well of me. I blinded her with my charm." Water ran out of his eyes. Sophie had no idea if he was really crying, or whether it was simply his cold. But she noticed he was slithering out again.

"I was talking about the way you keep dropping ladies as soon as you've made them love you," she said. "Why do you *do* it?"

Howl pointed a shaky hand up toward the canopy of his bed. "That's why I love spiders. 'If at first you don't succeed, try, try, try again.' I keep trying," he said with great sadness. "But I brought it on myself by making a bargain some years ago, and I know I shall never be able to love anyone properly now."

The water running out of Howl's eyes was definitely tears now. Sophie was concerned. "Now, you mustn't cry—"

There was a pattering outside. Sophie looked round to see the dog-man oozing himself past the door in a neat half-circle. She reached out and caught a handful of his red coat, thinking he was certainly coming to bite Howl. But all the dog did was to lean against her legs, so that she had to stagger back to the peeling wall.

"What's this?" said Howl.

"My new dog," Sophie said, hanging on to its curly hair. Now she was against the wall, she could see out of the bedroom window. It ought to have looked out on the yard, but instead it showed a view of a neat, square garden with a child's metal swing in the middle. The setting sun was firing raindrops hanging on the swing to blue and red. As Sophie stood and stared, Howl's niece, Mari, came running across the wet grass. Howl's sister, Megan, followed Mari. She was evidently shouting that Mari should not sit on the wet swing, but no sound seemed to come through. "Is that the place called Wales?" Sophie asked.

Howl laughed and pounded on the coverlet. Dust climbed like smoke. "Bother that dog!" he croaked. "I had a bet on with myself that I could keep you from snooping out of the window all the time you were in here!"

"Did you now?" said Sophie, and she let go of the dog, hoping he would bite Howl hard. But the dog only went on leaning on her, shoving her toward the door now. "So all that song and dance was just a game, was it?" she said. "I might have known!"

Howl lay back on his gray pillows, looking wronged and injured. "Sometimes," he said reproachfully, "you sound just like Megan."

"Sometimes," Sophie answered, shooing the dog out of the room in front of her, "I understand how Megan got the way she is." And she shut the door on the spiders, the dust, and the garden, with a loud bang.

Chapter 15:

━━━◆━◆━◆━━━

In which Howl goes to
a funeral in disguise

The dog-man curled up heavily on Sophie's toes when she went back to her sewing. Perhaps he was hoping she would manage to lift the spell if he stayed close to her. When a big, red-bearded man burst into the room, carrying a box of things, and shed his velvet cloak to become Michael, still carrying a box of things, the dog-man rose up and wagged his tail. He let Michael pat him and rub his ears.

"I hope he stays," Michael said. "I've always wanted a dog."

Howl heard Michael's voice. He arrived downstairs wrapped in the brown patchwork cover off his bed. Sophie stopped sewing and took a careful grip on the dog. But the dog was courteous to Howl too. He did not object when Howl fetched a hand out of the coverlet and patted him.

"Well?" Howl croaked, dispersing clouds of dust as he conjured some more tissues.

"I got everything," said Michael. "And there's a real

piece of luck, Howl. There's an empty shop for sale down in Market Chipping. It used to be a hat shop. Do you think we could move the castle there?"

Howl sat on a tall stool like a robed Roman senator and considered. "It depends how much it costs," he said. "I'm quite tempted to move the Porthaven entrance there. That won't be easy, because it will mean moving Calcifer. Porthaven is where Calcifer actually *is*. What do you say, Calcifer?"

"It will take a very careful operation to move me," Calcifer said. He had become several shades paler at the thought. "I think you should leave me where I am."

So Fanny is selling the shop, Sophie thought as the other three went on discussing the move. And so much for the conscience Howl said he had! But the main thing on her mind was the puzzling behavior of the dog. In spite of Sophie telling him many times that she could not take the spell off him, he did not seem to want to leave. He did not want to bite Howl. He let Michael take him for a run on Porthaven Marshes that night and the following morning. His aim seemed to be to become part of the household.

"Though if I were you, I'd be in Upper Folding making sure to catch Lettie on the rebound," Sophie told him.

Howl was in and out of bed all the next day. When he was in bed, Michael had to tear up and down the stairs. When he was up, Michael had to race about, measuring the castle with him and fixing metal brackets to every single corner. In between, Howl kept appearing, robed in his quilt and clouds of dust, to ask questions and make announcements, mostly for Sophie's benefit.

"Sophie, since you whitewashed over all the marks we made when we invented the castle, perhaps you can tell me where the marks in Michael's room were?"

"No," said Sophie, sewing in her seventieth blue triangle. "I can't."

Howl sneezed sadly and retired. Shortly he emerged again. "Sophie, if we were to take that hat shop, what would we sell?"

Sophie found she had had enough of hats to last a lifetime. "Not hats," she said. "You can buy the shop, but not the business, you know."

"Apply your fiendish mind to the matter," said Howl. "Or even think, if you know how." And he marched away upstairs again.

Five minutes later, down he came again. "Sophie, have you any preferences about the other entrances? Where would you like us to live?"

Sophie instantly found her mind going to Mrs. Fairfax's house. "I'd like a nice house with lots of flowers," she said.

"I see," croaked Howl and marched away again.

Next time he appeared, he was dressed. That made three times that day, and Sophie thought nothing of it until Howl put on the velvet cloak Michael had used and became a pale, coughing, red-bearded man with a large red handkerchief held to his nose. She realized Howl was going out then. "You'll make your cold worse," she said.

"I shall die and then you'll all be sorry," the red-bearded man said, and went out through the door with the knob green-down.

For an hour after that, Michael had time to work on his spell. Sophie got as far as her eighty-fourth blue triangle. Then the red-bearded man was back again. He shed the velvet cloak and became Howl, coughing harder than before and, if that was possible, more sorry for himself than ever.

"I took the shop," he told Michael. "It's got a useful shed at the back and a house at the side, and I took the lot. I'm not sure what I shall pay for it all with, though."

"What about the money you get if you find Prince Justin?" Michael asked.

"You forget," croaked Howl, "the whole object of this operation is *not* to look for Prince Justin. We are going to vanish." And he went coughing upstairs to bed, where he shortly began shaking the beams sneezing for attention again.

Michael had to leave the spell and rush upstairs. Sophie might have gone, except the dog-man got in the way when she tried. This was another part of his odd behavior. He did not like Sophie to do anything for Howl. Sophie felt this was fairly reasonable. She began on her eighty-fifth triangle.

Michael came cheerfully down and worked on his spell again. He was so happy that he was joining in Calcifer's saucepan song and chatting to the skull just as Sophie did, while he worked. "We're going to live in Market Chipping," he told the skull. "I can go and see my Lettie every day."

"Is that why you told Howl about the shop?" Sophie asked, threading her needle. By this time she was on her eighty-ninth triangle.

"Yes," Michael said happily. "Lettie told me about it when we were wondering how we'd ever see one another again. I told her—"

He was interrupted by Howl, trailing downstairs in his quilt again. "This is positively my last appearance," Howl croaked. "I forgot to say that Mrs. Pentstemmon is being buried tomorrow on her estate near Porthaven and I shall need this suit cleaned." He brought the gray-and-scarlet suit out from inside his coverlet and dropped it on Sophie's lap. "You're attending to the wrong suit," he told Sophie. "This is the one I like, but I haven't the energy to clean it myself."

"You don't need to go to the funeral, do you?" Michael said anxiously.

"I wouldn't dream of staying away," said Howl.

"Mrs. Pentstemmon made me the wizard I am. I have to pay my respects."

"But your cold's worse," said Michael.

"He's *made* it worse," said Sophie, "by getting up and chasing around."

Howl at once put on his noblest expression. "I'll be all right," he croaked, "as long as I keep out of the sea wind. It's a bitter place, the Pentstemmon estate. The trees are all bent sideways and there's no shelter for miles."

Sophie knew he was just playing for sympathy. She snorted.

"And what about the Witch?" Michael asked.

Howl coughed piteously. "I shall go in disguise, probably as another corpse," he said, trailing back toward the stairs.

"Then you need a winding sheet and not this suit," Sophie called after him. Howl trailed away upstairs without answering and Sophie did not protest. She now had the charmed suit in her hands and it was too good a chance to miss. She took up her scissors and hacked the gray-and-scarlet suit into seven jagged pieces. That ought to discourage Howl from wearing it. Then she got to work on the last triangles of the blue-and-silver suit, mostly little fragments from round the neck. It was now very small indeed. It looked as if it might be a size too small even for Mrs. Pentstemmon's page boy.

"Michael," she said. "Hurry up with that spell. It's urgent."

"I won't be long now," Michael said.

Half an hour later he checked things off on his list and said he thought he was ready. He came over to Sophie carrying a tiny bowl with a very small amount of green powder in the bottom. "Where do you want it?"

"Here," said Sophie, snipping off the last threads. She pushed the sleeping dog-man aside and laid the child-sized suit carefully on the floor. Michael, quite as carefully, tipped the bowl and sprinkled powder on every inch of it.

Then they both waited, rather anxiously.

A moment passed. Michael sighed with relief. The suit was gently spreading out larger. They watched it spread, and spread, until one side of it piled up against the dog-man and Sophie had to pull it further away to give it room.

After about five minutes they both agreed that the suit looked Howl's size again. Michael gathered it up and carefully shook the excess powder off into the grate. Calcifer flared and snarled. The dog-man jumped in his sleep.

"Watch it!" said Calcifer. "That was strong."

Sophie took the suit and hobbled upstairs on tip-toe with it. Howl was asleep on his gray pillows, with his spiders busily making new webs around him. He looked noble and sad in his sleep. Sophie hobbled to put the blue-and-silver suit on the old chest by the window, trying to tell herself that the suit had got no larger since she picked it up. "Still, if it stops you going to the funeral, that's no loss," she murmured as she took a look out of the window.

The sun was low across the neat garden. A large, dark man was out there, enthusiastically throwing a red ball toward Howl's nephew, Neil, who was standing with a look of patient suffering, holding a bat. Sophie could see the man was Neil's father.

"Snooping again," Howl said suddenly behind her. Sophie swung round guiltily, to find that Howl was only half awake really. He may even have thought it was the day before, because he said, "'Teach me to keep off envy's stinging'—that's all part of past years now. I love Wales, but it doesn't love me. Megan's full of envy because she's respectable and I'm not." Then he woke up a little more and asked, "What are you doing?"

"Just putting out your suit for you," Sophie said, and hobbled hastily away.

Howl must have gone back to sleep. He did not emerge again that night. There was no sign of him stirring when Sophie and Michael got up next morning. They were careful not to disturb him. Neither of them felt that going to Mrs. Pentstemmon's funeral was a good idea. Michael crept out on the hills to take the dog-man for a run. Sophie tiptoed about, getting breakfast, hoping Howl would oversleep. There was still no sign of Howl when Michael came back. The dog-man was starving hungry. Sophie and Michael were hunting in the closet for things a dog could eat when they heard Howl coming slowly downstairs.

"Sophie," Howl's voice said accusingly.

He was standing holding the door to the stairs open with an arm that was entirely hidden inside an immense blue-and-silver sleeve. His feet, on the bottom stair, were standing inside the top half of a gigantic blue-and-silver jacket. Howl's other arm did not come anywhere near the other huge sleeve. Sophie could see that arm in outline, making bulging gestures under a vast frill of collar. Behind Howl, the stairs were full of blue-and-silver suit trailing back all the way to his bedroom.

"Oh, dear!" said Michael. "Howl, it was my fault I—"

"Your fault? Garbage!" said Howl. "I can detect Sophie's hand a mile off. And there are several miles of this suit. Sophie dear, where is my other suit?"

Sophie hurriedly fetched the pieces of the gray-and-scarlet suit out of the broom cupboard, where she had hidden them.

Howl surveyed them. "Well, that's something," he said. "I'd been expecting it to be too small to see. Give it here, all seven of it." Sophie held the bundle of gray-and-scarlet cloth out toward him. Howl, with a bit of searching, succeeded in finding his hand inside the multiple folds of blue-and-silver sleeve and working it through a gap between two tremendous stitches. He grabbed the bundle off her. "I am now," he said, "going to get ready for the funeral. Please, both of you, refrain from doing anything whatsoever while I do. I can tell Sophie is in top form at the moment, and I want this room the usual size when I come back into it."

He set off with dignity to the bathroom, wading in blue-and-silver suit. The rest of the blue-and-silver suit followed him, dragging step by step down the stairs and rustling across the floor. By the time Howl was in the bathroom, most of the jacket was on the ground floor and the trousers were appearing on the stairs. Howl half shut the bathroom door and seemed to go on hauling the suit in hand over hand. Sophie and Michael and the dog-man stood and watched yard after yard of blue or silver fabric proceed across the floor, decorated with an occasional silver button the size of a millstone and enormous, regular, ropelike stitches. There may have been nearly a mile of it.

"I don't think I got that spell quite right," Michael said when the last huge scalloped edge had disappeared round the bathroom door.

"And didn't he let you know it!" said Calcifer. "Another log, please."

Michael gave Calcifer a log. Sophie fed the dog-man.

But neither of them dared do anything much else except stand around eating bread and honey for breakfast until Howl came out of the bathroom.

He came forth two hours later, out of a steam of verbena-scented spells. He was all in black. His suit was black, his boots were black, and his hair was black too, the same blue-raven black as Miss Angorian's. His earring was a long jet pendant. Sophie wondered if the black hair was in honor of Mrs. Pentstemmon. She agreed with Mrs. Pentstemmon that black hair suited Howl. His green-glass eyes went better with it. But she wondered very much which suit the black one really was.

Howl conjured himself a black tissue and blew his nose on it. The window rattled. He picked up one of the slices of bread and honey from the bench and beckoned the dog-man. The dog-man looked dubious. "I only want you where I can look at you," Howl croaked. His cold was still bad. "Come here, pooch." As the dog crawled reluctantly into the middle of the room, Howl added, "You won't find my other suit in the bathroom, Mrs. Snoop. You're not getting your hands on any of my clothes again."

Sophie stopped tiptoeing toward the bathroom and watched Howl walk round the dog-man, eating bread and honey and blowing his nose by turns.

"What do you think of this as a disguise?" he said. He flicked the black tissue at Calcifer and started to fall forward onto hands and knees. Almost as he started to move, he was gone. By the time he touched the floor, he was a curly red setter, just like the dog-man.

The dog-man was taken completely by surprise and his instincts got the better of him. His hackles came up, his ears lowered, and he growled. Howl played up—or else he felt the same. The two identical dogs walked round one another, glaring, growling, bristling, and getting ready to fight.

Sophie caught the tail of the one she thought was the dog-man. Michael grabbed for the one he thought was Howl. Howl rather hastily turned himself back. Sophie found a tall black person standing up in front of her and let go of the back of Howl's jacket. The dog-man sat down on Michael's feet, staring tragically.

"Good," said Howl. "If I can deceive another dog, I can fool everyone else. No one at the funeral is going to notice a stray dog lifting its leg against the gravestones." He went to the door and turned the knob blue-down.

"Wait a moment," said Sophie. "If you're going to the funeral as a red setter, why take all the trouble of getting yourself up in black?"

Howl lifted his chin and looked noble. "Respect to Mrs. Pentstemmon," he said, opening the door. "She liked one to think of all the details." He went out into the street of Porthaven.

Chapter 16:

◆─▶◀─◆

In which there is a great deal of witchcraft

Several hours passed. The dog-man was hungry again. Michael and Sophie decided to have lunch too. Sophie approached Calcifer with the frying pan.

"Why can't you have bread and cheese for once?" Calcifer grumbled.

All the same, he bent his head. Sophie was just putting the pan on top of the curly green flames when Howl's voice rang out hoarsely from nowhere.

"Brace yourself, Calcifer! She's found me!"

Calcifer sprang upright. The frying pan fell across Sophie's knees. "You'll have to wait!" Calcifer roared, flaming blindingly up the chimney. Almost at once he blurred into a dozen or so burning blue faces, as if he was being shaken violently about, and burned with a loud, throaty whirring.

"That must mean they're fighting," Michael whispered.

Sophie sucked a slightly burned finger and picked slices of bacon off her skirt with the other hand, staring at Calcifer. He was whipping from side to side of the fireplace. His blurred faces pulsed from deep blue to sky blue and then almost to white. One moment he had multiple orange eyes, the next, rows of starry silver ones. She had never imagined anything like it.

Something swept overhead with a blast and a boom which shook everything in the room. A second something followed, with a long, shrill roar. Calcifer pulsed nearly blue-black, and Sophie's skin fizzed with the backblast from the magic.

Michael scrambled for the window. "They're quite near!"

Sophie hobbled to the window too. The storm of magic seemed to have affected half the things in the room. The skull was yattering its jaw so hard that it was traveling round in circles. Packets were jumping. Powder was seething in jars. A book dropped heavily out of the shelves and lay open on the floor, fanning its pages back and forth. At one end of the room, scented steam boiled out of the bathroom: at the other, Howl's guitar made out-of-tune twangings. And Calcifer whipped about harder than ever.

Michael put the skull in the sink to stop it from yattering itself onto the floor while he opened the window and craned out. Whatever was happening was maddeningly just out of sight. People in the houses opposite were at doors and windows, pointing to something more or less overhead. Sophie and Michael ran to the broom cupboard, where they seized a velvet cloak each and flung them on. Sophie got the one that turned its wearer into a red-bearded man. Now she knew why Calcifer had laughed at her in the other one. Michael was a horse. But there was no time to laugh just then. Sophie dragged the door open and sped into the street, followed by the dog-man, who seemed surprisingly calm about the whole thing. Michael trotted out after her with a clatter of non-existent hooves, leaving Calcifer whipping from blue to white behind them.

The street was full of people looking upward. No one had time to notice things like horses coming out of houses. Sophie and Michael looked too, and found a huge cloud boiling and twisting just above the chimney tops. It was black and rotating on itself violently. White flashes that were not quite like light stabbed through the murk of it. But almost as soon as Michael and Sophie arrived, the clot of magic took on the shape of a misty bundle of fighting snakes. Then it tore in two with a noise like an enormous cat fight. One part sped yowling across the roofs and out to sea, and the second went screaming after it.

Some people retreated indoors then. Sophie and Michael joined the rush of braver people down the sloping lanes to the dockside. There everyone seemed to think the best view was to be had along the curve of the harbor wall. Sophie hobbled to get out along it too, but there was no need to go beyond the shelter of the harbor master's hut. Two clouds were hanging in the air, some way out to sea, on the other side of the harbor wall, the only two clouds in the calm blue sky. It was quite easy to see them. It was equally easy to see the dark patch of storm raging on the sea between the clouds, flinging up great, white-topped waves. There was an unfortunate ship caught in that storm. Its masts were beating back and forth. They could see spouts of water hitting it on all sides. The crew were desperately trying to take in the sails, but one at least had torn to flying gray rags.

"Can't they have a care for that ship!" someone said indignantly.

Then the wind and the waves from the storm hit the harbor wall. White water lashed over and the brave persons out on the wall came crowding hurriedly back to the quayside, where the moored ships were heaving and grinding at their moorings. Among all this was a great deal of screaming in high, singing voices. Sophie put her face out into the wind beyond the hut, where the screaming came from, and discovered that the raging magic had disturbed more than the sea and the wretched ship. A number of wet, slithery-looking ladies with flying green-brown hair were dragging themselves up onto the harbor wall, screaming and holding long, wet arms out to more screaming ladies tossing in the waves. Every one of them had a fishtail instead of legs.

"Confound it!" said Sophie. "The mermaids from the curse!" That meant only two more impossible things to come true now.

She looked up at the two clouds. Howl was kneeling on the lefthand one, much larger and nearer than she would have expected. He was still dressed in black. Typically enough, he was staring over his shoulder at the frantic mermaids. He was not looking at them as if he remembered they were part of the curse at all.

"Keep your mind on the Witch!" the horse beside Sophie yelled.

The Witch sprang into being, standing on the righthand cloud, in a whirl of flame-colored robe and streaming red hair, with her arms raised to invoke further magic. As Howl turned and looked at her, her arms came down. Howl's cloud erupted into a fountain of rose-colored flame. Heat from it swept across the harbor, and the stones of the wall steamed.

"It's all right!" gasped the horse.

Howl was on the tossing, nearly sinking ship below. He was a tiny black figure now, leaning against the bucking mainmast. He let the Witch know she had missed by waving at her cheekily. The Witch saw him the instant he waved. Cloud, Witch, and all at once became a savagely swooping red bird, diving at the ship.

The ship vanished. The mermaids sang a doleful scream. There was nothing but sulkily tossing water where the ship had been. But the diving bird was going too fast to stop. It plunged into the sea with a huge splash.

Everyone on the quayside cheered. "I knew that wasn't a real ship really!" someone behind Sophie said.

"Yes, it must have been an illusion," the horse said wisely. "It was too small."

As proof that the ship had been much nearer than it looked, the waves from the splash reached the harbor wall before Michael had stopped speaking. A twenty-foot green hill of water rode smoothly sideways across it, sweeping the screaming mermaids into the harbor, rolling every moored ship violently sideways, and thudding in swirls round the harbor master's hut. An arm came out of the side of the horse and hauled Sophie back toward the quay. Sophie gasped and stumbled in knee-high gray water. The dog-man bounded beside them, soaked to the ears.

They had just reached the quay, and the boats in the harbor had all just rolled upright, when a second mountain of water rolled over the harbor wall. Out of its smooth side burst a monster. It was a long, black, clawed thing, half cat, half sea lion, and it came racing down the wall toward the quay. Another burst out of the wave as it smashed into the harbor, long and low too, but scalier, and came racing after the first monster.

Everyone realized that the fight was not over yet and splashed backward hurriedly against the sheds and houses on the quayside. Sophie fell over a rope and then a doorstep. The arm came out of the horse and dragged her upright as the two monsters streaked past in a scatter of salt water. Another wave swirled over the harbor wall, and two more monsters burst out of that. They were identical to the first two, except the scaly one was closer to the catlike one. And the next rolling wave brought two more, closer together yet.

"What's going on?" Sophie squawked as this third pair raced past, shaking the stones of the jetty as they ran.

"Illusions," Michael's voice said out of the horse. "Some of them. They're both trying to fool one another into chasing the wrong one."

"Which is who?" said Sophie.

"No idea," said the horse.

Some of the onlookers found the monsters too terrifying. Many went home. Others jumped down into the rolling ships to fend them off from the quay. Sophie and Michael joined the hard core of watchers who set off through the streets of Porthaven after the monsters. First they followed a river of sea water, then huge, wet paw prints, and finally white gouges and scratches where the claws of the creatures had dug into the stones of the street. These led everyone out at the back of the town to the marshes where Sophie and Michael had chased the shooting star.

By this time all six creatures were bounding black dots, vanishing into the flat distance. The crowd spread out into a ragged line on the bank, staring, hoping for more, and afraid of what they might see. After a while no one could see anything but empty marsh. Nothing happened. Quite a few people were turning away to leave when of course everyone else shouted, *"Look!"* A ball of pale fire rolled lazily up in the distance. It must have been enormous. The bang that went with it only reached the watchers when the fireball had become a spreading tower of smoke. The line of people all winced at the blunt thunder of it. They watched the smoke spread until it became part of the mist on the marshes. They went on watching after that. But there was simply peace and silence. The wind rattled the marsh weeds, and birds began to dare to cry again.

"I reckon they must have done for one another," people said. The crowd gradually split into separate figures hurrying away to jobs they had left half done.

Sophie and Michael waited until the very last, when it was clear that it was indeed all over. Then they turned slowly back into Porthaven. Neither of them felt like speaking. Only the dog-man seemed happy. He sauntered beside them so friskily that Sophie was sure he thought Howl was done for. He was so pleased with life that when they turned into the street where Howl's house was and there happened to be a stray cat crossing the road, the dog-man uttered a joyful bark and galloped after it. He chased it with a dash and a skitter straight to the castle doorstep, where it turned and glared.

"Geroff!" it mewed. "This is all I needed!"

The dog backed away, looking ashamed.

Michael clattered up to the door. "Howl!" he shouted.

The cat shrank to kitten size and looked very sorry for itself. "And you both look ridiculous!" it said. "Open the door. I'm exhausted."

Sophie opened the door and the cat crawled inside. The cat crawled to the hearth, where Calcifer was down to the merest blue flicker, and, with an effort, got its front paws up onto the chair seat. There it grew rather slowly into Howl, bent double.

"Did you kill the Witch?" Michael asked eagerly, taking off his cloak and becoming himself too.

"No," said Howl. He turned round and flopped into the chair, where he lay looking very tired indeed. "All that on top of a cold!" he croaked. "Sophie, for pity's sake take off that horrible red beard and find the bottle of brandy in the closet—unless you've drunk it or turned it into turpentine, of course."

Sophie took off her cloak and found the brandy and a glass. Howl drank one glass off as if it were water. Then he poured out a second glass, and instead of drinking it, he dripped it carefully on Calcifer. Calcifer flared and sizzled and seemed to revive a little. Howl poured a third glass and lay back sipping it. "Don't stand staring at me!" he said. "I don't know who won. The Witch is mighty hard to come at. She relies mostly on her fire demon and stays behind out of trouble. But I think we gave her something to think about, eh, Calcifer?"

"It's old," Calcifer said in a weak fizzle from under his logs. "I'm stronger, but it knows things I never thought of. She's had it a hundred years. And it's half killed me!" He fizzled a bit, then climbed further out of his logs to grumble, "You might have warned me!"

"I did, you old fraud!" Howl said wearily. "You know everything I know."

Howl lay sipping brandy while Michael found bread and sausage for them to eat. Food revived them all, except perhaps the dog-man, who seemed subdued now Howl was back after all. Calcifer began to burn up and look his usual blue self.

"This won't do!" Howl said. He hauled himself to his feet. "Look sharp, Michael. The Witch knows we're in Porthaven. We're not only going to have to move the castle and the Kingsbury entrance now. I shall have to transfer Calcifer to the house that goes with that hat shop."

"Move *me?*" Calcifer crackled. He was azure with apprehension.

"That's right," said Howl. "You have a choice between Market Chipping or the Witch. Don't go and be difficult."

"Curses!" wailed Calcifer and dived to the bottom of the grate.

Chapter 17:

⟶ ⟩⟨◆⟩⟨ ⟵

In which the moving castle
moves house

Howl set to work as hard as if he had just had a week's rest. If Sophie had not seen him fight a grueling magic battle an hour ago, she would never have believed it. He and Michael dashed about, calling measurements to one another and chalking strange signs in the places where they had earlier put up metal brackets. They seemed to have to chalk every corner, including the backyard. Sophie's cubbyhole under the stairs and the odd-shaped place in the bathroom ceiling gave them quite a bit of trouble. Sophie and the dog-man were pushed this way and that, and then pushed aside completely so that Michael could crawl about chalking a five-pointed star inside a circle on the floor.

Michael had done this and was brushing dust and chalk off his knees when Howl came racing in with patches of whitewash all over his black clothes. Sophie and the dog-man were pushed aside again so that Howl could crawl about writing signs in and around both star and circle. Sophie and the dog-man went to sit on the stairs. The dog-man was shivering. This did not seem to be magic he liked.

Howl and Michael raced out to the yard. Howl raced back. "Sophie!" he shouted. "Quickly! What are we going to sell in that shop?"

"Flowers," Sophie said, thinking of Mrs. Fairfax again.

"Perfect," said Howl, and hurried over to the door with a pot of paint and a small brush. He dipped the brush in the pot and carefully painted the blue blob yellow. He dipped again. This time the brush came out purple. He painted the green blob with it. At the third dip the paint was orange, and the orange went over the red blob. Howl did not touch the black blob. He turned away, and the end of his sleeve went into the paint pot along with the brush. "Botheration!" said Howl, dragging it out. The trailing tip of the sleeve was all colors of the rainbow. Howl shook it, and it was black again.

"Which suit is that really?" Sophie asked.

"I've forgotten. Don't interrupt. The difficult part is just coming up," Howl said, rushing the paint pot back to the bench. He picked up a small jar of powder. "Michael! Where's the silver shovel?"

Michael raced in from the yard with a big, gleaming spade. The handle was wood, but the blade did seem to be solid silver. "All set out there!" he said.

Howl rested the shovel on his knee in order to chalk a sign on both handle and blade. He sprinkled red powder from the jar on it. He put a pinch of the same grains carefully in each point of the star and tipped all the rest into the middle. "Stand clear, Michael," he said. "Everyone stay clear. Are you ready, Calcifer?"

Calcifer emerged from between his logs in a long thread of blue flame. "As ready as I shall ever be," he said. "You know this could kill me, don't you?"

"Look on the bright side," said Howl. "It could be me it kills. Hold on tight. One, two, three." He dug the shovel into the grate, very steadily and slowly, keeping it straight and level with the bars. For a second he juggled it gently to get it under Calcifer. Then, even more steadily and gently, he raised it. Michael was quite obviously holding his breath. "Done it!" said Howl. Logs toppled sideways. They did not seem to be burning. Howl stood up and turned round, carrying Calcifer on the shovel.

The room filled with smoke. The dog-man whined and shivered. Howl coughed. He had a little trouble holding the shovel steady. Sophie's eyes were watering and it was hard to see clearly, but, as far as she could tell, Calcifer—just as he had said to her— did not have feet, or legs either. He was a long, pointed blue face rooted in a faintly glowing black lump. The black lump had a dent in the front of it, which suggested at first sight that Calcifer was kneeling on tiny, folded legs. But Sophie saw that was not so when the lump rocked slightly, showing it was rounded underneath. Calcifer obviously felt terribly unsafe. His orange eyes were round with fear, and he kept shooting feeble little arm-shaped flames out on either side, in a useless attempt to take hold of the sides of the shovel.

"Won't be long!" Howl choked, trying to be soothing. But he had to shut his mouth hard and stand for a moment trying not to cough. The shovel wobbled and Calcifer looked terrified. Howl recovered. He took a long, careful step into the chalked circle, and then another into the center of the five-pointed star. There, holding the shovel out level, he turned slowly round, one complete turn, and Calcifer turned with him, sky-blue and staring with panic.

It felt as if the whole room turned with them. The dog-man crouched close to Sophie. Michael staggered. Sophie felt as if their piece of the world had come loose and was swinging and jigging round in a circle, sickeningly. She did not blame Calcifer for looking so frightened. Everything was still swinging and swaying as Howl took the same long, careful steps out of the star and out of the circle. He knelt down by the hearth and, with enormous care, slid Calcifer back into the grate again and packed the logs back round him. Calcifer flopped green flames uppermost. Howl leaned on the shovel and coughed.

The room rocked and settled. For a few instants, while the smoke still hung everywhere, Sophie saw to her amazement the well-known outlines of the parlor in the house where she had been born. She knew it even though its floor was bare boards and there were no pictures on the walls. The castle room seemed to wriggle itself into place inside the parlor, pushing it out here, pulling it in there, bringing the ceiling down to match its own beamed ceiling, until the two melted together and became the castle room again, except perhaps it was now a bit higher and squarer than it had been.

"Have you done it, Calcifer?" coughed Howl.

"I think so," Calcifer said, rising up the chimney. He looked none the worse for his ride on the shovel. "You'd better check me, though."

Howl helped himself up on the shovel and opened the door with the yellow blob downward. Outside was the street in Market Chipping that Sophie had known all her life. People she knew were walking past in the evening, taking a stroll before supper, the way a lot of people did in summer. Howl nodded at Calcifer, shut the door, turned the knob orange-down, and opened it again.

A wide, weedy drive wound away from the door now, among clumps of trees most picturesquely lit sideways by the low sun. In the distance stood a grand stone gateway with statues on it. "Where *is* this?" said Howl.

"An empty mansion at the end of the valley," Calcifer said rather defensively. "It's the nice house you told me to find. It's quite fine."

"I'm sure it is," Howl said. "I simply hope the real owners won't object." He shut the door and turned the knob round to purple-down. "Now for the moving castle," he said as he opened it again.

It was nearly dusk out there. A warm wind full of different scents blew in. Sophie saw a bank of dark leaves drift by, loaded with big purple flowers among the leaves. It spun slowly away and its place was taken by a stand of dim white lilies and a glimpse of sunset on water beyond. The smell was so heavenly that Sophie was halfway across the room before she was aware.

"No, your long nose stays out of there until tomorrow," Howl said, and he shut the door with a snap. "That part's right on the edge of the Waste. Well done, Calcifer. Perfect. A nice house and lots of flowers, as ordered." He flung the shovel down and went to bed. And he must have been tired. There were no groans, no shouts, and almost no coughing.

Sophie and Michael were tired too. Michael flopped into the chair and sat stroking the dog-man, staring. Sophie perched on the stool, feeling strange. They had moved. It felt the same, but different, quite confusingly. And why was the moving castle now on the edge of the Waste? Was it the curse pulling Howl toward the Witch? Or had Howl slithered out so hard that he had come out right behind himself and turned out what most people would call honest?

Sophie looked at Michael to see what he thought. Michael was asleep, and so was the dog-man. Sophie looked at Calcifer instead, sleepily flickering among rosy logs with his orange eyes almost shut. She thought of Calcifer pulsing almost white, with white eyes, and then of Calcifer staring anxiously as he wobbled on the shovel. He reminded her of something. The whole shape of him did.

"Calcifer," she said, "were you ever a falling star?"

Calcifer opened one orange eye at her. "Of course," he said. "I can talk about that if you know. The contract allows me to."

"And Howl caught you?" said Sophie.

"Five years ago," said Calcifer, "out on Porthaven Marshes, just after he set up as Jenkin the Sorcerer. He chased me in seven-league boots. I was terrified of him. I was terrified anyway, because when you fall you know you're going to die. I'd have done anything rather than die. When Howl offered to keep me alive the way humans stay alive, I suggested a contract on the spot. Neither of us knew what we were getting into. I was grateful, and Howl only offered because he was sorry for me."

"Just like Michael," said Sophie.

"What's that?" Michael said, waking up. "Sophie, I wish we weren't right on the edge of the Waste. I didn't know we would be. I don't feel safe."

"Nobody's safe in a wizard's house," Calcifer said feelingly.

Next morning the door was set to black-blob-down and, to Sophie's great annoyance, it would not open at any setting. She wanted to see those flowers, Witch or no Witch. So she took out her impatience by fetching a bucket of water and scrubbing the chalked signs off the floor.

Howl came in while she was doing it. "Work, work, work," he said, stepping over Sophie as she scrubbed. He looked a little strange. His suit was still dense black, but he had turned his hair fair again. It looked white against the black. Sophie glanced at him and thought of the curse. Howl may have been think-ing of it too. He picked the skull out of the sink and held it in one hand, mournfully. "Alas, poor Yorick!" he said. "She heard mermaids, so it follows there is something rotten in the state of Denmark. I have caught an everlasting cold, but luckily I am terribly dishonest. I cling to that." He coughed pathetically. But his cold was getting better and it did not sound very convincing.

Sophie exchanged looks with the dog-man, who

was sitting watching her, looking as doleful as Howl. "You should go back to Lettie," she murmured. "What's the matter?" she said to Howl. "Miss Angorian not going well?"

"Dreadfully," said Howl. "Lily Angorian has a heart like a boiled stone." He put the skull back in the sink and shouted for Michael. "Food! Work!" he yelled.

After breakfast they took everything out of the broom cupboard. Then Michael and Howl knocked a hole in the side wall of it. Dust flew out of the cupboard door and strange thumpings occurred. At last they both shouted for Sophie. Sophie came, meaningly carrying a broom. And there was an archway where the wall had been, leading to the steps that had always connected the shop and the house. Howl beckoned her to come and look at the shop. It was empty and echoing. Its floor was now tiled in black and white squares, like Mrs. Pentstemmon's hall, and the shelves which had once held hats had a vase of waxed-silk roses and a small posy of velvet cowslips on them. Sophie realized she was expected to admire it, so she managed not to say anything.

"I found the flowers in the workshed out at the back," said Howl. "Come and look at the outside."

He opened the door into the street, and the same shop bell tinkled that Sophie had heard all her life. Sophie hobbled out into the empty early-morning street. The shop front had been newly painted green and yellow. Curly letters over the window said: H. JENKINS FRESH FLOWERS DAILY.

"Changed your mind about common names, haven't you?" said Sophie.

"For reasons of disguise only," said Howl. "I prefer Pendragon."

"And where do the fresh flowers come from?" Sophie asked. "You can't say that and then sell wax roses off hats."

"Wait and see," said Howl, leading the way back into the shop.

They went through and out into the yard Sophie had known all her life. It was only half the size now, because Howl's yard from the moving castle took up one side of it. Sophie looked up beyond the brick walls of Howl's yard to her own old house. It looked rather odd because of the new window in it that belonged to Howl's bedroom, and it made Sophie feel odder still when she realized that Howl's window did not look out onto the things she saw now. She could see the window of her own old bedroom, up above the shop. That made her feel odd too, because there did not seem to be any way to get up into it now.

As Sophie hobbled after Howl indoors again and up the stairs to the broom cupboard, she realized she was being very gruff. Seeing her own old home this way was giving her fearsome mixed feelings. "I think it's all very nice," she said.

"Really?" Howl said coldly. His feelings were hurt. He did so like to be appreciated, Sophie thought, sighing, as Howl went to the castle door and turned the knob to purple-down. On the other hand, she did not think she ever praised Howl, any more than Calcifer, and she wondered why she should start now.

The door opened. Big bushes loaded with flowers drifted gently past and stopped so that Sophie could climb down among them. Between the bushes, lanes of long, bright green grass led in all directions. Howl and Sophie walked down the nearest, and the castle followed them, brushing petals off as it went. The castle, tall and black and misshapen though it was, blowing its peculiar little wisps of smoke from one turret or another, did not look out of place here. Magic had been at work here. Sophie knew it had. And the castle fitted somehow.

The air was hot and steamy and filled with the scent of flowers, thousands of them. Sophie nearly said the smell reminded her of the bathroom after Howl had been in it, but she bit it back. The place was truly marvelous. Between the bushes and their loads of purple, red, and white flowers, the wet grass was full of smaller flowers: pink ones with only three petals, giant pansies, wild phlox, lupines of all colors, orange lilies, tall white lilies, irises, and myriad others. There were creepers growing flowers big enough for hats, cornflowers, poppies, and plants with strange shapes and stranger colors of leaves. Though it was not much like Sophie's dream of a garden like Mrs. Fairfax's, she forgot her gruffness and became delighted.

"You see," said Howl. He swung out an arm and his black sleeve disturbed several hundred blue butterflies feasting on a bush of yellow roses. "We can cut flowers by the armload every morning and sell them in Market Chipping with the dew still on them."

At the end of that green lane the grass became squashy. Vast orchids sprouted under the bushes. Howl and Sophie came suddenly to a steaming pool crowded with water lilies. The castle veered off sideways round the pool and drifted down another avenue lined with different flowers.

"If you come out here alone, bring your stick to test the ground with," Howl said. "It's full of springs and bogs. And don't go any further that way."

He pointed southeast, where the sun was a fierce white disk in the misty air. "That's the Waste over there—very hot and barren and full of Witch."

"Who made these flowers, right on the edge of the Waste?" Sophie said.

"Wizard Suliman started it a year ago," Howl said, turning toward the castle. "I think his notion was to make the Waste flower and abolish the Witch that way. He brought hot springs to the surface and got it growing. He was doing very nicely until the Witch caught him."

"Mrs. Pentstemmon said some other name," Sophie said. "He came from the same place as you, didn't he?"

"More or less," said Howl. "I never met him, though. I came and had another go at the place a few months later. It seemed a good idea. That's how I came to meet the Witch. She objected to it."

"Why?" said Sophie.

The castle was waiting for them. "She likes to think of herself as a flower," Howl said, opening the door. "A solitary orchid, blooming in the Waste. Pathetic, really."

Sophie took another look at the crowded flowers as she followed Howl inside. There were roses, thousands of them. "Won't the Witch know you're here?"

"I tried to do the thing she'd least expect," Howl said.

"And *are* you trying to find Prince Justin?" Sophie asked. But Howl slithered out of answering by racing through the broom cupboard, shouting for Michael.

Chapter 18:

—◦—◦—◦—

In which the scarecrow and Miss Angorian reappear

They opened the flower shop the next day. As Howl had pointed out, it could not have been simpler. Every early morning, all they had to do was to open the door with the knob purple-down and go out into the swimming green haze to gather flowers. It soon became a routine. Sophie took her stick and her scissors and stumped about, chatting to her stick, using it to test the squashy ground or hook down sprays of high-up choice roses. Michael took an invention of his own which he was very proud of. It was a large tin tub with water in it, which floated in the air and followed Michael wherever he went among the bushes. The dog-man went too. He had a wonderful time rushing about the wet green lanes, chasing butterflies or trying to catch the tiny, bright birds that fed on the flowers. While he dashed about, Sophie cut armloads of long irises, or lilies, or frondy orange flowers, or branches of blue hibiscus, and Michael loaded the bath with orchids, roses, starry white flowers, shiny vermilion ones, or anything that caught his fancy. They all enjoyed this time.

Then, before the heat in the bushes grew too intense, they took the day's flowers back to the shop and arranged them in a motley collection of jugs and buckets which Howl had dug out of the yard. Two of the buckets were actually the seven-league boots. Nothing, Sophie thought as she arranged shocks of gladiolus in them, could show how completely Howl had lost interest in Lettie. He did not care now if Sophie used them or not.

Howl was nearly always missing while they gathered flowers. And the doorknob was always turned black-down. He was usually back for a late breakfast, looking dreamy, still in his black clothes. He would never tell Sophie which suit the black one really was. "I'm in mourning for Mrs. Pentstemmon," was all he would say. And if Sophie or Michael asked why Howl was always away at that time, Howl would look injured and say, "If you want to talk to a school-teacher, you have to catch her before school starts." Then he would disappear into the bathroom for the next two hours.

Meanwhile Sophie and Michael put on their fine clothes and opened the shop. Howl insisted on the fine clothes. He said it would attract custom. Sophie insisted they all wore aprons. And after the first few days, when the people of Market Chipping simply stared through the window and did not come into the shop, the shop became very popular. Word had gone round that Jenkins had flowers like no flowers ever seen before. People Sophie had known all her life came and bought flowers by the bundle. None of them recognized her, and that made her feel very odd. They all thought she was Howl's old mother. But Sophie had had enough of being Howl's old mother. "I'm his aunt," she told Mrs. Cesari. She became known as Aunt Jenkins.

By the time Howl arrived in the shop, in a black apron to match his suit, he usually found it quite busy. He made it busier still. This was when Sophie began to be sure that the black suit was really the charmed gray-and-scarlet one. Any lady Howl served was sure to go away with at least twice the number of flowers she asked for. Most of the time Howl charmed them into buying ten times as much. Before long, Sophie noticed ladies peering in and deciding not to come into the shop when they saw Howl there. She did not blame them. If you just want a rose for a buttonhole, you do not want to be forced to buy three dozen orchids. She did not discourage Howl when Howl took to spending long hours in the workshed across the yard.

"I'm setting up defenses against the Witch, before you ask," he said. "By the time I've finished, there will be no way she can get into any part of this place."

There was sometimes a problem with leftover flowers. Sophie could not bear to see them wilting overnight. She found she could keep them fairly fresh if she talked to them. After that, she talked to flowers a lot. She got Michael to make her a plant-nutrition spell, and she experimented in buckets in the sink, and in tubs in the alcove where she used to trim hats. She found she could keep some plants fresh for days. So of course she experimented some more. She got the soot out of the yard and planted things in it, muttering busily. She grew a navy-blue rose like that, which pleased her greatly. Its buds were coal black, and its flowers opened bluer and bluer until they became almost the same blue as Calcifer. Sophie was so delighted with it that she took roots from all the bags hanging on the beams and experimented with those. She told herself she had never been happier in her life.

This was not true. Something was wrong, and Sophie could not understand what. Sometimes she thought it was the way no one in Market Chipping recognized her. She did not dare go and see Martha, for fear Martha would not know her either. She did not dare tip the flowers out of the seven-league boots and go and see Lettie for the same reason. She just could not bear either of her sisters to see her as an old woman.

Michael went off with bunches of spare flowers to

see Martha all the time. Sometimes Sophie thought that was what was the matter with her. Michael was so cheerful, and she was left on her own in the shop more and more often. But that did not seem to be quite it. Sophie enjoyed selling flowers on her own.

Sometimes the trouble seemed to be Calcifer. Calcifer was bored. He had nothing to do except to keep the castle gently drifting along the lanes of grass and round the various pools and lakes, and to make sure that they arrived in a new spot, with new flowers, every morning. His blue face was always leaning eagerly out of the grate when Sophie and Michael came in with their flowers. "I want to see what it's like out there," he said. Sophie brought him tasty smelling leaves to burn, which made the castle room smell as strongly as the bathroom, but Calcifer said what he really wanted was company. They went into the shop all day and left him alone.

So Sophie made Michael serve in the shop for at least an hour every morning while she went and talked to Calcifer. She invented guessing games to keep Calcifer occupied when she was busy. But Calcifer was still discontented. "When are you going to break my contract with Howl?" he asked more and more often.

And Sophie put Calcifer off. "I'm working on it," she said. "It won't be long now." This was not quite true. Sophie had stopped thinking of it unless she had to. When she put together what Mrs. Pentstemmon had said with all the things Howl and Calcifer had said, she found she had some strong and rather terrible ideas about that contract. She was sure that breaking it would be the end of both Howl and Calcifer. Howl might deserve it, but Calcifer did not. And since Howl seemed to be working quite hard in order to slither out of the rest of the Witch's curse, Sophie wanted to do nothing unless she could help.

Sometimes Sophie thought it was simply that the dog-man was getting her down. He was such a doleful creature. The only time he seemed to enjoy himself was when he chased down the green lanes between the bushes every morning. For the rest of the day he trudged gloomily about after Sophie, sighing deeply. As Sophie could do nothing about him either, she was rather glad when the weather grew hotter and hotter toward Midsummer Day and the dog-man took to lying in patches of shade out in the yard, panting.

Meanwhile the roots Sophie had planted had become quite interesting. The onion had become a small palm tree and was sprouting little onion-scented nuts. Another root grew into a sort of pink sunflower. Only one was slow to grow. When at last it put out two round green leaves, Sophie could hardly wait to see what it would grow into. The next day it looked as if it might be an orchid. It had pointed leaves spotted with mauve and a long stalk growing out of the middle with a large bud on it. The day after that, Sophie left the fresh flowers in the tin bath and hurried eagerly to the alcove to see how it was getting on.

The bud had opened into a pink flower like an orchid that had been through a mangle. It was flat, and joined to the stalk just below a round tip. There were four petals sprouting from a plump pink middle, two pointing downward and two more halfway up that stuck out sideways. While Sophie stared at it, a strong scent of spring flowers warned her that Howl had come in and was standing behind her.

"What is that thing?" he said. "If you were expecting an ultraviolet violet or an infra-red geranium, you got it wrong, Mrs. Mad Scientist."

"It looks to me like a squashed-baby flower," Michael said, coming to look.

It did too. Howl shot Michael an alarmed look and picked up the flower in its pot. He slid it out of the pot into his hand, where he carefully separated the white, thready roots and the soot and the remains of the manure spell, until he uncovered the brown, forked root Sophie had grown it from. "I might have guessed," he said. "It's mandrake root. Sophie strikes again. You do have a touch, don't you, Sophie?" He put the plant carefully back, passed it to Sophie, and went away, looking rather pale.

So that was almost all the curse come true, Sophie thought as she went to arrange the fresh flowers in the shopwindow. The mandrake root had had a baby. That only left one more thing: the wind to advance an honest mind. If that meant *Howl's* mind had to be honest, Sophie thought, there was a chance that the curse might never come true. She told herself it served Howl right anyway, for going courting Miss Angorian every morning in a charmed suit, but she still felt alarmed and guilty. She arranged a sheaf of white lilies in a seven-league boot. She crawled into the window to get them just so, and she heard a regular clump, clump, clump from outside in the street. It was not the sound of a horse. It was the sound of a stick hitting the stones.

Sophie's heart was behaving oddly even before she dared look out of the window. There, sure enough, came the scarecrow, hopping slowly and purposefully down the center of the street. The rags trailing from its outstretched arms were fewer and grayer, and the turnip of its face was withered into a look of determination, as if it had hopped ever since Howl hurled it away, until at last it had hopped its way back.

Sophie was not the only one to be scared. The few people about that early were running away from the scarecrow as hard as they could run. But the scarecrow took no notice and hopped on.

Sophie hid her face from it. "We're not here!" she

told it in a fierce whisper. "You don't know we're here! You can't find us. Hop away fast!"

The clump, clump of the hopping stick slowed as the scarecrow neared the shop. Sophie wanted to scream for Howl, but all she seemed to be able to do was to go on repeating, "We're not here. Go away quickly!"

And the hop-hopping speeded up, just as she told it to, and the scarecrow hopped its way past the shop and on through Market Chipping. Sophie thought she was going to come over queer. But she seemed just to have been holding her breath. She took a deep breath and felt shaky with relief. If the scarecrow came back, she could send it away again.

Howl had gone out when Sophie went into the castle room. "He seemed awfully upset," Michael said. Sophie looked at the door. The knob was black-down. Not that upset! she thought.

Michael went out too, to Cesari's, that morning, and Sophie was alone in the shop. It was very hot. The flowers wilted in spite of the spells, and very few people seemed to want to buy any. What with this, and the mandrake root, and the scarecrow, all Sophie's feelings seemed to come to a head. She was downright miserable.

"It may be the curse hovering to catch up with Howl," she sighed to the flowers, "but I think it's being the eldest, really. Look at me! I set out to seek my fortune and I end up exactly where I started, and old as the hills still!"

Here the dog-man put his glossy red snout round the door to the yard and whined. Sophie sighed. Never an hour passed without the creature checking up on her. "Yes, I'm still here," she said. "Where did you expect me to be?"

The dog came inside the shop. He sat up and stretched his paws out stiffly in front of him. Sophie realized he was trying to turn into a man. Poor creature. She tried to be nice to him because he was, after all, worse off than she was.

"Try harder," she said. "Put your back into it. You can be a man if you want."

The dog stretched and straightened his back, and strained and strained. And just as Sophie was sure he was going to have to give up or topple over backward, he managed to rise to his hind legs and heave himself up into a distraught, ginger-haired man.

"I envy—Howl!" he panted. "Does that—so easily. I was—dog in the hedge—you helped. Told Lettie—I knew you—I'd keep watch. I was—here before in—" He began to double up again into a dog and howled with annoyance. "With Witch in shop!" he wailed, and fell forward onto his hands, growing a great deal of gray and white hair as he did so.

Sophie stared at the large, shaggy dog that now stood there. "You were with the Witch!" she said. She remembered now. The anxious ginger-haired man who had stared at her in horror. "Then you know who I am and you know I'm under a spell. Does Lettie know too?"

The huge, shaggy head nodded.

"And she called you Gaston," Sophie remembered. "Oh, my friend, she has made it hard for you! Fancy having all that hair in this weather! You'd better go somewhere cool."

The dog nodded again and shambled miserably into the yard.

"But *why* did Lettie send you?" Sophie wondered. She felt thoroughly put out and disturbed by this discovery. She went up the stairs and through the broom cupboard to talk to Calcifer.

Calcifer was not much help. "It doesn't make any difference how many people know you're under a spell," he said. "It hasn't helped the dog much, has it?"

"No, but—" Sophie began, but, just then, the castle door clicked and opened. Sophie and Calcifer looked. They saw the doorknob was still set to black-down, and they expected Howl to come through it. It was hard to say which of them was more astonished when the person who slid rather cautiously round the door turned out to be Miss Angorian.

Miss Angorian was equally astonished. "Oh, I beg your pardon!" she said. "I thought Mr. Jenkins might be here."

"He's out," Sophie said stiffly, and she wondered where Howl had gone, if not to see Miss Angorian.

Miss Angorian let go of the door, which she had been clutching in her surprise. She left it swinging open on nothing and came pleadingly toward Sophie. Sophie found she had got up herself and come across the room. It seemed as if she was trying to block Miss Angorian off. "Please," said Miss Angorian, "don't tell Mr. Jenkins I was here. To tell you the truth, I only encouraged him in hope of getting news of my fiancé—Ben Sullivan, you know. I'm positive Ben disappeared to the same place Mr. Jenkins keeps disappearing to. Only Ben didn't come back."

"There's no Mr. Sullivan here," Sophie said. And she thought, That's Wizard Suliman's name! I don't believe a word of it!

"Oh, I know that," Miss Angorian said. "But this feels like the right place. Do you mind if I just look round a little to give myself some idea of the sort of life Ben's leading now?" She hooked her sheet of black hair behind one ear and tried to walk further into the room. Sophie stood in the way. This forced Miss Angorian to tiptoe pleadingly away sideways toward the workbench. "How very quaint!" she said, looking at the bottles and the jars. "What a quaint little town!" she said, looking out of the window.

"It's called Market Chipping," Sophie said, and she moved round and herded Miss Angorian backward toward the door.

"And what's up those stairs?" Miss Angorian asked, pointing to the open door to the stairs.

"Howl's private room," Sophie said firmly, walking Miss Angorian away backward.

"And what's through that other open door?" Miss Angorian asked.

"A flower shop," said Sophie. Nosy Parker! she thought.

By this time Miss Angorian either had to back into the chair or out through the door again. She stared at Calcifer in a vague, frowning way, as if she was not sure what she was seeing, and Calcifer simply stared back without saying a word. This made Sophie feel better about being so very unfriendly. Only people who understood Calcifer were really welcome in Howl's house.

But now Miss Angorian made a dive round the chair and noticed Howl's guitar leaning in its corner. She snatched it up with a gasp and turned round, holding it to her chest possessively. "Where did you get this?" she demanded in a low, emotional voice. "Ben had a guitar like this! It could be Ben's!"

"I heard Howl bought it last winter," Sophie said. And she walked forward again, trying to scoop Miss Angorian out of her corner and through the door.

"Something's happened to Ben!" Miss Angorian said throbbingly. "He would never have parted from his guitar! Where is he? I know he can't be dead. I'd *know* in my heart if he were!"

Sophie wondered whether to tell Miss Angorian that the Witch had caught Wizard Suliman. She looked across to see where the human skull was. She had half a mind to wave it in Miss Angorian's face and say it was Wizard Suliman's. But the skull was in the sink, hidden behind a bucket of spare ferns and lilies, and she knew that if she went over there, Miss Angorian would ooze out into the room again. Besides, it would be unkind.

"May I take this guitar?" Miss Angorian said huskily, clutching it to her. "To remind me of Ben."

The throb in Miss Angorian's voice annoyed Sophie. "No," she said. "There's no need to be so intense about it. You've no proof it was his." She hobbled close to Miss Angorian and seized the guitar by its neck. Miss Angorian stared at her over it with wide, anguished eyes. Sophie dragged. Miss Angorian hung on. The guitar gave out horrible, out-of-tune jangles. Sophie jerked it out of Miss Angorian's arms. "Don't be silly," she said. "You've no right to walk into people's castles and take their guitars. I've told you Mr. Sullivan's not here. Now go back to Wales. Go on." And she used the guitar to push Miss Angorian backward through the open door.

Miss Angorian backed into the nothingness until

half of her vanished. "You're hard," she said reproachfully.

"Yes, I am!" said Sophie and slammed the door on her. She turned the knob to orange-down to prevent Miss Angorian coming back and dumped the guitar back in its corner with a firm twang. "And don't you dare tell Howl she was here!" she said unreasonably to Calcifer. "I bet she came to see Howl. The rest was just a pack of lies. Wizard Suliman was *settled* here, years ago. He probably came to get away from her beastly throbbing voice!"

Calcifer chuckled. "I've never seen anyone got rid of so fast!" he said.

This made Sophie feel both unkind and guilty. After all, she herself had walked into the castle in much the same way, and she had been twice as nosy as Miss Angorian. "Gah!" she said. She stumped into the bathroom and stared at her withered old face in the mirrors. She picked up one of the packets labeled SKIN and then tossed it down again. Even young and fresh, she did not think her face compared particularly well with Miss Angorian's. "Gah!" she said. "Doh!" She hobbled rapidly back and seized ferns and lilies from the sink. She hobbled them, dripping, to the shop, where she rammed them into a bucket of nutrition spell. "Be daffodils!" she told them in a mad, angry, croaking voice. "Be daffodils in June, you beastly things!"

The dog-man put his shaggy face round the yard door. When he saw the mood Sophie was in, he backed out again hurriedly. When Michael came merrily in with a large pie a minute later, Sophie gave him such a glare that Michael instantly remembered a spell Howl had asked him to make up and fled away through the broom cupboard.

"Gah!" Sophie snarled after him. She bent over her bucket again. "Be daffodils! Be daffodils!" she croaked. It did not make her feel any better that she knew it was a silly way to behave.

Chapter 19:

·—◆·▬◆▬·◆—·

In which Sophie expresses
her feelings with weed-killer

Howl opened the shop door toward the end of the afternoon and sauntered in, whistling. He seemed to have
got over the mandrake root. It did not make Sophie
feel any better to find he had not gone to Wales after
all. She gave him her very fiercest glare.

"Merciful heavens!" Howl said. "I think that
turned me to stone! What's the matter?"

Sophie only snarled, "What suit are you wearing?"

Howl looked down at his black garments. "Does
it matter?"

"*Yes!*" growled Sophie. "And don't give me that
about being in mourning! Which one is it *really?*"

Howl shrugged and held up one trailing sleeve as
if he were not sure which it was. He stared at it, looking puzzled. The black color of it ran downward from
his shoulder into the pointed, hanging tip. His shoulder and the top of his sleeve grew brown, then gray,
while the pointed tip turned inkier and inkier, until
Howl was wearing a black suit with one blue-and-

silver sleeve whose end seemed to have been dipped in tar. "That one," he said, and let the black spread back up to his shoulder again.

Sophie was somehow more annoyed than ever. She gave a wordless grump of rage.

"Sophie!" Howl said in his most laughing, pleading way.

The dog-man pushed open the yard door and shambled in. He never would let Howl talk to Sophie for long.

Howl stared at it. "You've got an Old English sheepdog now," he said, as if he was glad of the distraction. "Two dogs are going to take a lot of feeding."

"There's only one dog," Sophie said crossly. "He's under a spell."

"He is?" said Howl, and he set off toward the dog with a speed that showed he was quite glad to get away from Sophie. This of course was the last thing the dog-man wanted. He backed away. Howl pounced, and caught him by two handfuls of shaggy hair before he could reach the door. "So he is!" he said, and knelt down to look into what could be seen of the sheepdog's eyes. "Sophie," he said, "what do you mean by not telling me about this? This dog is a man! And he's in a terrible state!" Howl whirled round on one knee, still holding the dog. Sophie looked into Howl's glass-marble glare and realized that Howl was angry now, really angry.

Good. Sophie felt like a fight. "You could have noticed for yourself," she said, glaring back, daring Howl to do his worst with green slime. "Anyway, the dog didn't want—"

Howl was too angry to listen. He jumped up and hauled the dog across the tiles. "And so I would have done, if I hadn't had things on my mind," he said. "Come on. I want you in front of Calcifer." The dog braced all four shaggy feet. Howl lugged at it, braced and sliding. "Michael!" he yelled.

There was a particular sound to that yell which brought Michael running.

"And did *you* know this dog was really a man?" Howl asked as he and Michael dragged the reluctant mountain of dog up the stairs.

"He's not, is he?" Michael asked, shocked and surprised.

"Then I let you off and just blame Sophie," Howl said, hauling the dog through the broom cupboard. "Anything like this is always Sophie! But *you* knew, didn't you, Calcifer?" he said as the two of them dragged the dog in front of the hearth.

Calcifer retreated until he was bent backward against the chimney. "You never asked," he said.

"Do I *have* to ask you?" Howl said. "All right, I should have noticed myself! But you disgust me, Calcifer! Compared with the way the Witch treats *her* demon, you live a revoltingly easy life, and all I ask in return is that you tell me things I need to know. This is twice you've let me down! Now help me get this creature to its own shape this minute!"

Calcifer was an unusually sickly shade of blue. "All right," he said sulkily.

The dog-man tried to get away, but Howl got his shoulder under its chest and shoved, so that it went up onto its hind legs, willy-nilly. Then he and Michael held it there. "What's the silly creature holding out for?" Howl panted. "This feels like one of the Witch of the Waste's again, doesn't it?"

"Yes. There are several layers of it," said Calcifer.

"Let's get the dog part off anyway," said Howl.

Calcifer surged to a deep, roaring blue. Sophie, watching prudently from the door of the broom cupboard, saw the shaggy dog shape fade away inside the man shape. It faded to dog again, then back to man, blurred, then hardened. Finally, Howl and Michael were each holding the arm of a ginger-haired man in a crumpled brown suit. Sophie was not surprised she had not recognized him. Apart from his anxious look, his face was almost totally lacking in personality.

"Now, who are you, my friend?" Howl asked him.

The man put his hands up and shakily felt his face. "I—I'm not sure."

Calcifer said, "The most recent name he answered to was Percival."

The man looked at Calcifer as if he wished Calcifer

did not know this. "Did I?" he said.

"Then we'll call you Percival for now," Howl said. He turned the ex-dog round and sat him in the chair. "Sit there and take it easy, and tell us what you do remember. By the feel of you, the Witch had you for some time."

"Yes," said Percival, rubbing his face again. "She took my head off. I—I remember being on a shelf, looking at the rest of me."

Michael was astonished. "But you'd be dead!" he protested.

"Not necessarily," said Howl. "You haven't got to that sort of witchcraft yet, but I could take any piece of you I wanted and leave the rest of you alive, if I went about it the right way." He frowned at the ex-dog. "But I'm not sure the Witch put this one back together properly."

Calcifer, who was obviously trying to prove that he was working hard for Howl, said, "This man is incomplete, and he has parts from some other man too."

Percival looked more distraught than ever.

"Don't alarm him, Calcifer," Howl said. "He must feel bad enough anyway. Do you know why the Witch took your head off, my friend?" he asked Percival.

"No," said Percival. "I don't remember anything."

Sophie knew that could not be true. She snorted rather.

274

Michael was suddenly seized with the most exciting idea. He leaned over Percival and asked, "Did you ever answer to the name of Justin—or Your Royal Highness?"

Sophie snorted again. She knew this was ridiculous even before Percival said, "No. The Witch called me Gaston, but that isn't my name."

"Don't crowd him, Michael," said Howl. "And don't make Sophie snort again. The mood she's in, she'll bring down the castle next time."

Though that seemed to mean Howl was no longer angry, Sophie found she was angrier than ever. She stumped off into the shop, where she banged about, shutting the shop and putting things away for the night. She went to look at her daffodils. Something had gone horribly wrong with them. They were wet brown things trailing out of a bucket full of the most poisonous-smelling liquid she had ever come across.

"Oh, confound it all!" Sophie yelled.

"What's all this, now?" said Howl, arriving in the shop. He bent over the bucket and sniffed. "You seem to have some rather efficient weed-killer here. How about trying it on those weeds on the drive of the mansion?"

"I will," said Sophie. "I feel like killing something!" She slammed around until she had found a watering can, and stumped through into the castle with the can and the bucket, where she hurled open the door, orange-down, onto the mansion drive. Percival looked up anxiously. They had given him the guitar, rather as you gave a baby a rattle, and he was sitting making horrible twangings.

"You go with her, Percival," Howl said. "The mood she's in, she'll be killing all the trees too."

So Percival laid down the guitar and took the bucket carefully out of Sophie's hand. Sophie stumped out into a golden summer evening at the end of the valley. Everyone had been too busy up to now to pay much attention to the mansion. It was much grander than Sophie had realized. It had a weedy terrace with statues along the edge, and steps down to the drive. When Sophie looked back—on the pretext of telling Percival to hurry up—she saw the house was very big, with more statues along the roof, and rows of windows. But it was derelict. Green mildew ran down the peeling wall from every window. Many of the windows were broken, and the shutters that should have folded against the wall beside them were gray and blistered and hanging sideways.

"Huh!" said Sophie. "I think the least Howl could do is to make the place look a bit more lived in. But no! He's far too busy gadding off to Wales! Don't just stand there, Percival! Pour some of that stuff into the can and then come along behind me."

Percival meekly did as she said. He was no fun at

all to bully. Sophie suspected that was why Howl had sent him with her. She snorted, and took her anger out on the weeds. Whatever the stuff was that had killed the daffodils, it was strong. The weeds in the drive died as soon as it touched them. So did the grass at the sides of the drive, until Sophie calmed down a little. The evening calmed her. The fresh air was blowing off the distant hills, and clumps of trees planted at the sides of the drive rustled majestically in it.

Sophie weed-killed her way down a quarter of the drive. "You remember a great deal more than you let on," she accused Percival while he refilled her can. "What did the Witch really want with you? Why did she bring you into the shop with her that time?"

"She wanted to find out about Howl," Percival said.

"Howl?" said Sophie. "But you didn't know him, did you?"

"No, but I must have known something. It had to do with the curse she'd put on him," Percival explained, "but I've no idea what it was. She took it, you see, after we came to the shop. I feel bad about that. I was trying to stop her knowing, because a curse is an evil thing, and I did it by thinking about Lettie. Lettie was just in my head. I don't know how I knew her, because Lettie said she'd never seen me when I went to Upper Folding. But I knew all about her— enough so that when the Witch made me tell her about Lettie, I said she kept a hat shop in Market Chipping. So the Witch went there to teach us both a lesson. And you were there. She thought you were Lettie. I was horrified, because I didn't know Lettie had a sister."

Sophie picked up the can and weed-killed generously, wishing the weeds were the Witch. "And she turned you into a dog straight after that?"

"Just outside the town," said Percival. "As soon as I'd let her know what she wanted, she opened the carriage door and said, 'Off you run. I'll call you when I need you.' And I ran, because I could feel some sort of spell following me. It caught up just as I'd got to a farm, and the people there saw me change into a dog and thought I was a werewolf and tried to kill me. I had to bite one to get away. But I couldn't get rid of the stick, and it stuck in the hedge when I tried to get through."

Sophie weed-killed her way down another curve of the drive as she listened. "Then you went to Mrs. Fairfax's?"

"Yes. I was looking for Lettie. They were both very kind to me," Percival said, "even though they'd never seen me before. And Wizard Howl kept visiting to court Lettie. Lettie didn't want him, and she asked me to bite him to get rid of him, until Howl suddenly began asking her about you and——"

Sophie narrowly missed weed-killing her shoes.

Since the gravel was smoking where the stuff met it, this was probably just as well. *"What?"*

"He said, 'I know someone called Sophie who looks a little like you.' And Lettie said, 'That's my sister,' without thinking," Percival said. "And she got terribly worried then, particularly as Howl went on asking about her sister. Lettie said she could have bitten her tongue off. The day you came there, she was being nice to Howl in order to find out how he knew you. Howl said you were an old woman. And Mrs. Fairfax said she'd seen you. Lettie cried and cried. She said, 'Something terrible has happened to Sophie! And the worst of it is she'll think she's safe from Howl. Sophie's too kind herself to see how heartless Howl is!' And she was so upset that I managed to turn into a man long enough to say I'd go and keep an eye on you."

Sophie spread weed-killer in a great, smoking arc. "Bother Lettie! It's very kind of her, and I love her dearly for it. I've been quite as worried about her. But I do *not* need a watchdog!"

"Yes you do," said Percival. "Or you did. I arrived far too late."

Sophie swung round, weed-killer and all. Percival had to leap into the grass and run for his life behind the nearest tree. The grass died in a long brown swathe behind him as he ran. "Curse everyone!" Sophie cried out. "I've done with the lot of you!" She dumped the smoking watering can in the middle of the drive and marched off through the weeds toward the stone gateway. "Too late!" she muttered as she marched. "What nonsense! Howl's not only heartless, he's *impossible!* Besides," she added, "I *am* an old woman."

But she could not deny that something had been wrong ever since the moving castle moved, or even before that. And it seemed to tie up with the way Sophie seemed so mysteriously unable to face either of her sisters.

"And all the things I told the King are *true!*" she went on. She was going to march seven leagues on her own two feet and not come back. Show everyone! Who cared that poor Mrs. Pentstemmon had relied on Sophie to stop Howl from going to the bad! Sophie was a failure anyway. It came of being the eldest. And Mrs. Pentstemmon had thought Sophie was Howl's loving old mother anyway. Hadn't she? Or *had* she? Uneasily, Sophie realized that a lady whose trained eye could detect a charm sewn into a suit could surely even more easily detect the stronger magic of the Witch's spell.

"Oh, confound that gray-and-scarlet suit!" Sophie said. "I refuse to believe that I was the one that got caught with it!" The trouble was the blue-and-silver suit seemed to have worked just the same. She stumped a few steps further. "Anyway," she said with great relief, "Howl doesn't like me!"

This reassuring thought would have been enough to keep Sophie walking all night, had not a sudden familiar uneasiness swept over her. Her ears had caught a distant tock, tock, tock. She looked sharply under the low sun. And there, on the road which wound away behind the stone gate, was a distant figure with outstretched arms, hopping, hopping.

Sophie picked up her skirts, whirled round, and sped back the way she had come. Dust and gravel flew up round her in clouds. Percival was standing forlornly in the drive beside the bucket and the watering can. Sophie seized him and dragged him behind the nearest trees.

"Is something wrong?" he said.

"Quiet! It's that dratted scarecrow again," Sophie gasped. She shut her eyes. "We're not here," she said. "You can't find us. Go away. Go away fast, fast, fast!"

"But why—?" said Percival.

"Shut *up!* Not here, not here, not here!" Sophie said desperately. She opened one eye. The scarecrow, almost between the gateposts, was standing still, swaying uncertainly. "That's right," said Sophie. "We're not here. Go away fast. Twice as fast, three times as fast, ten times as fast. Go *away!*"

And the scarecrow hesitantly swayed round on its stick and began to hop back up the road. After the first few hops it was going in giant leaps, faster and faster, just as Sophie had told it to. Sophie hardly breathed, and did not let go of Percival's sleeve until the scarecrow was out of sight.

"What's wrong with it?" said Percival. "Why didn't you want it?"

Sophie shuddered. Since the scarecrow was out on the road, she did not dare leave now. She picked up the watering can and stumped back to the mansion. A fluttering caught her eye as she went. She looked up at the building. The flutter was from long white curtains blowing from an open French window beyond the statues of the terrace. The statues were now clean white stone, and she could see curtains at most of the windows, and glass too. The shutters were now folded properly beside them, newly painted white. Not a green stain nor a blister marked the new creamy plaster of the house front. The front door was a masterpiece of black paint and gold scrollwork, centering on a gilded lion with a ring in its mouth for a doorknocker.

"Huh!" said Sophie.

She resisted the temptation to go in through the open window and explore. That was what Howl wanted her to do. She marched straight to the front door, seized the golden doorknob, and threw the door open with a crash. Howl and Michael were at the bench hastily dismantling a spell. Part of it must have been to change the mansion, but the rest, as

Sophie well knew, had to be a listening-in spell of some kind. As Sophie stormed in, both their faces shot nervously round toward her. Calcifer instantly plunged down under his logs.

"Keep behind me, Michael," said Howl.

"Eavesdropper!" Sophie shouted. "Snooper!"

"What's wrong?" Howl said. "Do you want the shutters black and gold too?"

"You barefaced—" Sophie stuttered. "That wasn't the only thing you heard! You—you—How long have you known I was—I am—?"

"Under a spell?" said Howl. "Well, now—"

"I told him," Michael said, looking nervously round Howl. "My Lettie—"

"*You!*" Sophie shrieked.

"The other Lettie let the cat out of the bag too," Howl said quickly. "You know she did. And Mrs. Fairfax talked a great deal that day. There was a time when everyone seemed to be telling me. Even Calcifer did—when I asked him. But do you honestly think I don't know my own business well enough not to spot a strong spell like that when I see it? I had several goes at taking it off you when you weren't looking. But nothing seems to work. I took you to Mrs. Pentstemmon, hoping she could do something, but she evidently couldn't. I came to the conclusion that you liked being in disguise."

"*Disguise!*" Sophie yelled.

Howl laughed at her. "It must be, since you're doing it yourself," he said. "What a strange family you are! Is *your* name really Lettie too?"

This was too much for Sophie. Percival edged nervously in just then, carrying the half-full bucket of weed-killer. Sophie dropped her can, seized the bucket from him, and threw it at Howl. Howl ducked. Michael dodged the bucket. The weed-killer went up in a sheet of sizzling green flame from floor to ceiling. The bucket clanged into the sink, where all the remaining flowers died instantly.

"Ow!" said Calcifer from under his logs. "That was strong."

Howl carefully picked the skull out from under the smoking brown remains of the flowers and dried it on one of his sleeves. "Of course it was strong," he said. "Sophie never does things by halves." The skull, as Howl wiped it, became bright new white, and the sleeve he was using developed a faded blue-and-silver patch. Howl set the skull on the bench and looked at his sleeve ruefully.

Sophie had half a mind to stump straight out of the castle again, and away down the drive. But there was that scarecrow. She settled for stumping to the chair instead, where she sat and fell into a deep sulk. I'm not going to speak to any of them! she thought.

"Sophie," Howl said, "I did my best. Haven't you noticed that your aches and pains have been better lately? Or do you enjoy having those too?" Sophie did not answer. Howl gave her up and turned to Percival. "I'm glad to see that you have some brain after all," he said. "You had me worried."

"I really don't remember very much," Percival said. But he stopped behaving like a half-wit. He picked the guitar up and tuned it. He had it sounding much nicer in seconds.

"My sorrow revealed," Howl said pathetically. "I was born an unmusical Welshman. Did you tell Sophie all of it? Or do you really know what the Witch was trying to find out?"

"She wanted to know about Wales," said Percival.

"I thought that was it," Howl said soberly. "Ah, well." He went away into the bathroom, where he was gone for the next two hours. During that time Percival played a number of tunes on the guitar in a slow, thoughtful way, as if he was teaching himself how to, while Michael crawled about the floor with a smoking rag, trying to get rid of the weed-killer. Sophie sat in the chair and said not a word. Calcifer kept bobbing up and peeping at her, and going down again under his logs.

Howl came out of the bathroom with his suit glossy black, his hair glossy white, in a cloud of steam smelling of gentians. "I may be back quite late," he said to Michael. "It's going to be Midsummer Day after midnight, and the Witch may well try something.

So keep all the defenses up, and remember all I told you, please."

"All right," Michael said, putting the steaming remains of the rag in the sink.

Howl turned to Percival. "I think I know what's happened to you," he said. "It's going to be a fair job sorting you out, but I'll have a go tomorrow after I get back." Howl went to the door and stopped with his hand on the knob. "Sophie, are you still not talking to me?" he asked miserably.

Sophie knew Howl could sound unhappy in heaven if it suited him. And he had just used her to get information out of Percival. "No!" she snarled.

Howl sighed and went out. Sophie looked up and saw that the knob was pointing black-down. That does it! she thought. I don't care if it *is* Midsummer Day tomorrow! I'm leaving.

Chapter 20:

◆—⫻—◆

In which Sophie finds farther difficulties in leaving the castle

Midsummer Day dawned. About the same moment that it did, Howl crashed in through the door with such a noise that Sophie shot up in her cubbyhole, convinced that the Witch was hot on his heels.

"They think so much about me that they always play without me!" Howl bellowed. Sophie realized that he was only trying to sing Calcifer's saucepan song and lay down again, whereupon Howl fell over the chair and caught his foot in the stool so that it shot across the room. After that, he tried to go upstairs through the broom cupboard, and then the yard. This seemed to puzzle him a little. But finally he discovered the stairs, all except the bottom one, and fell up them on his face. The whole castle shook.

"What's the matter?" Sophie asked, sticking her head through the banister.

"Rugby Club Reunion," Howl replied with thick dignity. "Didn't know I used to fly up the wing for my university, did you, Mrs. Nose?"

"If you were trying to fly, you must have forgotten how," Sophie said.

"I was born to strange sights," said Howl, "things invisible to see, and I was just on my way to bed when you interrupted me. I know where all past years are, and who cleft the Devil's foot."

"Go to bed, you fool," Calcifer said sleepily. "You're drunk."

"Who, me?" said Howl. "I assure you, my friends, I am cone sold stober." He got up and stalked upstairs, feeling for the wall as if he thought it might escape him unless he kept in touch with it. His bedroom door did escape him. "What a lie that was!" Howl remarked as he walked into the wall. "My shining dishonesty will be the salvation of me." He walked into the wall several times more, in several different places, before he discovered his bedroom door and crashed his way through it. Sophie could hear him falling about, saying that his bed was dodging.

"He is quite impossible!" Sophie said, and she decided to leave at once.

Unfortunately, the noise Howl made woke Michael up, and Percival, who was sleeping on the floor in Michael's room. Michael came downstairs saying that they were so thoroughly awake that they might as well go out and gather the flowers for the Midsummer garlands while the day was still cool. Sophie was not sorry to go out into the place of flowers for one last time. There was a warm, milky haze out there, filled with scent and half-hidden colors. Sophie thumped along, testing the squashy ground with her stick and listening to the whirrings and twitters of the thousands of birds, feeling truly regretful. She stroked a moist satin lily and fingered one of the ragged purple flowers with long, powdery stamens. She looked back at the tall black castle breasting the mist behind them. She sighed.

"He made it much better," Percival remarked as he put an armful of hibiscus into Michael's floating bath.

"Who did?" said Michael.

"Howl," said Percival. "There were only bushes at first, and they were quite small and dry."

"You remember being here before?" Michael asked excitedly. He had by no means given up his idea that Percival might be Prince Justin.

"I think I was here with the Witch," Percival said doubtfully.

They fetched two bathloads of flowers. Sophie noticed that when they came in the second time, Michael spun the knob over the door several times. That must have had something to do with keeping the Witch out. Then of course there were the Midsummer garlands to make. That took a long time. Sophie had meant to leave Michael and Percival to do that, but Michael was too busy asking Percival cunning questions and Percival was very slow at the work. Sophie knew what made Michael excited. There *was* a sort of air about Percival, as if he expected something to happen soon. It made Sophie wonder just how much in the power of the Witch he still was. She had to make most of the garlands. Any thoughts she might have had about staying and helping Howl against the Witch vanished. Howl, who could have made all the garlands just by waving his hand, was now snoring so loudly she could hear him right through in the shop.

They were so long making the garlands that it was time to open the shop before they had finished. Michael fetched them bread and honey, and they ate while they dealt with the tremendous first rush of customers. Although Midsummer Day, in the way of holidays, had turned out to be a gray and chilly day in Market Chipping, half the town came, dressed in fine holiday clothes, to buy flowers and garlands for the festival. There was the usual jostling crowd out in the street. So many people came into the shop that it was getting on for midday before Sophie finally stole away up the stairs and through the broom cupboard. They had taken so much money, Sophie thought as she stole about, packing up some food and her old clothes in a bundle, that Michael's hoard under the hearthstone would be ten times the size.

"Have you come to talk to me?" asked Calcifer.

"In a moment," Sophie said, crossing the room with her bundle behind her back. She did not want Calcifer raising an outcry about that contract.

She stretched out her hand to unhook her stick from the chair, and somebody knocked at the door. Sophie stuck, with her hand stretched out, looking inquiringly at Calcifer.

"It's the mansion door," said Calcifer. "Flesh and blood and harmless."

The knocking came again. This always happens when I try to leave! Sophie thought. She turned the knob orange-down and opened the door.

There was a carriage in the drive beyond the statues, pulled by a goodish pair of horses. Sophie could see it round the edges of the very large footman who had been doing the knocking.

"Mrs. Sacheverell Smith to call upon the new occupants," said the footman.

How very awkward! Sophie thought. It was the result of Howl's new paint and curtains. "We're not at h—" she began. But Mrs. Sacheverell Smith swept the footman aside and came in.

"Wait with the carriage, Theobald," she said to the footman as she sailed past Sophie, folding her parasol.

It was Fanny—Fanny looking wonderfully prosperous in cream silk. She was wearing a cream silk hat trimmed with roses, which Sophie remembered only too well. She remembered what she had said to that hat as she trimmed it: "You are going to have to marry money." And it was quite clear from the look of her that Fanny had.

"Oh, dear!" said Fanny, looking round. "There must be some mistake. This is the servants' quarters!"

"Well—er—we're not really quite moved in yet, Madam," Sophie said, and wondered how Fanny would feel if she knew that the old hat shop was only just beyond the broom cupboard.

Fanny turned round and gaped at Sophie. "Sophie!" she exclaimed. "Oh, good gracious, child, what's happened to you? You look about ninety! Have you been very ill?" And, to Sophie's surprise, Fanny threw aside her hat and her parasol and all of her grand manner and flung her arms round Sophie and wept. "Oh, I didn't know *what* had happened to you!" she sobbed. "I went to Martha and I sent to Lettie, and neither of them knew. They changed places, silly girls, did you know? But nobody knew a thing about you! I've a reward out still. And here you are, working as a servant, when you could be living in luxury up the hill with me and Mr. Smith!"

Sophie found she was crying as well. She hurriedly dropped her bundle and led Fanny to the chair. She pulled the stool up and sat beside Fanny, holding her hand. By this time they were both laughing as well as crying. They were most powerfully glad to see one another again.

"It's a long story," Sophie said after Fanny had asked her six times what had happened to her. "When I looked in the mirror and saw myself like this, it was such a shock that I sort of wandered away——"

"Overwork," Fanny said wretchedly. "How I've blamed myself!"

"Not really," said Sophie. "And you mustn't worry, because Wizard Howl took me in——"

"Wizard Howl!" exclaimed Fanny. "That wicked, wicked man! Has *he* done this to you? Where is he? Let me at him!"

She seized her parasol and became so very warlike that Sophie had to hold her down. Sophie did not care to think how Howl might react if Fanny woke him by stabbing him with her parasol. "No, no!" she said. "Howl has been very kind to me." And this was true, Sophie realized. Howl showed his kindness rather strangely, but, considering all Sophie had done to annoy him, he had been very good to her indeed.

"But they say he eats women alive!" Fanny said, still struggling to get up.

Sophie held down her waving parasol. "He doesn't really," she said. "Do listen. He's not wicked at all!" There was a bit of a fizz from the grate at this, where Calcifer was watching with some interest. "He isn't!" Sophie said, to Calcifer as much as to Fanny. "In all the time I've been here, I've not seen him work a single evil spell!" Which again was true, she knew.

"Then I have to believe you," Fanny said, relaxing, "though I'm sure it must be your doing if he's reformed. You always did have a way with you, Sophie. You could stop Martha's tantrums when I couldn't do a thing with her. And I always said it was thanks to you that Lettie only got her own way *half* of the time instead of *all* the time! But you should have told me where you were, love!"

Sophie knew she should have. She had taken Martha's view of Fanny, whole and entire, when she should have known Fanny better. She was ashamed.

Fanny could not wait to tell Sophie about Mr. Sacheverell Smith. She launched into a long and excited account of how she had met Mr. Smith the very week Sophie had left, and married him before the week was out. Sophie watched her as she talked. Being old gave her an entirely new view of Fanny. She was a lady who was still young and pretty, and she had found the hat shop as boring as Sophie did. But she had stuck with it and done her best, both with the shop and with the three girls—until Mr. Hatter died. Then she had suddenly been afraid she was just like Sophie: old, with no reason, and nothing to show for it.

"And then, with you not being there to pass it on to, there seemed no reason not to sell the shop," Fanny was saying, when there was a clatter of feet in the broom cupboard.

Michael came through, saying, "We've shut the shop. And look who's here!" He was holding Martha's hand.

Martha was thinner and fairer and almost looked like herself again. She let go of Michael and rushed at Sophie, shouting, "Sophie, you should have told me!" while she flung her arms round her. Then she flung her arms round Fanny, just as if she had never said all those things about her.

But this was not all. Lettie and Mrs. Fairfax came through the cupboard after Martha, carrying a hamper between them, and after them came Percival, who looked livelier than Sophie had ever seen him. "We came over by carrier at first light," Mrs. Fairfax said, "and we brought—Bless me! It's Fanny!" She dropped her end of the hamper and ran to hug Fanny. Lettie dropped her end and ran to hug Sophie.

In fact, there was such general hugging and exclaiming and shouting that Sophie thought it was a marvel Howl did not wake up. But she could hear him snoring even through the shouting. I shall have to leave this evening, she thought. She was too glad to see everyone to consider going before that.

Lettie was very fond of Percival. While Michael carried the hamper to the bench and unpacked cold chickens and wines and honey puddings from it, Lettie hung on to Percival's arm in an ownerlike way that Sophie could not quite approve of, and made him tell her all that he remembered. Percival did not seem to mind. Lettie looked so lovely that Sophie did not blame him.

"He just arrived and kept turning into a man and then into different dogs and insisting that he knew me," Lettie said to Sophie. "I knew I'd never seen him before, but it didn't matter." She patted Percival's shoulder as if he were still a dog.

"But you had met Prince Justin?" Sophie said.

"Oh, yes," Lettie said offhandedly. "Mind you, he was in disguise in a green uniform, but it was obviously him. He was so smooth and courtly, even when he was annoyed about the finding spells. I had to make him up two lots because they would keep showing that Wizard Suliman was somewhere between us and Market Chipping, and he swore that couldn't be true. And all the time I was doing them, he kept interrupting me, calling me 'sweet lady' in a sarcastic sort of way, and asking me who I was and where my family lived and how old I was. I thought it was cheek! I'd rather have Wizard Howl, and that's saying something!"

By this time everyone was milling about, eating chicken and sipping wine. Calcifer seemed to be shy. He had gone down to green flickers and nobody seemed to notice him. Sophie wanted him to meet Lettie. She tried to coax him out.

"Is that really the demon who has charge of Howl's life?" Lettie said, looking down at the green flickers rather disbelievingly.

Sophie looked up to assure Lettie that Calcifer was real and saw Miss Angorian standing by the door, looking shy and uncertain. "Oh, do excuse me. I've come at a bad time, haven't I?" Miss Angorian said. "I just wanted to talk to Howell."

Sophie stood up, not quite sure what to do. She was ashamed of the way she had driven Miss Angorian out before. It was only because she knew Howl was courting Miss Angorian. On the other hand, that did not mean she had to like her.

Michael took things out of Sophie's hands by greeting Miss Angorian with a beaming smile and a shout of welcome. "Howl's asleep at the moment," he said. "Come and have a glass of wine while you wait."

"How kind," said Miss Angorian.

But it was plain that Miss Angorian was not happy. She refused wine and wandered nervously about, nibbling at a leg of chicken. The room was full of people who all knew one another very well and she was the outsider. Fanny did not help by turning from nonstop talk with Mrs. Fairfax and saying, "What peculiar clothes!" Martha did not help either. She had seen how admiringly Michael greeted Miss Angorian. She went and made sure that Michael did not talk to anyone but herself and Sophie. And Lettie ignored

Miss Angorian and went to sit on the stairs with Percival.

Miss Angorian seemed rather quickly to decide that she had had enough. Sophie saw her at the door, trying to open it. She hurried over, feeling very guilty. After all, Miss Angorian must have felt very strongly about Howl to have come here at all. "Please don't go yet," Sophie said. "I'll go and wake Howl up."

"Oh, no, you mustn't do that," Miss Angorian said, smiling nervously. "I've got the day off, and I'm quite happy to wait. I thought I'd go and explore outside. It's rather stuffy in here with that funny green fire burning."

This seemed to Sophie the perfect way to get rid of Miss Angorian without really getting rid of her. She politely opened the door for her. Somehow—maybe it had to do with the defenses Howl had asked Michael to keep up—the knob had got turned round to purple-down. Outside was a misty blaze of sun and the drifting banks of red and purple flowers.

"What gorgeous rhododendrons!" Miss Angorian exclaimed in her huskiest and most throbbing voice. "I *must* look!" She sprang eagerly down into the marshy grass.

"Don't go toward the southeast," Sophie called after her.

The castle was drifting off sideways. Miss Angorian buried her beautiful face in a cluster of white flowers. "I won't go far at all," she said.

"Good gracious!" Fanny said, coming up behind Sophie. "Whatever has happened to my carriage?"

Sophie explained, as far as she could. But Fanny was so worried that Sophie had to turn the door orange-down and open it to show the mansion drive in a much grayer day, where the footman and Fanny's coachman were sitting on the roof of the carriage eating cold sausage and playing cards. Only then would Fanny believe that her carriage had not been mysteriously spirited away. Sophie was trying to explain, without really knowing herself, how one door could open on several different places, when Calcifer surged up from his logs, roaring.

"Howl!" he roared, filling the chimney with blue flame. "*Howl!* Howell Jenkins, the Witch has found your sister's family!"

There were two violent thumps overhead. Howl's bedroom door crashed, and Howl came tearing downstairs. Lettie and Percival were hurled out of his way. Fanny screamed faintly at the sight of him. Howl's hair was like a haystack and there were red rims round his eyes. "Got me on my weak flank, blast her!" he shouted as he shot across the room with his black sleeves flying. "I was afraid she would! Thanks, Calcifer!" He shoved Fanny aside and hurled open the door.

Sophie heard the door bang behind Howl as she

hobbled upstairs. She knew it was nosy, but she had to see what happened. As she hobbled through Howl's bedroom, she heard everyone else following her.

"What a filthy room!" Fanny exclaimed.

Sophie looked out of the window. It was drizzling in the neat garden. The swing was hung with drops. The Witch's waving mane of red hair was all dewed with it. She stood leaning against the swing, tall and commanding in her red robes, beckoning and beckoning again. Howl's niece, Mari, was shuffling over the wet grass toward the Witch. She did not look as if she wanted to go, but she seemed to have no choice. Behind her, Howl's nephew, Neil, was shuffling toward the Witch even more slowly, glowering in his most ferocious way. And Howl's sister, Megan, was behind the two children. Sophie could see Megan's arms gesturing and Megan's mouth opening and shutting. She was clearly giving the Witch a piece of her mind, but she was being drawn toward the Witch too.

Howl burst out onto the lawn. He had not bothered to alter his clothes. He did not bother to do any magic. He just charged straight at the Witch. The Witch made a grab for Mari, but Mari was still too far away. Howl got to Mari first, slung her behind him, and charged on. And the Witch ran. She ran, like a cat with a dog after it, across the lawn and over the neat fence, in a flurry of flame-colored robes, with

Howl, like the chasing dog, a foot or so behind and closing. The Witch vanished over the fence in a red blur. Howl went after her in a black blur with trailing sleeves. Then the fence hid both of them from sight.

"I hope he catches her," said Martha. "The little girl's crying."

Down below, Megan put her arm round Mari and took both children indoors. There was no knowing what had happened to Howl and the Witch. Lettie and Percival and Martha and Michael went back downstairs. Fanny and Mrs. Fairfax were transfixed with disgust at the state of Howl's bedroom.

"Look at those spiders!" Mrs. Fairfax said.

"And the dust on these curtains!" said Fanny. "Annabel, I saw some brooms in that passage you came through."

"Let's get them," said Mrs. Fairfax. "I'll pin that dress up for you, Fanny, and we'll get to work. I can't bear a room to be in this state!"

Oh, poor Howl! Sophie thought. He does love those spiders! She hovered on the stairs, wondering how to stop Mrs. Fairfax and Fanny.

From downstairs, Michael called, "Sophie! We're going to look round the mansion. Want to come?"

That seemed the ideal thing to stop the two ladies from cleaning. Sophie called to Fanny and hobbled hurriedly downstairs. Lettie and Percival were already opening the door. Lettie had not listened when Sophie explained it to Fanny. And it was clear that Percival did not understand either. Sophie saw they were opening it purple-down by mistake. They got it open as Sophie hobbled across the room to put them right.

The scarecrow loomed up in the doorway against the flowers.

"*Shut* it!" Sophie screamed. She saw what had happened. She had actually helped the scarecrow last night by telling it to go ten times as fast. It had simply sped to the castle entrance and tried to get in there. But Miss Angorian was out there. Sophie wondered if she was lying in the bushes in a dead faint. "No, don't," she said weakly.

No one was attending to her anyway. Lettie's face was the color of Fanny's dress, and she was clutching Martha. Percival was standing staring, and Michael was trying to catch the skull, which was yattering its teeth so hard that it was threatening to fall off the bench and take a wine bottle with it. And the skull seemed to have a strange effect on the guitar too. It was giving out long, humming twangs: Noumm Harrummm! Noumm Harrummm!

Calcifer flamed up the chimney again. "The thing is speaking," he said to Sophie. "It is saying it means no harm. I think it is speaking the truth. It is waiting for your permission to come in."

Certainly the scarecrow was just standing there. It

was not trying to barge inside as it had before. And Calcifer must have trusted it. He had stopped the castle moving. Sophie looked at the turnip face and the fluttering rags. It was not so frightening after all. She had once had fellow feeling for it. She rather suspected that she had just made it into a convenient excuse for not leaving the castle because she had really wanted to stay. Now there was no point. Sophie had to leave anyway: Howl preferred Miss Angorian.

"Please come in," she said, a little croakily.

"Ahmmnng!" said the guitar. The scarecrow surged into the room with one powerful sideways hop. It stood swinging about on its one leg as if it was looking for something. The smell of flowers it had brought in with it did not hide its own smell of dust and rotting turnip.

The skull yattered under Michael's fingers again. The scarecrow spun round, gladly, and fell sideways toward it. Michael made one attempt to rescue the skull and then got hastily out of the way. For as the scarecrow fell across the bench, there came the fizzing jolt of strong magic and the skull melted into the scarecrow's turnip head. It seemed to get inside the turnip and fill it out. There was now a strong suggestion of a rather craggy face on the turnip. The trouble was, it was on the back of the scarecrow. The scarecrow gave a wooden scramble, hopped upright uncertainly, and then swiftly spun its body round so that the front of it was under the craggy turnip face. Slowly it eased its outstretched arms down to its sides.

"Now I can speak," it said in a somewhat mushy voice.

"I may faint," Fanny announced, on the stairs.

"Nonsense," Mrs. Fairfax said, behind Fanny. "The thing's only a magician's golem. It has to do what it was sent to do. They're quite harmless."

Lettie, all the same, looked ready to faint. But the only one who did faint was Percival. He flopped to the floor, quite quietly, and lay curled up as if he were asleep. Lettie, in spite of her terror, ran toward him, only to back away as the scarecrow gave another hop and stood itself in front of Percival.

"This is one of the parts I was sent to find," it said in its mushy voice. It swung on its stick until it was facing Sophie. "I must thank you," it said. "My skull was far away and I ran out of strength before I reached it. I would have lain in that hedge forever if you had not come and talked life into me." It swiveled to Mrs. Fairfax and then to Lettie. "I thank you both too," it said.

"Who sent you? What are you supposed to do?" Sophie said.

The scarecrow swung about uncertainly. "More than this," it said. "There are still parts missing." Everyone waited, most of them too shaken to speak, while the scarecrow rotated this way and that, seemingly thinking.

"What is Percival a part of?" Sophie said.

"Let it collect itself," said Calcifer. "No one's asked it to explain itself bef—" He suddenly stopped speaking and shrank until barely a green flame showed. Michael and Sophie exchanged alarmed glances.

Then a new voice spoke, out of nowhere. It was enlarged and muffled, as if it were speaking in a box, but it was unmistakably the voice of the Witch. "Michael Fisher," it said, "tell your master, Howl, that he fell for my decoy. I now have the woman called Lily Angorian in my fortress in the Waste. Tell him I will only let her go if he comes himself to fetch her. Is that clear, Michael Fisher?"

The scarecrow whirled round and hopped for the open door.

"Oh, no!" Michael cried out. "Stop it! The Witch must have sent it so that she could get in here!"

Chapter 21:

— ·—◆◆◆—· —

In which a contract is concluded before witnesses

Most people ran after the scarecrow. Sophie ran the other way, through the broom cupboard and into the shop, grabbing her stick as she went.

"This is my fault!" she muttered. "I have a genius for doing things wrong! I could have kept Miss Angorian indoors. I only needed to talk to her politely, poor thing! Howl may have forgiven me a lot of things, but he's not going to forgive me for this in a hurry!"

In the flower shop she hauled the seven-league boots out of the window display and emptied hibiscus, roses, and water out of them onto the floor. She unlocked the shop door and towed the wet boots out onto the crowded pavement. "Excuse me," she said to various shoes and trailing sleeves that were walking in her way. She looked up at the sun, which was not easy to find in the cloudy gray sky. "Let's see. Southeast. That way. Excuse me, excuse me," she said, clearing a small space for the boots among the holiday-makers.

She put them down pointing the right way. Then she stepped into them and began to stride.

Zip-zip, zip-zip, zip-zip, zip-zip, zip-zip, zip-zip, zip-zip. It was as quick as that, and even more blurred and breathless in both boots than in one. Sophie had brief glimpses between long double strides: of the mansion down at the end of the valley, gleaming between trees, with Fanny's carriage at the door; of bracken on a hillside; of a small river racing down into a green valley; of the same river sliding in a much broader valley; of the same valley turned so wide it seemed endless and blue in the distance, and a towery pile far, far off that might have been Kingsbury; of the plain narrowing toward mountains again; of a mountain which slanted so steeply under her boot that she stumbled in spite of her stick, which stumble brought her to the edge of a deep, blue-misted gorge, with the tops of trees far below, where she had to take another stride or fall in.

And she landed on crumbly yellow sand. She dug her stick in and looked carefully round. Behind her right shoulder, some miles off, a white, steamy mist almost hid the mountains she had just zipped through. Below the mist was a band of dark green. Sophie nodded. Though she could not see the moving castle this far away, she was sure the mist marked the place of flowers. She took another careful stride. Zip. It was fearsomely hot. The clay-yellow sand stretched in all directions now, shimmering in the heat. Rocks lay about in a messy way. The only growing things were occasional dismal gray bushes. The mountains looked like clouds coming up on the horizon.

"If this is the Waste," Sophie said, with sweat running in all her wrinkles, "then I feel sorry for the Witch having to live here."

She took another stride. The wind of it did not cool her down at all. The rocks and bushes were the same, but the sand was grayer, and the mountains seemed to have sunk down the sky. Sophie peered into the quivering gray glare ahead, where she thought she could see something rather higher than rock. She took one more stride.

Now it was like an oven. But there was a peculiar-shaped pile about a quarter of a mile off, standing on a slight rise in the rock-littered land. It was a fantastical shape of twisted little towers, rising to one main tower that pointed slightly askew, like a knotty old finger. Sophie climbed out of the boots. It was too hot to carry anything so heavy, so she trudged off to investigate with only her stick.

The thing seemed to be made of the yellow-gray grit of the Waste. At first Sophie wondered if it might be some strange kind of ants' nest. But as she got nearer, she could see that it was as if something had fused together thousands of grainy yellow flowerpots into a tapering heap. She grinned. The moving castle had often struck her as being remarkably like the inside of a chimney. This building was really a collection of chimney pots. It had to be a fire demon's work.

As Sophie panted up the rise, there was suddenly no doubt that this was the Witch's fortress. Two small orange figures came out of a dark space at the bottom and stood waiting for her. She recognized the Witch's two page boys. Hot and breathless as she was, she tried to speak to them politely, to show she had no quarrel with them. "Good afternoon," she said.

They just gave her sulky looks. One bowed and held out his hand, pointing toward the misshapen dark archway between the bent columns of chimney pots. Sophie shrugged and followed him inside. The other page walked after her. And of course the entrance vanished as soon as she was through. Sophie shrugged again. She would have to deal with that problem when she came back.

She rearranged her lace shawl, straightened her draggled skirts, and walked forward. It was a little like going through the castle door with the knob black-down. There was a moment of nothingness, followed by murky light. The light came from greenish yellow flames that burned and flickered all round, but in a shadowy way which gave no heat and very little light either. When Sophie looked at them, the flames were never where she was looking, but always to the side. But that was the way of magic. Sophie shrugged again and followed the page this way and that among skinny pillars of the same chimney-pot kind as the rest of the building.

At length the pages led her to a sort of central den. Or maybe it was just a space between pillars. Sophie was confused by then. The fortress seemed enormous, though she suspected that it was deceptive, just as the castle was. The Witch was standing there waiting. Again, it was hard to tell how Sophie knew—except that it could be no one else. The Witch was hugely tall and skinny now and her hair was fair, in a ropelike pigtail over one bony shoulder. She wore a white dress. When Sophie walked straight up to her, brandishing her stick, the Witch backed away.

"I am not to be threatened!" the Witch said, sounding tired and frail.

"Then give me Miss Angorian and you won't be," said Sophie. "I'll take her and go away."

The Witch backed away further, gesturing with both hands. And the page boys both melted into sticky orange blobs which rose into the air and flew toward Sophie. "Yucky! Get off!" Sophie cried, beating at them with her stick. The orange blobs did not seem to care for her stick. They dodged it, and wove about, and then darted behind Sophie. She was just thinking she had got the better of them when she found herself glued to a chimney-pot pillar by them. Orange sticky stuff stranded between her ankles when she tried to move and plucked at her hair quite painfully.

"I'd almost rather have green slime!" Sophie said. "I hope those weren't real boys."

"Only emanations," said the Witch.

"Let me go," said Sophie.

"No," said the Witch. She turned away and seemed to lose interest in Sophie entirely.

Sophie began to fear that, as usual, she had made a mess of things. The sticky stuff seemed to be getting harder and more elastic every second. When she tried to move, it snapped her back against the pottery pillar. "Where's Miss Angorian?" she said.

"You will not find her," said the Witch. "We will wait until Howl comes."

"He's not coming," said Sophie. "He's got more sense. And your curse hasn't all worked anyway."

"It will," said the Witch, smiling slightly. "Now that you have fallen for our deception and come here. Howl will have to be honest for once." She made another gesture, toward the murky flames this time, and a sort of throne trundled out from between two pillars and stopped in front of the Witch. There was a man sitting in it, wearing a green uniform and long, shiny boots. Sophie thought he was asleep at first, with his head out of sight sideways. But the Witch gestured again. The man sat up straight. And he had no head on his shoulders at all. Sophie realized she was looking at all that was left of Prince Justin.

"If I was Fanny," Sophie said, "I'd threaten to faint. Put his head back on at once! He looks terrible like that!"

"I disposed of both heads months ago," said the Witch. "I sold Wizard Suliman's skull when I sold his guitar. Prince Justin's head is walking around somewhere with the other leftover parts. This body is a perfect mixture of Prince Justin and Wizard Suliman. It is waiting for Howl's head, to make it our perfect human. When we have Howl's head, we shall have the new King of Ingary, and I shall rule as Queen."

"You're mad!" Sophie said. "You've no right to make jigsaws of people! And I shouldn't think Howl's head will do a thing you want. It'll slither out somehow."

"Howl will do exactly as we say," the Witch said with a sly, secretive smile. "We shall control his fire demon."

Sophie realized she was very scared indeed. She knew she had made a mess of things now. "Where is Miss Angorian?" she said, waving her stick.

The Witch did not like Sophie to wave her stick. She stepped backward. "I am very tired," she said. "You people keep spoiling my plans. First Wizard Suliman would not come near the Waste, so that I had to threaten Princess Valeria in order to make the King order him out here. Then, when he came, he grew trees. Then the King would not let Prince Justin follow

Suliman for months, and when he did follow, the silly fool went up north somewhere for some reason, and I had to use all my arts to get him here. Howl has caused me even more trouble. He got away once. I've had to use a curse to bring him in, and while I was finding out enough about him to lay the curse, *you* got into what was left of Suliman's brain and caused me more trouble. And now when I bring you here, you wave your stick and argue. I have worked very hard for this moment, and I am not to be argued with." She turned away and wandered off into the murk.

Sophie stared after the tall white figure moving among the dim flames. I think her age has caught up with her! she thought. She's crazy! I must get loose and rescue Miss Angorian from her somehow! Remembering that the orange stuff had avoided her stick, just as the Witch had, Sophie reached back over her shoulders with her stick and wagged it back and forth where the sticky stuff met the pottery pillar. "Get out of it!" she said. "Let me go!" Her hair dragged painfully, but stringy orange bits began to fly away sideways. Sophie wagged the stick harder.

She had worked her head and shoulders loose when there came a dull booming sound. The pale flames wavered and the pillar behind Sophie shook. Then, with a crash like a thousand tea sets falling downstairs, a piece of the fortress wall blew out. Light blinded in through a long, jagged hole, and a figure came leaping in through the opening. Sophie turned eagerly, hoping it was Howl. But the black outline had only one leg. It was the scarecrow again.

The Witch gave a yowl of rage and rushed toward it with her fair pigtail flying and her bony arms stretched out. The scarecrow leaped at her. There was another violent bang and the two of them were wrapped in a magic cloud, like the cloud over Porthaven when Howl and the Witch had fought. The cloud battered this way and that, filling the dusty air with shrieks and booms. Sophie's hair frizzed. The cloud was only yards away, going this way and that among pottery pillars. And the break in the wall was quite near too. As Sophie had thought, the fortress was really not big. Every time the cloud moved across the blinding white gap, she could see through it, and see the two skinny figures battling in its midst. She stared, and kept wagging her stick behind her back.

She was loose all except her legs when the cloud screamed across in front of the light one more time. Sophie saw another person leap through the gap behind it. This one had flying black sleeves. It was Howl. Sophie could see the outline of him clearly, standing with his arms folded, watching the battle. For a moment it looked as if he was going to let the Witch and the scarecrow get on with it. Then the long sleeves flapped as Howl raised his arms. Above the screaming and booming, Howl's voice shouted one strange, long word, and a long roll of thunder came with it. The scarecrow and the Witch both jolted. Claps of sound rang round the pottery pillars, echo after echo, and each echo carried some of the cloud of magic away with it. It vanished in wisps and swirled away in murky eddies. When it had become the thinnest white haze, the tall figure with the pigtail began to totter. The Witch seemed to fold in on herself, thinner and whiter than ever. Finally, as the haze faded clean away, she fell in a heap with a small clatter. As the million soft echoes died, Howl and the scarecrow were left thoughtfully facing one another across a pile of bones.

Good! thought Sophie. She slashed her legs free and went across to the headless figure in the throne. It was getting on her nerves.

"No, my friend," Howl said to the scarecrow. The scarecrow had hopped right among the bones and was pushing them this way and that with its leg. "No, you won't find her heart here. Her fire demon will have got that. I think it's had the upper hand of her for a long time now. Sad, really." As Sophie took off her shawl and arranged it decently across Prince Justin's headless shoulders, Howl said, "I think the rest of what you were looking for is over here." He walked toward the throne, with the scarecrow hopping beside him. "Typical!" he said to Sophie. "I break my neck to get here, and I find you peacefully tidying up!"

Sophie looked up at him. As she had feared, the

hard black-and-white daylight coming through the broken wall showed her that Howl had not bothered to shave or tidy his hair. His eyes were still red-rimmed and his black sleeves were torn in several places. There was not much to choose between Howl and the scarecrow. Oh, dear! Sophie thought. He must love Miss Angorian very much. "I came for Miss Angorian," she explained.

"And I thought if I arranged for your family to visit you, it would keep you quiet for once!" Howl said disgustedly. "But no——"

Here the scarecrow hopped in front of Sophie. "I was sent by Wizard Suliman," it said in its mushy voice. "I was guarding his bushes from the birds in the Waste when the Witch caught him. He cast all of his magic that he could spare on me, and ordered me to come to his rescue. But the Witch had taken him to pieces by then and the pieces were in various places. It has been a hard task. If you had not come and talked me to life again, I would have failed."

It was answering the questions Sophie had asked it before they both rushed off.

"So when Prince Justin ordered finding spells, they must have kept pointing to *you*," she said. "Why was that?"

"To me or to his skull," said the scarecrow. "Between us, we are the best part of him."

"And Percival is made of Wizard Suliman and

Prince Justin?" Sophie said. She was not sure Lettie was going to like this.

The scarecrow nodded its craggy turnip face. "Both parts told me that the Witch and her fire demon were no longer together and I could defeat the Witch on her own," it said. "I thank you for giving me ten times my former speed."

Howl waved it aside. "Bring that body with you to the castle," he said. "I'll sort you out there. Sophie and I have to get back before that fire demon finds a way of getting inside my defenses." He took hold of Sophie's skinny wrist. "Come on. Where are those seven-league boots?"

Sophie hung back. "But Miss Angorian——!"

"Don't you understand?" Howl said, dragging at her. "Miss Angorian *is* the fire demon. If it gets inside the castle, then Calcifer's had it and so have I!"

Sophie put both hands over her mouth. "I *knew* I'd made a mess of it!" she said. "It's been in twice already. But she——it went out."

"Oh, lord!" groaned Howl. "Did it touch anything?"

"The guitar," Sophie admitted.

"Then it's still in there," said Howl. "Come *on!*" He pulled Sophie over to the smashed wall. "Follow us carefully," he shouted back to the scarecrow. "I'm going to have to raise a wind! No time to look for those boots," he said to Sophie as they climbed over the jagged edges into the hot sunlight. "Just run. And keep running, or I won't be able to move you."

Sophie helped herself along with her stick and managed to break into a hobbling run, stumbling among the stones. Howl ran beside her, pulling her. Wind leaped up, whistling, then roaring, hot and gritty, and gray sand climbed around them in a storm that pinged on the pottery fortress. By that time they were not running, but skimming forward in a sort of slow-motion lope. The stony ground sped past underneath. Dust and grit thundered around them, high overhead and streaming far away behind. It was very noisy and not at all comfortable, but the Waste rocketed past.

"It's not Calcifer's fault!" Sophie yelled. "I told him not to say."

"He wouldn't anyway," Howl shouted back. "I knew he'd never give away a fellow fire demon. He was always my weakest flank."

"I thought Wales was!" Sophie screamed.

"No! I left that deliberately!" Howl bellowed. "I knew I'd be angry enough to stop her if she tried anything there. I had to leave her an opening, see? The only chance I had of coming at Prince Justin was to use that curse she'd put on me to get near *her*."

"So you *were* going to rescue the Prince!" Sophie shouted. "Why did you pretend to run away? To deceive the Witch?"

"Not likely!" Howl yelled. "I'm a coward. Only

way I can do something this frightening is to tell myself I'm *not* doing it!"

Oh, dear! Sophie thought, looking round at the swirling grit. He's being honest! And this is a wind. The last bit of the curse has come true!

The hot grit hit her thunderously and Howl's grip hurt. "Keep running!" Howl bawled. "You'll get hurt at this speed!" Sophie gasped and made her legs work again. She could see the mountains clearly now and a line of green below that was the flowering bushes. Even though yellow sand kept swirling in the way, the mountains seemed to grow and the green line rushed toward them until it was hedge high. "All my flanks were weak!" Howl shouted. "I was relying on Suliman being alive. Then when all that seemed to be left of him was Percival, I was so scared I had to go out and get drunk. And then you go and play into the Witch's hands!"

"I'm the eldest!" Sophie shrieked. "I'm a failure!"

"Garbage!" Howl shouted. "You just never stop to think!" Howl was slowing down. Dust kicked up round them in dense clouds. Sophie only knew the bushes were quite near because she could hear the rush and rattle of the gritty wind in the leaves. They plunged in among them with a crash, still going so fast that Howl had to swerve and drag Sophie in a long, skimming run across a lake. "And you're too nice," he added, above the lap-lap of the water and the patter of sand on the water-lily leaves. "I was relying on you being too jealous to let that demon near the place."

They hit the steamy shore at a slow run. The bushes on either side of the green lane thrashed and heaved as they passed, throwing birds and petals into a whirlwind behind them. The castle was drifting swiftly down the lane toward them, with its smoke streaming back in the wind. Howl slowed down enough to crash the door open, and shot Sophie and himself inside.

"Michael!" he shouted.

"It wasn't me who let the scarecrow in!" Michael said guiltily.

Everything seemed to be normal. Sophie was surprised to discover what a short time she had really been away. Someone had pulled her bed out from under the stairs and Percival was lying on it, still unconscious. Lettie and Martha and Michael were gathered round it. Overhead, Sophie could hear Mrs. Fairfax's voice and Fanny's, combined with ominous swishings and thumpings that suggested that Howl's spiders were having a hard time.

Howl let go of Sophie and dived toward the guitar. Before he could touch it, it burst with a long, melodious *boom*. Strings flailed. Splinters of wood showered Howl. He was forced to back away with one tattered sleeve over his face.

And Miss Angorian was suddenly standing beside the hearth, smiling. Howl had been right. She must have been in the guitar all this time, waiting for her moment.

"Your Witch is dead," Howl said to her.

"Isn't that too bad!" Miss Angorian said, quite unconcerned. "Now I can make myself a new human who will be much better. The curse is fulfilled. I can lay hands on your heart now." And she reached down into the grate and plucked Calcifer out of it. Calcifer wobbled on top of her clenched fist, looking terrified. "Nobody move," Miss Angorian said warningly.

Nobody dared stir. Howl stood stillest of all. "Help!" Calcifer said weakly.

"Nobody can help you," said Miss Angorian. "*You* are going to help *me* control my new human. Let me show you. I have only to tighten my grip." Her hand that was holding Calcifer squeezed until its knuckles showed pale yellow.

Howl and Calcifer both screamed. Calcifer beat this way and that in agony. Howl's face turned bluish and he crashed to the floor like a tree falling, where he lay as unconscious as Percival. Sophie did not think he was breathing.

Miss Angorian was astonished. She stared at Howl. "He's faking," she said.

"No he's *not!*" Calcifer screamed, twisted into a writhing spiral shape. "His heart's really quite soft! Let go!"

Sophie raised her stick, slowly and gently. This

time she thought for an instant before she acted. "Stick," she muttered. "Beat Miss Angorian, but don't hurt anyone else." Then she swung the stick and hit Miss Angorian's tight knuckles the biggest crack she could.

Miss Angorian let out a squealing hiss like a wet log burning and dropped Calcifer. Poor Calcifer rolled helplessly on the floor, flaming sideways across the flagstones and roaring huskily with terror. Miss Angorian raised a foot to stamp on him. Sophie had to let go of her stick and dive to rescue Calcifer. Her stick, to her surprise, hit Miss Angorian again on its own, and again, and again. But of course it would! Sophie thought. She had talked life into that stick. Mrs. Pentstemmon had told her so.

Miss Angorian hissed and staggered. Sophie stood up holding Calcifer, to find her stick drubbing away at Miss Angorian and smoking with the heat of her. By contrast, Calcifer did not seem very hot. He was milky blue with shock. Sophie could feel that the dark lump of Howl's heart was only beating very faintly between her fingers. It had to be Howl's heart she was holding. He had given it away to Calcifer as his part of the contract, to keep Calcifer alive. He must have been sorry for Calcifer, but, all the same, what a silly thing to do!

Fanny and Mrs. Fairfax hurried through the door from the stairs, carrying brooms. The sight of them seemed to convince Miss Angorian that she had failed.

She ran for the door, with Sophie's stick hovering over her, still clouting at her.

"Stop her!" Sophie shouted. "Don't let her get out! Guard all the doors!"

Everyone raced to obey. Mrs. Fairfax put herself in the broom cupboard with her broom raised. Fanny stood on the stairs. Lettie jumped up and guarded the door to the yard and Martha stood by the bathroom. Michael ran for the castle door. But Percival leaped up off the bed and ran for the door too. His face was white and his eyes were shut, but he ran even faster than Michael. He got there first, and he opened the door.

With Calcifer so helpless, the castle had stopped moving. Miss Angorian saw the bushes standing still in the haze outside and raced for the door with inhuman speed. Before she reached it, it was blocked by the scarecrow, looming up with Prince Justin hung across its shoulders, still draped in Sophie's lace shawl. It spread its stick arms across the door, barring the way. Miss Angorian backed away from it.

The stick beating at her was on fire now. Its metal end was glowing. Sophie realized it could not last much longer. Luckily, Miss Angorian hated it so much that she seized hold of Michael and dragged him in its way. The stick had been told not to hurt Michael. It hovered, flaming. Martha dashed up and tried to pull Michael away. The stick had to avoid her too. Sophie had got it wrong as usual.

There was no time to waste.

"Calcifer," Sophie said, "I shall have to break your contract. Will it kill you?"

"It would if anyone else broke it," Calcifer said hoarsely. "That's why I asked you to do it. I could tell you could talk life into things. Look what you did for the scarecrow and the skull."

"Then have another thousand years!" Sophie said, and willed very hard as she said it, in case just talking was not enough. This had been worrying her very much. She took hold of Calcifer and carefully nipped him off the black lump, just as she would nip a dead bud off a stalk. Calcifer whirled loose and hovered by her shoulder as a blue teardrop.

"I feel so light!" he said. Then it dawned on him what had happened. "I'm free!" he shouted. He whirled to the chimney and plunged up it, out of sight. "I'm free!" Sophie heard him shout overhead faintly as he came out through the chimney pot of the hat shop.

Sophie turned to Howl with the almost-dead black lump, feeling doubtful in spite of her hurry. She had to get this right, and she was not sure how you did. "Well, here goes," she said. Kneeling down beside Howl, she carefully put the black lump on his chest in the leftish sort of place she had felt hers in when it troubled her, and pushed. "Go in," she told it. "Get in there and work!" And she pushed and pushed. The heart began to sink in, and to beat more strongly as it went. Sophie tried to ignore the flames and scuffles by the door and to keep up a steady, firm pressure. Her hair kept getting in her way. It fell across her face in reddish fair hanks, but she tried to ignore that too. She pushed.

The heart went in. As soon as it had disappeared, Howl stirred about. He gave a loud groan and rolled over onto his face. "Hell's teeth!" he said. "I've got a hangover!"

"No, you hit your head on the floor," Sophie said.

Howl rose up on his hands and knees with a scramble. "I can't stay," he said. "I've got to rescue that fool Sophie."

"I'm here!" Sophie said, shaking his shoulder. "But so is Miss Angorian! Get up and do something about her! Quickly!"

The stick was entirely flames by now. Martha's hair was frizzling. And it had dawned on Miss Angorian that the scarecrow would burn. She was maneuvering to get the hovering stick into the doorway. As usual, Sophie thought, I didn't think it through!

Howl only needed to take one look. He stood up in a hurry. He held out one hand and spoke a sentence of those words that lost themselves in claps of thunder. Plaster fell from the ceiling. Everything trembled. But the stick vanished and Howl stepped back with a small, hard, black thing in his hand. It could have been a lump of cinder, except that it was the same shape as the thing Sophie had just pushed into Howl's chest. Miss Angorian whined like a wet fire and held out her arms imploringly.

"I'm afraid not," Howl said. "You've had your time. By the look of this, you were trying to get a new heart too. You were going to take my heart and let Calcifer die, weren't you?" He held the black thing between both palms and pushed his hands together. The Witch's old heart crumbled into black sand, and soot, and nothing. Miss Angorian faded away as it crumbled. As Howl opened his hands empty, the doorway was empty of Miss Angorian too.

Another thing happened as well. The moment Miss Angorian was gone, the scarecrow was no longer there either. If Sophie had cared to look, she would have seen two tall men standing in the doorway, smiling at one another. The one with the craggy face had ginger hair. The one with a green uniform had vaguer features and a lace shawl draped round the shoulders of his uniform. But Howl turned to Sophie just then. "Gray doesn't really suit you," he said. "I thought that when I first saw you."

"Calcifer's gone," Sophie said. "I had to break your contract."

Howl looked a little sad, but he said, "We were both hoping you would. Neither of us wanted to end up like the Witch and Miss Angorian. Would you call your hair ginger?"

"Red gold," Sophie said. Not much had changed about Howl that she could see, now he had his heart back, except maybe that his eyes seemed a deeper color—more like eyes and less like glass marbles. "Unlike some people's," she said, "it's natural."

"I've never seen why people put such value on things being natural," Howl said, and Sophie knew then that he was scarcely changed at all.

If Sophie had had any attention to spare, she would have seen Prince Justin and Wizard Suliman shaking hands and clapping one another delightedly on the back. "I'd better get back to my royal brother," Prince Justin said. He walked up to Fanny, as the most likely person, and made her a deep, courtly bow. "Am I addressing the lady of this house?"

"Er—not really," Fanny said, trying to hide her broom behind her back. "The lady of the house is Sophie."

"Or will be shortly," Mrs. Fairfax said, beaming benevolently.

Howl said to Sophie, "I've been wondering all along if you would turn out to be that lovely girl I met on May Day. Why were you so scared then?"

If Sophie had been attending, she would have seen Wizard Suliman go up to Lettie. Now he was himself, it was clear that Wizard Suliman was at least as strong-minded as Lettie was. Lettie looked quite nervous as

Suliman loomed craggily over her. "It seemed to be the Prince's memory I had of you and not my own at all," he said.

"That's quite all right," Lettie said bravely. "It was a mistake."

"But it wasn't!" protested Wizard Suliman. "Would you let me take you on as a pupil at least?" Lettie went fiery red at this and did not seem to know what to say.

That seemed to Sophie to be Lettie's problem. She had her own. Howl said, "I think we ought to live happily ever after," and she thought he meant it. Sophie knew that living happily ever after with Howl would be a good deal more eventful than any story made it sound, though she was determined to try. "It should be hair-raising," added Howl.

"And you'll exploit me," Sophie said.

"And then you'll cut up all my suits to teach me," said Howl.

If Sophie or Howl had had any attention to spare, they might have noticed that Prince Justin, Wizard Suliman, and Mrs. Fairfax were all trying to speak to Howl, and that Fanny, Martha, and Lettie were plucking at Sophie's sleeves, while Michael was dragging at Howl's jacket.

"That was the neatest use of words of power I ever saw from anyone," Mrs. Fairfax said. "I wouldn't have known what to do with that creature. As I often say . . . "

"Sophie," said Lettie, "I need your advice."

"Wizard Howl," said Wizard Suliman, "I must apologize for trying to bite you so often. In the normal way, I wouldn't dream of setting teeth in a fellow countryman."

"Sophie, I think this gentleman is a prince," said Fanny.

"Sir," said Prince Justin, "I believe I must thank you for rescuing me from the Witch."

"Sophie," said Martha, "the spell's off you! Did you hear?"

But Sophie and Howl were holding one another's hands and smiling and smiling, quite unable to stop. "Don't bother me now," said Howl. "I only did it for the money."

"Liar!" said Sophie.

"I said," Michael shouted, "that *Calcifer's come back!*"

That did get Howl's attention, and Sophie's too. They looked at the grate, where, sure enough, the familiar blue face was flickering among the logs.

"You didn't need to do that," Howl said.

"I don't mind, as long as I can come and go," Calcifer said. "Besides, it's raining out there in Market Chipping."